Praise for The Amoveo Legend series

"Sizzling sexual chemistry that is sure to please... I really can't wait to see where we go to next."

—*Yankee Romance Reviewers*

"A moving tale that captures both the sweetness and passion of romance."

—*Romance Junkies*, 5 Blue Ribbons

"A well-written, action-packed love story featuring two very strong characters."

—*Romance Book Scene*, 5 Hearts

"*Unleashed* earned its Best Book rating in spades... The characters haunted my dreams and I thought about this book constantly."

—*Long and Short Reviews*

"I loved this book. A paranormal top pick, and I'm looking forward to many more in this series."

—*Night Owl Romance* Reviewer Top Pick, 5 Stars

"Awesome... captivates the reader with action and romance."

—*Rom Fan Reviews*

"The love scenes are steamy... the plot is intriguing and... the reader will be entertained."

"Spectacular... A stunning new shifter series will thrill paranormal fans who love the genre. A fascinating world."

—*Bookaholics Romance Book Club*

"A fast-paced paranormal romance with fantastic world-building. I can't wait to read more from this author and in this series."

—*The Book Girl*, 5 Stars

"A great plot... I liked the new twist on shapeshifting."
—*Love Romance Passion*

"The characters are very strong and warm... There is enough action and danger to keep it interesting and the romance is sexy."

—*Book Reviews by Martha's Bookshelf*

"Sweet and passionate. An enthralling story... Ms. Humphreys has created a fantastic world [that] will leave you wanting more."

—*Anna's Book Blog*

"A blend of intriguing urban fantasy with rich romantic overtures."

—*That's What I'm Talking About*

"Loved learning about the Amoveo Legend and I can't wait till *Untouched* comes out!"

—*Paranormal and Romantic Suspense Reviews*

The Amoveo Legend

UNTOUCHED

SARA HUMPHREYS

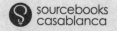

sourcebooks
casablanca

Published by Sourcebooks Casablanca, an imprint of Sourcebooks, Inc.
P.O. Box 4410, Naperville, Illinois 60567-4410
(630) 961-3900
FAX: (630) 961-2168
www.sourcebooks.com

Printed and bound in Canada
WC 10 9 8 7 6 5 4 3 2 1

"What we remember from childhood we remember forever: permanent ghosts, stamped, inked, imprinted, eternally seen."

—Cynthia Ozick

For my parents... who have inked
and stamped my life with love.

Chapter 1

"YOU ARE ONE SEXY BITCH." KERRY GRINNED BROADLY and shut the door to Samantha's bedroom. She leaned back and folded her arms to get a better look at the bride. "Seriously, does Malcolm know how freaking lucky he is?" she asked skeptically. Kerry bent down and smoothed out the train of Samantha's simple ivory gown.

"Oh he does, and so do I." Samantha smiled serenely and adjusted the bodice of her strapless silk wedding dress. Kerry stood behind her best friend and removed the one or two kinks in the delicate veil. She smiled at their contrasting reflections in the oval antique mirror. Kerry was a good head taller than Sam. Sam's hair, swept off her neck, was as blonde as Kerry's was black. Samantha had always been beautiful, but today she was truly radiant.

Tears stung at the back of Kerry's eyes. Her best friend, her only friend, was getting married. She took a deep breath, wrapped her arms around Sam's waist, and braced herself. It was always a gamble touching another human being. Samantha was the only person Kerry could bear to touch. Everyone, including Sam, thought it was a germ phobia. The truth was much more complicated.

It was far more frightening.

She embraced Sam and saw the one image that

always burst into her mind, an enormous gray wolf. As odd as it was, that unique image gave her comfort. Since they were children that was the only thing Kerry saw when she touched Sam. Unfortunately, that wasn't the case when she touched other people. Kerry let out a heavy sigh, a mixture of relief and comfort as Sam gave her arms a squeeze.

"I'm not going to Mars, you know. I'm just getting married." Sam laughed. "Now I'll be two houses down the beach instead of one. At the very most I'm a phone call away."

"That's what they all say." Kerry sniffled and released Sam from the embrace. She turned quickly and wiped the tears away, feeling foolish for such a display.

"Besides, you're the famous model," Sam said with a teasing lilt in her voice. "You know... always jet-setting around the world on photo shoots. We only get to see each other a couple of times a year anyway. Who knows? We may see each other more now."

Sam took Kerry's hand and gave it a reassuring squeeze. The wolf image burst into Kerry's head, but at least there was no pain. She could almost tolerate the visions. It was the crippling pain that terrified her. Kerry's body stilled, and she prayed her friend wouldn't notice.

"I promise nothing will change! Look at it this way, every time you come to your parents place for a break at the beach, you can count on me being here."

"He better not be one of those Neanderthal types that won't let you have a girls' night out. I mean I don't even know this guy. Are you sure this is it? You've only known him for a month."

Even as the words escaped her lips she knew what

the answer was. In truth, she'd never seen her friend this happy. Ever since Samantha met Malcolm, she glowed. Kerry had heard about that but hadn't witnessed it until now. Her lips curved. She had always been envious of Sam because she'd been raised in a household with real love and affection. Sam's family was a far cry from the icy environment of her own childhood.

Sometimes she wondered if her parents' cool behavior was a reaction to her unusual... sensitivity. They hadn't tried to embrace her or touch her in years. They had tried a few times when she was a child, but whenever they did she screamed bloody murder and wouldn't speak for days. Soon they just stopped trying. It saddened her to know that they never would've adopted her if they'd known how different she was.

To top it all off, she didn't exactly fit the preppy, upper-crusty mold that the Smithsons were cut from. She towered over everyone in the family and was built more like an Amazon than a delicate WASP. In every picture she stuck out like a sore thumb. Tall, big-boned, dark-haired, dark-eyed... loner. They didn't know human contact brought not only horrifying images, but excruciating pain.

Except for when she touched Samantha. There was something special about Sam. Thank God.

"Hey!" Sam snapped her fingers and brought Kerry out of her trance. "Hello in there? You okay?" Sam knitted her brow worriedly at Kerry. "Maybe we should've postponed the wedding? I don't think you're quite yourself since..."

Kerry put her hand up in protest before Samantha could finish her thought. "Don't even think about bringing up that ugliness, especially today! I'm fine. I don't even remember any of it. I mean it!" She clapped her hands and quickly changed the subject. "Hey, why are we standing around here? You've got a big hunk of man waiting to marry you underneath that beautiful tent on the beach."

Sam smiled and gave a quick nod, knowing her friend well enough to know the subject was closed. She picked up her bouquet of red roses and headed out the door toward her new life. Kerry held Sam's train off of the floor, a traditional maid of honor duty, and followed her down the stairs. She tried to concentrate on the smooth fabric between her fingers, instead of the fact that she'd just lied to her best friend.

She did remember.

She had a vivid memory of one thing from the day she was attacked. A pair of eyes had been fixed on her, eyes that glowed like embers in a fire, accompanied by a deep guttural growl. Every night since the attack, her dreams were haunted by that memory. As she walked into the bright September sunlight, she couldn't help but wonder if she would ever sleep soundly again.

The music from the lively band flowed lightly around Kerry and the rest of the wedding guests. She sipped the cool, crisp champagne as she watched Samantha dance with her new husband and could practically feel their happiness mixed with the late summer breeze. Her gaze drifted over the intimate group of guests gathered around the bride and groom. They all had that same serene look while they watched Malcolm and Samantha share their first dance as husband and wife. He towered over her as he twirled her around the dance floor, and the sound of her laughter peppered the air.

The two of them hadn't taken their eyes off each other for one second. If Kerry didn't know any better, she'd swear they were reading each other's minds. She chuckled quietly and sipped her champagne from the delicate crystal flute. The guests were limited to only thirty or so close friends and family members. Her own parents had sent their regrets from Europe, which was something of a relief. Kerry could only handle them in limited doses and didn't want their chilly demeanor ruining such a beautiful day for Sam.

"May I have this dance?"

The deep voice rolled over her like sudden thunder in the distance. She jumped with a yelp and splashed champagne onto her red satin gown. "Shit," she hissed under her breath. Kerry brushed at the droplets, which were now making dark stains on her dress, and shot an irritated glance at Malcolm's best man, Dante. "I don't dance." Something about this guy threw her off balance. Kerry prided herself on her ability to stay in control, and this guy rattled her.

"I'm sorry. I didn't realize I'd have that effect on you."

The amusement in his voice made her want to punch him square in the mouth.

Or kiss him. Shit, she was in trouble.

She glared at him through narrowed eyes and put on her most stuck-up and obnoxious tone, hoping she could frighten him away. "Don't flatter yourself, Tarzan. I got startled. That's all."

He had moved in next to her without a sound. How

long had he been standing there? He didn't go away, but instead, he moved in closer, just a breath away from her. The warmth of his body whispered along her bare arm and all the little hairs stood on end. She was terrified he'd touch her and at the same time worried he wouldn't. She quickly turned her attention back to Malcolm and Sam, trying to ignore him, but failing miserably.

He was a difficult man to ignore. At five foot ten, she was usually taller than most men, and this guy towered over her, even in her Jimmy Choos. He was massive, well over six feet tall—a solid wall of muscle. He had a handsome, masculine face with the most enormous amber eyes she'd ever seen. His thick auburn hair was almost the exact same color as his eyes.

Not that she'd noticed him or anything.

Kerry scolded herself. There was absolutely no point in getting all hot and bothered over some guy she'd never be able to touch. *I must be the oldest living virgin that isn't officially a nun*. She drained what was left of her drink.

Her goal was to be as horrible to him as possible and get him to go away. Dante smiled as though he knew she was doing her best to upset him, and she could feel his gaze wander down the length of her body.

"You'll dance with me. Maybe not today," he whispered seductively into her ear. "But eventually… you and I will dance."

Kerry turned to give the arrogant bastard a piece of her mind, but he was gone. Vanished, it seemed, into thin air. Her breath came quickly, and her eyes darted around the tent. Her body still quivered from the soft whisper, laden with innuendo. She was horrified that everyone in the tent would see how he'd thrown her entire body into overdrive. Her cheeks burned with anger, fear, and lust—a potent combination. Kerry straightened her back in an effort to calm her quaking limbs as a welcome voice wafted over her.

"Well now, missy. I hope you're going to keep coming to visit me even though our girl is married off."

Kerry let out the breath she'd been holding and smiled at Sam's grandmother Nonie. "C'mon Nonie, you're not getting rid of me that easily." Kerry placed the empty flute on a passing waiter's tray and quickly scooped up a fresh glass. Perhaps a little more booze would calm her nerves.

"Well, you know you've always been like a granddaughter to me. You and Samantha are practically sisters, so you can't blame an old lady for worrying." She smiled up at Kerry with twinkling eyes that reminded her of the summer ocean.

"Well, since Sam and Malcolm aren't even going on a honeymoon, and they're living right next door to you… I don't think you'll be that lonely." Kerry took a fresh swig of the champagne and hoped she didn't sound as jealous as she felt. "I have to leave tomorrow for a photo shoot in New Orleans, but I'll be back after that. To be very honest," she said with a sigh, "I'm getting really burnt out and sick of traveling."

"You're going on a shoot already? Well now, don't you think you're jumping back into things awfully fast?" Nonie's voice hovered somewhere between panic and anger. Kerry couldn't quite tell which was going to win out. She couldn't bring herself to look at Nonie, so she kept her eyes trained on the happy couple.

"I'm fine, Nonie. Sheesh, did you and Sam go to the same worrywart school? I'm not in any more danger from AJ. My cousin was obsessed with Sam, remember? I just got in his way," she said flippantly. "He's long gone from here anyway. Every cop in Rhode Island has his picture, and Westerly is a small town. I mean, for Christ's sake, Millie's even got his picture up at the diner with a big *danger* sign plastered above it. I'd be more worried about Samantha."

Nonie's mouth set in a grim line. "Samantha will be fine. She's stronger than you think, and besides she has Malcolm. I worry about *you*, Kerry. You shouldn't be traveling by yourself. You just never know what can happen, and I would think you've learned that as a result of recent events."

Kerry rolled her eyes at the scolding tone and turned to face Nonie. She looked into her worry-filled eyes set in a soft, wrinkled face, and any irritation she felt melted away with the ocean breeze. She had the overwhelming urge to scoop the old woman up in a hug but knew the cost would be too great. Instead she swallowed the lump that had formed in her throat and turned quickly to face the calm, blue sea.

Nonie and Sam were the only two people in the world she really loved, and she'd almost lost them both because of AJ. He'd been completely obsessed with Samantha and had coerced Kerry into luring her into his sick trap. Her mind drifted to that awful night. She had fought back as much as she could, but he'd overpowered her. She was disgusted with herself because if she had touched him before that, just once, she would've seen what he was up to. She would've seen through the facade to the evil underneath, but she'd been too weak. Her stomach roiled at the memory of her cowardice.

Samantha's bright laughter tumbled through the air and brought a smile to her lips. Nonie was right. Sam would be fine. If it weren't for Malcolm, AJ would've killed them both. He'd scared the little worm off, and there'd been no trace of him in the weeks following the attack. It was as though he'd vanished from the face of the earth. Samantha had been hurt because of her, and she would never forgive herself for that.

Nonie stood silently by her side as they watched the waves roll gently onto the sand. Kerry wanted to tell Nonie and Sam the truth, but was terrified at what they would think. They were all that she had, and she couldn't afford to lose them. What was she supposed to say? *Hey, guess what? I have visions when I touch people. Oh, by the way, it's so painful I want to vomit. How about a hug?* They would think she's insane just like her twisted cousin AJ. She cringed at the very thought of it.

If she lost them, then she would really be alone. Kerry pulled the burgundy wrap tightly around her as the cool ocean breeze picked up. She shivered, knowing it wasn't from the wind. Taking a deep breath, she finally broke the silence.

"I'll be careful, Nonie. Listen. I'm going to New Orleans not Iraq. I'll be perfectly safe."

"Yes, you will." Samantha's all too chipper tone came over Kerry's other shoulder. "Malcolm and I have hired someone to make certain that is the case."

Kerry narrowed her eyes and looked warily at Samantha. "What are you babbling about? Has marriage made you lose your senses already?"

"Oh, I make her crazy. There's no doubt about that," Malcolm said softly. He stood behind Sam with his arms wrapped around her waist and nibbled on her ear.

"Malcolm," Sam giggled. "Cut it out. This is serious." Kerry rolled her eyes but couldn't resist smiling at them and fought the urge to look around for Dante. "You two are gonna frighten the guests. Get a room. Jeez."

"What my lovely bride is trying to tell you is that we've taken measures to be sure you're kept safe on this next trip. It's only been a few weeks since the unfortunate events of late. We just want to be certain that you have an extra measure of security. That's all."

Kerry eyed the three of them one at a time. Each of their faces held steely resolve, and she saw there was no point in arguing. "I can see that I'm being totally ganged up on. Aren't I?"

"Yes!" Samantha wriggled out of Malcolm's embrace, popped up on her toes, and planted a quick kiss on Kerry's cheek. The wolf image whisked fleetingly through Kerry's mind, leaving as quickly as it came, and she shook her head as Malcolm led Samantha back to the dance floor. "It better not be some crotchety old cop or something," she shouted after them.

"I'm not crotchety or a cop." Dante's deep, male voice rolled over her, and she was instantly aware of his body behind hers. So close. Too close. Kerry held her breath and whipped around to face him.

"No way!" She placed her hands firmly on her hips and glared up at him defiantly.

"Inferno Securities has the highest reputation. We've provided personal security for kings and queens. I'm sure I can handle a princess like you." Dante delivered

a wicked grin and remained stone still, unwilling to retreat. He smiled as her deep brown eyes flashed angrily
back at him.

He might be there to protect her, but little did she
know, she was the one who would be saving him.

—⁓—

He would be sorry. A satisfied giggle bubbled and threatened to boil over. Their betrayal and disloyalty would
finally be punished. They were traitors of the largest
proportions, and after all these years they would finally
pay for their actions. Imagine the audacity. Choosing
that woman over his own kind? Had he learned nothing
from the others? He had to know that sooner or later
he'd have to pay price. The ultimate punishment would
be delivered by the Punisher.

"I like that." The words came out in a rush. "I need
to call myself something while I play our little game.
Don't I?"

The question hung unanswered in the air. The sounds
of the city bustled outside the window as steam fogged
up the bathroom mirror.

"The Punisher. That's what I'll call myself, and that
is the name that they will fear. It will keep them up at
night and have them all looking around every corner."

The Punisher laughed loudly and reveled in the sound
as it bounced around the tiled room.

Death was coming.

Chapter 2

DANTE STAYED HIDDEN IN THE TALL BROWN AND green sea grass along the beach, and kept a watchful eye on her house. The inky black night provided additional cover, and his dark rust-colored fur blended well with his surroundings. The wedding guests were gone, and the beach was quiet once again. If a random beachcomber saw him, they would merely marvel at their incredible luck. Not many people saw the fox that lived in these grasses, but then again, Dante was not your average fox.

His furry body twitched, welcoming the salty breeze. It was a relief from the itchy grasses that fluttered along his thick russet coat. He watched her through the bedroom window, his gaze fixed on her lovely body silhouetted against the sheer curtains. His breath stilled as she came to the open window and pushed aside the thin fabric. He lifted his snout to the air and breathed deeply. His keen sense of smell caught her scent as it floated in the breeze. He inhaled the intoxicating mixture of lilac and spice. His heart raced at the very sight of her. He watched as she brushed her long ebony hair and wanted nothing more than to claim her as his. She was, after all, his mate.

He had dreamt of her for so many years. As with all Amoveo, he had been dreaming of his mate since adolescence. The problem was she hadn't been looking for him, and he'd almost given up hope of finding her.

Then just a few weeks ago, here at this very beach, he'd stumbled upon her. She was indeed unusual. He knew she had a psychic gift but was amazed that she never used it. In fact she seemed fearful of it.

A sudden rustling behind him in the grasses caught his attention. His large ears stood up, and his body tensed. The sound of Malcolm's laughter relaxed him instantly. He turned to see his friend standing behind him, hands on his hips and shaking his head. "Boy, oh boy, have you got it bad."

Dante whined and let out a low growl of annoyance. Closing his eyes, he silently whispered the ancient language. *Verto*. Dante visualized his human form, shimmered, and in seconds was standing shoulder to shoulder with his friend.

"What are you doing down here? Isn't this your wedding night?" He tried to hide his embarrassment for being caught spying on Kerry, but knew he'd failed miserably.

"We're enjoying our evening just fine. Believe me." He grinned. "Samantha sensed you were out here and wanted me to come and check on you. Are you ready for your trip tomorrow with Kerry?"

"I am, but I don't think she is. In fact at the wedding today she basically told me to take a flying leap. *That she didn't need a big oaf like me following her around*." Dante looked up at Kerry's window disappointed to find it empty.

"She's going to have quite a few changes to accept in the coming days." Malcolm sighed, and the lines in his face deepened apologetically. "I'm embarrassed that I didn't realize it sooner."

Dante cocked his head and turned slowly to Malcolm. "What do you mean?" He narrowed his eyes and held his breath. Could Malcolm suspect the same thing? Did he see it too?

"She is Amoveo," he said quietly. "She's a hybrid like Samantha. I just can't believe I didn't realize it sooner." He shrugged. "I suppose I was so caught up in Sam, I was blind to anything else."

The breath Dante had been holding came out in a rush of relief. "I thought I was going crazy." He ran a hand over his face. "Thank God you see it too. What about Samantha? Does she know?"

Malcolm nodded somberly. "She picked up on it before I did. Her abilities have grown significantly in the past month. I think that is what the Purists are worried about. They are threatened by Samantha." He cast a quick glance to Kerry's house. "And anyone else like her. That's why we hired you to go with her to New Orleans. If *we* have realized her heritage, it's likely others in our race will as well. She needs you, Dante." Malcolm placed a hand on his shoulder. "She is in real danger until we find the rest of the conspirators." He gave Dante's shoulder a squeeze and looked him square in the eyes. "Your father was not the only one."

Dante's anger flared hard and fast at the memory of his father's betrayal. His eyes shifted to the eyes of his clan and glowed brightly in the dark night. "I know full well of my father's deception. His actions almost killed my mate as well." He bit the words out through clenched teeth. "I do not need to be reminded of his treachery." His body went rigid, and his hands balled into tight fists at his side.

Malcolm dropped his hand, and his eyes softened. "I'm sorry. Brendan betrayed us all."

Dante turned away from his cousin and crossed his arms tightly across his chest. "My father paid for his foolishness with his life… and ultimately, my mother will pay the price as well." He took a deep breath and willed his eyes to their human state. "I'm furious that she will suffer because of him, and there's nothing I can do to stop it." His mind drifted to the stories he'd heard as a child, about the slow deaths that all Amoveo suffered when they lost their mates. His face grew darker still. "My only true regret is that I wasn't able to confront him myself." He shook his head and faced Malcolm once again. "Imagine what he would do if he knew his son was destined to be with a hybrid. That alone might've killed him."

"Indeed." Malcolm gave his friend a tight smile. "We do have Amoveo kin that live in New Orleans and one of the Vasullus family members as well." Dante nodded. "They have been alerted of your arrival, but they do not know about Kerry or her… special situation. I think it's safest for both of you if you try to keep that quiet for now."

"I don't think that should be a problem considering she can't stand me. Oh, and of course she has no idea that our people even exist." He ran his hand through his hair and let out a frustrated sigh. "How did you manage to convince Samantha?"

"She couldn't resist me. There was very little convincing needed." Malcolm puffed up his chest visibly. Moments later a bathrobe-clad Samantha materialized next to the two men, her hands placed firmly on her hips.

"Oh really?" She looked at Malcolm with an arched eyebrow and skeptical smirk. "Don't let him fool you for a minute, Dante. He had to do plenty of convincing." She swatted a contrite Malcolm and then turned her attention to Dante. "Kerry puts up a tough front, but it's all an act. She's really very fragile and deep down she's terrified. She doesn't understand her own gift, and she sees it as more of a curse."

She looked up at Malcolm who had moved in next to her and wrapped a protective arm around her waist. "We are both convinced that the more time she spends with you, the better she'll be able to manage her psychic touch. I've noticed in the past couple of weeks, since she's met you, she can tolerate more human contact. It's still very painful for her." Her sympathy for Kerry was written all over her face. "But I'm hoping when she connects fully with you, that will change. I think you're the missing piece to her puzzle."

Dante smiled down at Sam. It was easy to see why Malcolm loved her; she was lovely and had mastered her Amoveo abilities with surprising speed. He couldn't help but wonder if Kerry would be able to transition into their world as smoothly. Would she be able to accept the truth, or would she run screaming from him? He had to know because nothing could be worse than living in limbo.

"I hope you're right." He sighed. "It would help if I could scan her mind, but she's got one hell of a mental barrier up. I'd found her in the dream realm so many times. I couldn't see her, but she felt so close—right next to me. I sensed her there, but she had no awareness of me at all. It's been very frustrating. That defense mechanism of hers is practically impenetrable," he murmured softly.

Malcolm nodded in agreement. "I did notice that as well. She's a very strong psychic, and I'm quite sure she has no idea that she's blocking us. It's probably how she stayed hidden in plain sight, but if anyone can get through to her, you can."

"Yeah, well, we'll see about that. I don't need to scan her mind to know that she can't stand me at the moment. She's made that very clear with extremely colorful language."

Sam laughed lightly and placed a gentle kiss on his cheek. "I think you'll get through to her. Give it some time." She gave his arm a reassuring squeeze. "Like I said… she puts on a good front. Think about it, Dante, she's spent her entire life keeping people at arm's length. No human contact to speak of really. Don't give up on her. She'll come around."

She stepped back into the crook of Malcolm's arm. "Now if you don't mind, I'm going to take my husband back upstairs and take advantage of him." She winked, and the two newlyweds vanished into the night.

"Good thing the guest room is on the first floor," he mumbled.

Dante smiled and turned back to Kerry's house. Her light was out, the window was closed, and she was surely asleep. She was safe at the moment. However, he knew that as long as the Purists were out there, she'd never really be safe. The memory of her attack crept into his mind, and anger threatened to overtake him. He would never forgive himself for allowing her to be harmed. She'd almost died because he hadn't been there soon enough. He hadn't been able to protect her, and he swore to himself that would never happen again. She was the only one who could save him from the darkness.

She ran through the house, tears streaming down her face. He would find her. He always found her. Kerry's breath came in ragged gasps, and terror gripped her heart. The house was dark, lit only by the occasional lightning strike from the coming storm. Kerry tried every door. None of them would budge. She ran back down the hallway and fled down the stairs. She heard his sick laughter bouncing through the house.

He would find her, and he would kill her.

He came around the bottom of the stairs, and his fist slammed into her face. Stars burst behind her eyes, and the pain that ensued threatened to overtake her and crack her head like an egg. She hit the steps hard; pain shot through her body. He grabbed her arm and yanked her to her feet, dragging her into the living room. Pain seared her skull as gruesome images filled her mind. She saw all the vicious things he wanted to do to Samantha. Blood. Knives. Each image flashed harsher than the next, one more violent than the other, and all of them accompanied by white, hot pain. Her body convulsed wildly; her eyes rolled back in her head as he laughed wickedly at her pain.

"I'm going to kill that whore and that thing she's with. They're both going to die." AJ's face twisted in a mask of evil. He shoved her harshly into the wall and pointed a giant black crossbow at her, just inches from her heaving chest. Kerry tried desperately to keep from passing out. As soon as he released her, the pain

subsided and the visions stopped, but nausea and fear kept their grip on her. Blood flowed from the wound in her head; her cheek throbbed from where he'd struck her. Her body shook uncontrollably, and the tears flowed freely.

He took her cell phone out of his pocket and held it next to her head. "You're going to call your little girlfriend and tell her to come over here. Right now."

Kerry shook her head furiously in defiance. He grabbed her by the back of her head and pulled harshly on her long hair. Excruciating pain flashed behind her eyes, and more nightmarish images rippled relentlessly. He laughed and released her, all the while keeping that crossbow pointed directly at her heart. He gave her the phone and pushed the tip of the bow harder against her skin. "Call or die."

Kerry whimpered pathetically and with shaking hands called Samantha. She had barely gotten out a few pleading words before AJ took the phone and hung up. "Good girl. That should do it." He took the phone and threw it into a corner. "Now you can take a little nap, until I need you again." He slammed her in the head with the butt of the crossbow, sending her into a heap on the ground.

She lay there bleeding on the verge of passing out, the guilt of calling Samantha adding to her torment. Blood dripped into her swollen eyes, and her hair fell across her face. Her entire body ached, and her head throbbed mercilessly. She heard AJ walk away from her and prayed for a quick death.

Suddenly, a low deadly growl came from across the room. With a ridiculous amount of effort, she opened one eye a crack. Through blurred vision she saw a frightening set of glowing amber eyes that were fixed on her and filled with rage. The growling raged in her head as the scream ripped from her throat.

Kerry sat up in bed screaming and shaking uncontrollably. Her sweat-covered body soaked her sheets. Her breath came quickly, and she looked wildly around the room. It was morning. She was in her room. If it had just been a nightmare, she could've shaken it off, but it was much more than that. The night AJ attacked her had become the only thing she dreamt of anymore. She couldn't even escape in her sleep. Pain and fear had become her way of life.

Chapter 3

THE SUN BEAT DOWN ON DANTE AS HE STOOD WAITING at the front door of the Smithson house. The princess was taking her time answering the door. He stood ramrod straight, hands folded in front of him, and did his best not to tap his foot. Sweat was pouring down his back, and he cursed silently at himself for wearing a dark suit on such a hot day. Mate or not, at the moment she was his client, and he was damn well going to treat her like one.

Mindful of the time, Dante checked his watch. He did not want to miss their plane to New Orleans. He rang the doorbell for the third time and felt his patience slipping away by the second. Just as he was about to pound on the door, it swung open. The vision before him robbed him of his breath.

His body stilled, and he drank in the sight of her. Her thick ebony hair was swept up gracefully, exposing her long lovely neck. She wore a crisp white shirt unbuttoned just enough to reveal the top of her full breasts, and black pants hugged every delicious curve. His sharp gaze slowly wandered over her shapely form from head to toe, and he had to work hard to keep from licking his lips. She looked positively mouthwatering. He was very glad he kept his sunglasses on because the second he saw her, his eyes had shifted to his fox. However, the disapproving look on her face sent them back to normal.

"What the hell are you doing here? I told you I don't need or want a bodyguard. Especially one that resembles a Neanderthal," she said as she fumed.

"I'm sorry you feel that way," he said quietly. "However, I don't work for you. I was hired by Malcolm and Samantha. Therefore, until *they* relieve me of my duties, you're stuck with me."

Kerry let out a frustrated sigh and looked at her watch. "Where the hell is my car service? They were supposed to be here by now," she said, looking past him to the empty road.

"I took the liberty of sending them away. I'll be driving us to the airport, and I've arranged to have the seat next to you on the plane as well. Now if you'll just give me your bag, we can get moving."

Kerry's anger slammed into him. Even if he hadn't been able to feel her energy waves, there was no mistaking the look on her face. Her dark eyes flashed, and her fair skin developed a crimson tint. She was pissed. Dante got the feeling that she wasn't used to hearing "no" very often. It was kind of a turn on, and he did his best not to smile.

"You presumptuous son of a bitch," she seethed. "Who in the hell do you think you are?"

"I'm your bodyguard and I suggest we get going, or you're going to miss your plane." He kept his voice even and didn't take his eyes off hers. Dante removed his sunglasses and held her gaze. "Your bags, princess?"

Kerry made a sound of disgust and shoved her sunglasses on. "Fine."

Her voice was ice cold, but the heat that radiated from her body told a different story. Dante felt her conflicting reactions to him, and it gave him hope. *Me thinks the lady doth protest too much*, he thought. She stepped back and gestured brusquely to two mammoth bags in the foyer. Dante knew she kept her distance intentionally, avoiding any physical contact as she had for her entire life.

He'd let her avoid his touch… for now.

Effortlessly he scooped up the bags and brought them down to his waiting car as Kerry followed him reluctantly, mumbling unflattering comments about him under her breath. He tried to open the door for her, but she beat him to it. She got in and slammed the door shut, making her feelings about the entire situation quite clear. Dante slipped his sunglasses back on as he whistled his way back into the car.

The drive to Bradley Airport was made in stony silence, and he was surprisingly grateful for it. Having Kerry in such close proximity proved to be much more challenging for him than he'd anticipated. The intoxicating combination of her scent, along with the warmth of her body, had his head spinning and the rest of his body hard as hell.

He wanted nothing more than to pull the car over and take her right here in the front seat, but since she wasn't even speaking to him that was not likely to happen.

He glanced at her and felt his stomach flip-flop. He squirmed in his seat at the awkward and unfamiliar feeling. Women had always been easy marks and nothing more than pleasant diversions. Something altogether foreign was happening here, and for the first time in his life he felt unsure of himself.

A subtle change in her energy captured his attention. The fire and spark she had earlier was diminished, and sadness had swiftly replaced anger. She reminded him of a flower that had been left out in the sun too long, wilted and weary. Her energy drained and her guard down, she stared out the window at the passing scenery. He felt an odd squeeze in his chest. His heart ached as hers did. Dante opened his mouth to break the silence, and that was when he heard her.

Why can't I be normal? Her soft voice floated into his mind like a warm breeze as he heard her telepathically for the first time. His eyes shifted instinctively the moment she touched her mind to his, and his heart thundered in his chest ferociously. Dante gripped the steering wheel, turning his knuckles white. He struggled to keep his breathing steady as tiny beads of sweat formed on his brow. He strained listening for more, praying she would stroke his mind with hers just one more time, but there was none.

The deafening silence shrouded them once again.

Dante blinked and returned his eyes to their human state. This was the most promising development yet. All Amoveo were telepathic, however, telepathy between mates was particularly important. It was their most intimate form of communication and a crucial part of their mating process. He let out the breath he didn't even realize he'd been holding and trained his eyes on the road before them.

They made it to the airport just in time for their flight, which was fine with Dante. He wasn't much for sitting around in the waiting area. He was perfectly happy to check in and get onboard. Kerry, of course, expressed her dismay at the close timing. They made their way through airport security at a reasonable pace.

He took note of the fluidity with which she moved as she gracefully and subtly avoided all human contact. The entire trip through the airport Kerry hadn't allowed herself to so much as brush a stranger's arm as they passed by. It was like watching a dancer whose every move had been choreographed.

Her movements were sleek and sexy as hell.

She reminded him of Amoveo in the Cat Clans. Her lush, curvy body moved with fluid grace and absolute control. Between the way she moved and her feisty attitude, it was crystal clear she *was* from one of the Cat Clans, which one, however, still remained to be seen.

Dante kept a close eye on the people around her, ensuring no one approached her. He scanned the minds of the surrounding travelers as a precaution. His keen Amoveo senses read the emotions in the air, confirming no danger lurked nearby. Several people recognized her but had the decency to leave her alone. He watched closely as she collected her things from the conveyor belt. She smiled and nodded at the security agents who clearly had recognized her. Their whispers to each other wafted past as he and Kerry walked away toward the gate.

"You have some admirers back there. I think it made their day just to have seen you up close and in person." His voice remained low, and his eyes continued to scan their surroundings.

Kerry sighed, and her full lips curved. "It's funny, you know. They don't know me. Have never met me, but feel like they do know me." She shook her head and adjusted her shoulder bag, laughing softly. "Does that make any sense?"

They got in line to board their flight, and Dante turned to her, capturing her gaze with his. "I know just how they feel." His eyes remained locked with hers, and for several moments neither moved. It was a silent game of chicken. Who would look away first? Dante knew it wouldn't be him.

His mouth curved slowly into a lopsided grin as he inched his massive frame even closer to her. Her large brown Amoveo eyes widened as he invaded her space further, bringing their bodies just a breath apart. His blood hummed, and his heart beat rapidly, falling in time with hers. Her desire for him spilled over him in warm energy waves, and the temperature increased by the second. His body responded quickly, and his energy matched hers.

Static crackled between them in the air.

She licked her bottom lip nervously, and he wanted nothing more than to taste her. His mind filled with wicked images of her long, lush naked body writhing beneath him. Almost instantly there was a shift in her energy. It came faster and harder. Dante froze. Fear. She was frightened? The last thing in the world he wanted was her to fear him.

"We're holding up the line." She lifted her chin and quickly stepped ahead of him, breaking the trance.

"Of course," he murmured, following her onto the plane.

He expected her to be frightened when she learned of the Amoveo and of her unique heritage. However, he never thought she'd fear *him*, as a man. Her reaction reminded him of someone innocent, a young girl who had no experience with men. Then the realization hit him like a ton of bricks and stopped him dead in his tracks.

Of course she was innocent. How could she possibly have been intimate with anyone given her unique circumstances? The least bit of human contact had brought her nothing but pain. Dante scolded himself. How could he have been so stupid and so completely blind? He realized that all this time he had only been focused on how much he needed her. He'd only been fixated on how she would change *his* life. He was ashamed of himself for having given little thought to what their mating would mean for *her*.

She settled into her seat, and he watched her through a different lens. She was not the woman she pretended to be. Samantha was right. She was far more fragile and innocent than anyone would expect, including him. She had become an expert at living in a mental minefield. Even the seating she'd chosen on the airplane had been taken into consideration. She had the window seat in the first row of first class, which was about as isolated as you can get on a commercial flight. He admired her. She had learned to navigate her entire life from a very lonely place.

He knew that he needed to show her she was not alone.

"This is not going to work if you're going to ogle me like that." She straightened her back and stuck her nose in the air. "Stop staring. It's bad manners," she said briskly, while she flipped through the in-flight magazine.

"I'm sorry if I've made you uncomfortable," he said softly.

She made a short scoffing sound. "Listen." She shifted her body so they were now face-to-face. Her dark chocolate eyes narrowed with gritty determination. "I get stared at all day long by total strangers. The last thing I need is my bodyguard, or whatever you are, to be undressing me with your eyes. So why don't you do us both a favor and keep your big eyes to yourself. Okay?" She smiled tightly and crossed her arms under her breasts, which only served to accentuate her spectacular cleavage.

"I wasn't undressing you with my eyes or anything else for that matter." He leaned in closer with only the armrest between them. Her eyes widened, and her warm breath puffed across his cheek. Dante lowered his voice so only she would hear him. "Believe me, princess," he said with a smile. "When I undress you, I'll do it the old-fashioned way, with my hands." He winked.

Kerry's visibly shocked face reddened at his suggestion. "Just who the hell do you think you are?"

A long lock of ebony hair fell across her forehead, and Dante knew it was now or never. Before she could stop him he reached up, gently swept the hair from her face, and tucked it behind her ear. The pads of his fingers softly grazed the alabaster skin at her temple and skimmed along the top of her perfectly formed ears. The skin-to-skin contact may have been brief, but Dante knew the impact would have much longer lasting ramifications.

He sat back in his seat slowly and kept his gaze locked on her startled face. Kerry's body had gone completely still, but he sensed her heart beating wildly beneath the surface.

Her confused eyes searched his for answers, and all he wanted to do was touch her again, gather her in his arms, and tell her it was all going to be okay. His heart ached as ripples of confusion flowed from her body, and one large tear rolled down her face.

"You tell me, princess," he whispered. "Who am I?"

The pilot's voice boomed over the intercom, announcing the preparations for takeoff. Kerry sniffled, brushed the tear away quickly, and immediately turned her attention back to the magazine in her lap. "You're a Neanderthal."

Dante chuckled softly and settled back in his seat. "Whatever you say, princess."

Kerry pretended to ignore Dante for the rest of the flight. She needed to try and figure out what the hell was going on. The game had changed. Suddenly, her future, her path, nothing was clear.

Fear.

Shock.

Excitement.

Horror.

Lust.

Relief.

Joy.

Confusion.

Every single one of those emotions simultaneously flooded her body the moment Dante touched her, but what stunned her most was the glorious absence of pain. He'd touched her, and it had actually felt good. Good? Nope. That didn't cover it. Not even close. It wasn't just good… it was luscious, seductive, and breathtaking. His touch, however brief, sent unfamiliar luminous warmth radiating through her body.

And one image filled her mind.

A fox. A huge red fox.

What the hell was going on? There were so many

new sensations coming at her at once, she wasn't quite sure which to analyze first. Dante had her so far off balance that she'd actually let him touch her. He'd been too quick and the space in the plane too confined for her to avoid him, and she'd never been more grateful for anything in her entire life.

Her mind raced with the possibilities. Samantha was the only other person she'd been able to touch without the mind-splitting pain. She also saw a big furry animal when she touched Sam, but there was a very big difference between the two. Her face burned at the memory of what one light graze of his fingertips did to her. Sheesh. She almost had an orgasm from a little touch. What would happen if he held her hand? Or kissed her? Or...

Kerry stole a sidelong glance at Dante and was relieved to see he was asleep or at least polite enough to pretend to be asleep. She let her eyes wander down the length of his strong powerful body. The dark suit fit him perfectly, although she suspected he was more of a jeans and T-shirt guy. His large arms were crossed over his massive chest, which rose and fell in the deep breathing of sleep. His thick auburn hair curled enticingly at his collar, and she had to resist the sudden urge to run her fingers through it.

She had gone her entire life with almost no human contact—at least no normal human contact. If she did touch someone or they touched her, Kerry had become a master at disguising the pain. No one could put on a polite smile better than she could. Sometimes the physical pain was outdone by the emotional carnage. Seeing people's deepest secrets or the evil they harbored in their souls was even worse.

Once they stopped touching her, the mind-splitting pain would subside, but the brutal images lingered. There was no way to erase those horrors from her mind's eye. The male model at a shoot that had a secret fetish for young girls or her neighbor in the city who had fantasies about killing her husband, those scenarios loitered viciously and haunted her. It was difficult to make friends once you saw those kinds of things. Her physical limitations kept her isolated in more ways than one.

Now fate stepped in and delivered a smart-ass Adonis who seemed to hold the promise of everything she had secretly dreamed of. *Was this for real?* she wondered. Or was the universe dangling this big handsome carrot in front of her just so it could be ripped away? Fear gripped her heart. She nibbled on her lip. What if it was just a fluke?

She had to know.

Kerry drew in a slow deep breath and tentatively raised her hand. Her fingers hovered just above his and were immediately bathed in heat emanating from his golden skin. Her heart skipped a beat. She licked her lips and struggled to keep her breathing steady, praying for the nerve to touch him. She needed to see inside of him.

Dante shifted in his seat and mumbled something in his sleep. Kerry snatched her hand back and immediately pretended to be sleeping. The last thing she needed was to get caught trying to touch him. She cringed at the thought of it. That would be mortification of the highest order, especially after she'd been such a bitch to him. She had done her best to be horrible because she wanted him to believe she was the stuck-up diva the press wrote about.

She had definitely cultivated quite a reputation for herself in the industry. They called her *The Ice Queen*, and she really couldn't blame them. In Hollywood and the world of fashion, hugs and kisses were thrown around like candy. Her obvious avoidance of such things did not go unnoticed. The mere idea of kisses and her mind went right back to Dante. A hint of a smile played at her lips as she drifted to the cradling arms of sleep.

Then she began to dream.

The dream started the same as it had since the night she'd been attacked. Terror filled her mind. She hid behind the bed attempting to make herself as small as possible, which was no easy task considering her stature. Her lips trembled. She hugged her knees tightly and rocked back and forth, telling herself it was just a nightmare and repeatedly attempted to wake up, but no relief came. Fear gripped her heart as relentlessly as the wind that howled through the window. The storm raged outside. Wind and rain whipped through the room, spraying her shivering body.

He would find her. He always found her.

She heard footsteps in the hallway and knew he was coming for her. Kerry willed her shaking body to settle and peered over the top of the bed. The doorknob rattled as he tried to open it. She'd locked it to keep him at bay. Kerry hunkered back down behind the bed, squeezed her eyes shut, and squished herself into the corner behind the nightstand, hoping the long silk drapes would provide her some cover. She prayed he would leave or that she would wake up and be safely on the plane beside

Dante. Her pounding heart threatened to burst out of her chest. Her breath came in short ragged gasps.

Then she heard it.

Silence.

Kerry stilled and strained to hear noises around her, but there was nothing. No AJ bursting through the door. No more storm outside. Hope glimmered cruelly in her mind. Was it over? She latched on to that wispy bit of optimism and struggled to squelch the all too familiar fear that nagged at her. She opened one eye and found the room empty with a beam of sunlight streaming through the window. The blue silk drapes fluttered lightly by her feet. Kerry unfolded her stiff body and stood slowly on unsteady legs.

She leaned back into the corner, allowing herself time to register the sudden change to her surroundings. The room was once again serene. No evidence of the nightmare remained. Her breathing slowed, and she closed her eyes, listening to lull of the ocean. The cry of seagulls, familiar and soothing, calmed her soul and chased away the last shards of fear. The remaining bit of tension flowed from her tired body, while the warm sea air brushed long strands of hair across her face, and the beginnings of a smile played on her lips.

A dream, *she breathed.* Finally I'm having a dream. Not a nightmare. Thank you. *The words rushed from her lips in one huge sigh of relief.*

You're welcome. *The familiar voice, deep and male, floated around her in the ocean breeze.*

Her eyes flew open. Dante. She looked wildly around the room, but he wasn't there. She even went so far as to look under the bed and in the closet. He was nowhere in sight, but she knew he was there. She could feel his energy around her, enveloping her like a warm blanket. She wandered back to the open window and looked out at the beach below, and that's when she saw it. Sitting there on the sand was a giant red fox. The same fox she had seen when Dante touched her.

It sat perfectly still, staring back at her with enormous amber eyes, which burned brightly in the sunlight. Its thick red fur fluttered in the breeze, and its long bushy tail swished slowly. They stared at one another for what seemed like an eternity. She found herself inexplicably drawn to it, mesmerized by its gleaming eyes. She couldn't have looked away even if she wanted to—and she didn't want to. The warm ocean breeze brushed her long hair off of her face. The sky outside her window swirled with unnatural shades of lavenders and blues, and Kerry found herself blanketed by a serenity she'd never experienced. Peace. This must be what peace feels like.

The storm is over, Kerry. *Dante's seductive voice surrounded her as the unusual animal trotted away down the beach.* Sleep. *Kerry closed her eyes, lifted her face to the sun, and surrendered to the tranquility.*

Chapter 4

DANTE WOKE UP FROM HIS NAP ON THE PLANE FEELING hopeful for the first time in years. Finally, after so much time and so many failed efforts, she had recognized and acknowledged him in the dream realm. Not only had she seen him, but she'd heard him as well. It had been their first true connection. He'd hoped that when she woke up there would be some residual effects of their shared experience.

He awoke before she did, and his heart ached at the look of serenity on her lovely face. Her mouth curved in a delicate smile, and one lock of long dark hair rested along her high cheekbone. In that moment she reminded him of Snow White. He hated to wake her and disturb what was certainly her first peaceful sleep in weeks, but they were last people left on the plane. The flight crew hovered impatiently by the cockpit, obviously eager to clean and ready it for the next group of travelers.

He whispered her name softly, but she didn't stir. After several low whispers he decided to speak with her as he would any other Amoveo—telepathically. Would she hear him? She had a very strong mental barrier that he'd been barely able to crack. However, their connection in the dream realm proved she was beginning to let down her defenses. He took a deep breath and tentatively reached out to her mind with his.

Kerry. Her brow knitted together, and she moaned

softly. A smile crept over his face as he realized she could hear him. He let out the breath he'd been holding. *Kerry. It's time to wake up, princess.*

Kerry's eyes flew open wide, and her gaze immediately locked with his. She sat up quickly and pushed the hair from her face—a look of confusion swiftly replaced with obvious disdain for her traveling companion. She made a sound of disgust. "Don't call me princess."

Dante chuckled and stood up, gathering his belongings. She hadn't even realized she'd heard him in her mind. He glanced at the flight attendant with the plastered-on smile that couldn't hide her annoyance no matter how much she tried. Her energy waves filled the plane and were giving him a headache. Usually he was very good at filtering human emotions, but Kerry had him distracted in more ways than one. He stole a look at her, wondering if human emotion impacted her the way it did all Amoveo. The pained look he saw on her face was answer enough.

"Are you alright?" he asked quietly.

Kerry shook her head, waving him off. "Just sick of traveling I guess. I have a bit of a headache." She squeezed her eyes shut and rubbed at her temples, trying to relieve some of the discomfort.

Dante turned his attention to the sour-puss flight attendant. "Sorry we're holding you up ma'am," he said with the most charming smile he could muster. He knew the effect he had on most women, and now was as good a time as any to use it to his advantage. Dante flirted shamelessly with her, and almost immediately the energy she gave off changed. He felt his own headache ease and knew that Kerry would be feeling better as well.

"It's quite alright. You and Ms. Smithson take your time," she said with a coquettish grin. "I'll be at the door of the plane. If you need anything at all just let me know."

Dante turned around and was surprised to find Kerry standing right behind him. Her arms were crossed tightly over her breasts, and her intense eyes glittered with anger.

"If you're done flirting with the stewardess, would you mind getting the hell out of my way? I'd like to get off the plane sometime this century." The irritation in her voice matched the look on her face.

"No need to get jealous." He smirked, and before she could respond, he turned and led the way out of the plane. Kerry followed him into the terminal, while muttering some very painful suggestions about where he could stick his comments.

They made their way through the midafternoon Sunday travelers with surprising ease. They reached the baggage claim area, and Dante waved at Peter, who'd been waiting for him them as planned. Peter was the driver for Inferno Securities and Dante's right-hand man. He traveled wherever Dante needed him. As a former NYPD detective he had the best defensive driving skills Dante had ever seen.

Over the past few years he had become not only an asset to the business, but a good friend as well. He greeted them both with a big smile, and his gaze landed directly on Kerry. While he certainly couldn't blame Pete for staring at her, something dark inside of him began to stir. Jealousy? He was jealous? Shit.

"It's good to see you, sir." Although he spoke to Dante, he hadn't taken his eyes off of Kerry. The two men shook hands, and Dante positioned himself closely to Kerry.

"And who is this handsome devil?" Kerry smiled sweetly at Pete, and Dante felt the darkness bubble up. Peter was handsome and had a welcoming, easy smile that women loved. Dante straightened his back against the unfamiliar jealousy.

"Peter. I'd like you to meet Ms.—"

"Kerry Smithson. Of course. Every red-blooded man on the planet knows who this lovely lady is," he said with a smile and a nod. "It's a pleasure to meet you, ma'am." He hadn't tried to shake her hand. Her "germ phobia" was fuel for the tabloid fire, and as a result, very well known.

"The pleasure is all mine, Pete." She winked and delivered a smile that Dante wished had been for him. This was going to be nightmare if she insisted on flirting with every man in New Orleans. Dante had the overwhelming urge to punch Pete's lights out, throw Kerry over his shoulder, and take her out of here.

She was right. He was a Neanderthal.

Great.

"Pete, stop flirting with our client, and go pull the car around," he said as casually as possible, although he knew it sounded harsher than he wanted. "Ms. Smithson and I will get the bags and meet you out front."

"Yes sir, Mr. Coltari." He gave an exaggerated salute and nod before he left.

"Oh, cut the Mr. Coltari crap," he called after him.

Dante and Kerry walked over to the bag carousel to the sound of Pete chuckling his way out the door. Dante refocused his attention on the travelers around them, scanning their minds, assuring no hidden threat loomed. Nothing stood out except for the few people who had recognized her. He would never understand the human obsession with fame. He could, however, understand why someone would notice Kerry. The mixture of her stature and undeniable beauty conjured up the expression *tall drink of water*. For Dante, there couldn't have been a more appropriate way to describe her, since his thirst for her increased with every passing moment.

They stood there for a minute or two in silence, watching the bags of varying sizes ride round and round, waiting for someone to claim them. Very quickly Dante felt Kerry's eyes on him, studying him. He looked down into her dark eyes, and his heart flip-flopped.

He was in big trouble.

How the hell could he keep her safe if she had him all twisted up? The knowing smile on her face told him she knew exactly what kind of effect she had on him. He cleared his throat and turned his attention back to the bags passing on the conveyor belt.

"So, Mr. Coltari?" He shot Kerry a look of disapproval, but all it did was elicit an amused smile. "What's his deal?" She nodded toward the door.

"What do you mean?" He spotted her massive bags and hoisted them effortlessly from the conveyor belt.

"Single? Married?" she asked all too innocently.

Anger and jealousy came over him with shocking intensity. Dante spun around to face her and struggled to keep his eyes from shifting. The satisfied smile that played at her lips cooled his anger, but fueled his desire. She said that just to see if she'd get a reaction out of him. Someone was getting brave. The little minx was playing with him like a cat would play with a mouse. Well, he was no mouse.

"I don't think that's anything you need to worry about, Ms. Smithson." He kept his voice low and his body dangerously close to hers. Surprisingly, she didn't retreat. "Our employees do not fraternize with clients."

"Really?" Her voice, soft and tantalizing, threatened his control. His body hardened as her gaze boldly wandered down the length of him and back up again. Her eyes locked with his. She leaned in and whispered softly, "Now that's a damn shame." Smiling, she turned on her heels and headed toward the exit. Rendered speechless by her unexpected flirtation, Dante followed her out, carrying both the bags and a raging hard-on.

The ride to their hotel consisted of friendly chatter between Peter and Kerry about life in New York City. The subways, the crime, the best places to get great food were all touched on. Dante stayed quiet, afraid his jealousy at their easy banter would be revealed. Why couldn't he talk to her without it turning into some kind of sparring match? He *was* jealous of Pete. Not because he thought Kerry really wanted him, but because she was at ease with him so quickly.

For the first time since he found her, the energy she gave off seemed less encumbered and lighter. He wanted more than anything to be the source of her happiness. He couldn't blame her. Everyone felt comfortable around Pete. He was the guy that could talk to anyone, and he envied him for that. Dante didn't envy humans often, and he did not want to become familiar with it. In fact, he'd had about enough.

"Peter, while we're checking in and getting Ms.

Smithson settled, I want you to do a dry run to the shoot location. Make sure you have more than one route in and out."

"You got it, boss. Anything else?" Peter kept his eyes on the traffic ahead.

Dante shook his head. "No. The rest is on me."

"Oh great." Kerry voiced her displeasure from the backseat. "I still don't know why Sam and Malcolm hired you. I do not need a bodyguard. Sure, I get threats, but so does anyone with even the littlest bit of notoriety. I think this whole thing is ridiculous," she said, rolling her eyes.

Dante threw a glance over his shoulder. "What threats?" Dread crept up his belly.

"Oh, just the usual kooks sending weirdo love notes." She waved her hand dismissively. "Arthur, my rep from the agency, sends anything really weird to the cops. I've asked him to not even tell me about them anymore."

"I'll have to get good old Artie to bring me up to speed, won't I?"

"Oh please." Kerry laughed out loud. "Arthur is not happy about you. Not at all. And he'll really be pissed if you call him that. It's Arthur," she said, dragging out his name dramatically.

"Why would he have a problem with you having extra security and filling me in?" He kept his voice even, but felt his irritation rising by the second. As if another man, a human, could keep information from him about his own mate.

"Number one, the agency didn't pick you. Sam and Malcolm did. The agency is not a big fan of strangers coming in and telling them how to handle their clients.

Arthur definitely isn't." She shrugged. "What can I say? He's a control freak. But a damn good rep," she added quickly.

Dante turned all the way around in his seat and locked his large amber eyes onto her startled ones. It took every ounce of resolve he had to resist shifting into his clan form. "You may be his client, princess." He kept his voice low and steady. "But you're my responsibility. I don't care what this guy likes or doesn't like. Your safety is my single most important consideration. He will give me all of the information I need. Period." Dante turned around in his seat and shoved his mirrored aviators on as his eyes shifted.

"Jeez. Is he this bossy with everyone, Pete, or is it just me?" she asked with a short laugh.

"He's the boss," Pete replied with a friendly wink in the rearview mirror.

Dante expected her to say that he wasn't her boss, but she simply laughed softly. The light musical sound of her laughter instantly loosened the knots in his stomach. Then it dawned on him. Without realizing it, she sent him reassuring waves of energy. A hint of a smile played at his lips, and his eyes shifted back to their human state. Their connection grew stronger with each passing hour; with every smile and glance she came closer to being his. Could it be possible that he was the reason she felt better? He almost dared not entertain the thought.

The sleek black Lexus turned onto Royal Street and pulled up in front of the Hotel Monteleone. The Monteleone was one of the oldest hotels in the French Quarter with a rich history and even richer clientele. Dante hopped out of the car before it had even come to a full stop. The hot damp Louisiana air clung to him the moment he stepped onto the curb, and he once again cursed the dark suit that stuck to his skin like glue. He scanned the street around them. Satisfied the area was secure, Dante pulled the door open and was greeted by the sweet scent of her. Heat flared low in his belly from one whiff, all lilacs and spice. His heated gaze caught hers as he offered his hand to help her from the car.

Dante knew the odds were slim that she would risk touching him, but he had to give her the choice. She sat motionless for several seconds, her face set in a mask of concentration as though she were weighing her options. She sucked in her breath and fear flickered briefly across her face. Finally, after what seemed like an eternity, she accepted his offering and placed her delicate hand in his much larger one.

With great care and tenderness, Dante closed his fingers around hers and quickly helped her from the car. When they connected flesh to flesh her eyes widened, and for the briefest moment he saw a spark of recognition there. Kerry stepped onto the curb, instantly withdrew her hand, and held it to her chest. She licked her lips nervously and tore her gaze from his.

"Thank you, Mr. Coltari." Her voice wavered, and she slipped her large sunglasses on.

"You are welcome, Ms. Smithson." He gave a curt nod and followed her into the hotel, grateful for the strides they were making and hopeful for all that was to come.

Once they stepped inside the hotel, Kerry breathed an audible sigh of relief. She stood in the large foyer, allowing the cool air to refresh both her body and mind. The damp Louisiana air outside still stuck to her body, and Dante's touch stuck to her soul. When he'd offered his hand to her she almost refused, but there was something in his eyes that put her at ease—a sense of longing that was all too familiar. She had wanted to find out if their previous encounter had been a fluke, and he had given her that very opportunity.

When her fingers touched his, the same delicious sensation spread over her skin. Her flesh immediately bathed in sweet honey. There was no pain. There was just exquisite sweetness. Thick and warm, it washed over her. The vision that accompanied it felt happily familiar as it flashed into her mind. Kerry wasn't afraid to see it. On the contrary, she had been hoping to see it.

It was the fox. The same fox from her dream this afternoon.

Her nap on the plane had been the first time since the attack that she'd had a dream, opposed to a nightmare. The undisturbed sleep had rejuvenated her for the days ahead, but her curiosity about Dante was quickly becoming something of an obsession. Who could blame her? Anyone would be primed and ready after thirty years of pent-up sexual frustration.

Kerry waited for the desk clerk to complete her check-in and stole a look at Dante. He possessed a magnificent, albeit somewhat frightening, presence. He stood in front of a massive ivory column, turning his head almost imperceptibly, presumably tracking everyone in the room. His dark suit and entire demeanor were in stark contrast to the creamy white pillars and scrolled designs of the extravagant lobby. He held himself ramrod straight with his hands folded in front of him and had on those ridiculous mirrored sunglasses.

Kerry stifled a giggle.

He looked like a cross between The Terminator and a secret service agent—a really *hot* secret service agent. The man looked as though he had not an ounce of body fat under that suit. She suspected there was nothing under there but muscle and sinewy strength. A far cry from her own soft body, she mused. Model or not, she had insecurities like any other woman. Early in her career she'd tried to maintain that skinny, hanger-like body for modeling, but that just wasn't in the cards. Once she embraced her fuller figure and her curves, things just started to pop.

She smiled. She'd like to pop Dante.

Heat crept up her cheeks at the memory of how blatantly she flirted with him at the airport. She had practically propositioned him, and by no means did she flirt like that with men. *Ever*. What was the point since it could never go anywhere?

Dante, however, was a different story entirely.

She couldn't take her eyes off of him. Everything about him enticed her. He conducted himself in an almost regal manner. His confidence bordered on arrogance, but she sensed tenderness there as well, although she imagined that most people never saw it. She watched the muscles in his jaw clench, and even that flickering movement conjured up vivid images of what the rest of him must look like under that suit.

Her mind rapidly filled with all kinds of things she'd like to do with him. All those things she'd seen in movies and heard about from girlfriends, things she never ever thought she'd be able to do.

Until now. Meeting Dante had changed all the rules.

Her pornographic daydream was interrupted by the sound of the desk clerk clearing his throat. Startled, she jumped, horrified that everyone in that lobby knew exactly what she'd been thinking. She brushed at her chin, afraid that there might actually be drool on it. Her head snapped back, and she found herself looking at the clerk, who couldn't have been more than twenty-one. His big, brown puppy dog eyes looked at her expectantly.

"Ms. Smithson?" The young man looked around as though he was telling her state secrets and kept his voice just barely above a whisper. "We have you all checked into the Tennessee Williams suite. The bottled water and fresh flowers are already up there, as requested."

Kerry rolled her eyes and slid her sunglasses onto her head, pushing those few pesky strands of hair off her face. She smiled broadly and leaned into the starstruck boy. "What's your name, sweetie?"

"Brent, ma'am." He swallowed, and she couldn't help but notice that little beads of sweat had begun to form at his brow. "I'm new here," he added quickly. "My girlfriend, Penelope, is one of your biggest fans. Me too, of course."

Kerry couldn't help but take pity on the poor kid. After all, her reputation as being a coldhearted bitch was the only thing people had heard or read about her. His eyes grew even rounder, and he looked as though he would piss his pants right there at the desk.

"Okay, Brent." She kept her voice as light as possible. "I don't need special water or fresh flowers brought to my room every day. That's my agency's style, not mine.

I just want to have my privacy and enjoy The Big Easy for the few days that I'm here. Sound good?"

Brent nodded, and a big smile spread across his sweet round face. Kerry winked, gathered her things, and made her way over to Dante. A bellman approached to help with the bags, but Dante quickly dismissed him and led the way to the elevators.

They rode up to the fourteenth floor in silence, and Kerry found herself feeling awkward and unsure. She felt like a high school girl on a date for the first time. She cringed at her own foolishness. Jeez, what a dork.

The ding of the elevator signified arrival to their floor and broke the silence.

"So why is it called the Tennessee Williams suite?" he asked while they made their way down the corridor.

"All of the suites are named after authors." Kerry fished the card key out of the paper folder and slid it into the door.

He grunted what must have been his version of saying he understood as he pushed past her into the massive suite. The large living room was well appointed with a sofa and armchairs in varying hues of cream and beige. A dining table loomed largely on the left side of the room with an enormous crystal chandelier dangling overhead. The towering windows were elegantly adorned in floral drapes fringed with tassels.

Kerry closed the door behind them and made her way into the similarly decorated and cavernous bedroom. The king-size bed looked exceptionally welcoming. She shook her head as Dante proceeded to look around every corner and in every closet. He even checked the bathroom, but for what she wasn't sure.

Although it was certainly big enough for someone to hide in, he found nothing, and made his way back to the living room.

"While I'm getting settled here," she called from the bathroom, "why don't you go on downstairs and get yourself checked in. I'm sure you've managed to get the suite next door," she mumbled under her breath.

"No. I'll be staying here," he said absentmindedly, looking out the window at the bustling street below.

Kerry dropped her makeup bag onto the smooth granite counter and looked at herself in the mirror. "Is he crazy?" she whispered to her own reflection. She stormed into the living room to ask him the same question. "Are you crazy? You're not staying in my room with me." Her body trembled with outrage, and as much as she hated to admit it, some excitement. She crossed her arms in an effort to quiet her shaking limbs.

He didn't even turn around, just continued staring out the damn window.

"I can't very well protect you while staying in another room at the hotel." His voice was irritatingly calm. When he finally turned around, she noticed he'd taken off his stupid sunglasses. "I'll sleep out here on the sofa," he said, gesturing to it. "Besides, I don't sleep much anyway. I'm really more of a night creature." A smile spread slowly across his face as he closed the distance between them. "Don't worry, princess. You'll be perfectly safe."

His hulking frame loomed largely in front of her, and she felt positively tiny. She never felt tiny. *Ever*. Would every single encounter with this man bring a new sensation? Kerry's tongue darted out, nervously licking her lips. Her breath caught in her chest, and her heart raced wildly. She brushed that pesky stray lock of hair off her face and struggled to keep her expression neutral.

When Kerry opened her mouth to protest, Dante placed a fingertip on her lips and shook his head slowly. She sucked in her breath, and her body shuddered faintly at the exquisite effect of his touch. Sweet, honeyed warmth radiated from her lips, flickered over skin, and flashed through the rest of her body. Did every woman feel this way when a man touched her? Is this how it's supposed to be?

God, she hoped so.

Kerry's eyes fluttered closed as he gently stroked her bottom lip with his thumb, and his fingers brushed her cheek. The vision of the fox floated gently into her mind. Its amber eyes glowed brighter, and with every featherlight stroke, exquisite pleasure rippled through her body. Too tired to fight it and exhausted from years of isolation, she allowed herself to give in. Eyes closed, she leaned into his hand and surrendered to the seductive sensations swirling through her.

She didn't know why he could touch her this way. She didn't care. All she knew was that she never wanted it to end. As if he'd read her mind, Dante held her face with both hands and stroked her cheeks softly. He treaded lightly over the virgin flesh. The rough texture of his fingers against her soft skin created delicious friction.

"You have nothing to fear from me," he said. The sound of his voice washed over her, enticing and erotic. He leaned in, and his breath blew hotly against her ear. She moaned softly in response, sinking deeper into the sweet honey of his touch. She hung there, blissfully succumbing to it, until one word floated into her mind and ripped her from the soft sensations. *Princess*.

Her body stilled. Her eyes flew open, and she launched herself away from him.

"What the fuck?" she whispered through trembling lips. She backed away blindly and nearly fell over the large armchair. He didn't move or try to come after her, but kept his expression neutral. Dante stood there as though speaking to her with his mind was a totally normal thing to do.

"Did you just—?" She stammered helplessly and pointed at him accusingly. "Say something, for Christ's sake! Don't just stand there looking at me like I'm crazy."

He stayed stone still. His deep amber eyes stared back at her as he held her in his unrelenting gaze. She stood her ground, hands planted firmly on her hips, waiting for him, daring him to deny it. The silence that pulsed between them seemed almost palpable. She wanted to scream and pound him in the chest, make him tell her she wasn't crazy—and then she heard it.

Yes.

That one word slammed into her mind. His lips hadn't moved, but she had heard him. One word. She never thought that one word could ever sound that loud.

The son of a bitch was telepathic.

She had heard of telepathy but never personally experienced it. Her whole life had just gone from weird to completely fucking nuts in a matter of minutes.

"You, of all people, should know that the world is full of surprises, and not everyone is who or what they seem to be." His voice, calm and even, shattered the silence of the hotel room.

He sounded so nonchalant that Kerry wanted to punch him in the nose. Before she could batter him with questions, they were abruptly interrupted by a loud knock at the door, which elicited a yelp from Kerry. Dante cursed under his breath but kept his penetrating stare trained on Kerry. For a moment neither moved, but when the persistent visitor knocked a second time, Dante reluctantly stalked over to answer the door.

He peered through the keyhole. "Who is it?" Dante barked.

"It's Arthur, Kerry's representative from the agency," he snapped impatiently. As if everyone on the planet should know who he is. Typical Arthur. "Open the door!"

Kerry smirked and shook her head as Dante opened the door for him. His mouth was set in a grim line as he looked down at a visibly annoyed Arthur, who stood all of five foot seven and couldn't have weighed more than a hundred and fifty pounds. The man hadn't had a carb since the new millennium. His perfectly coiffed salt-and-pepper hair glistened with sweat, and the look on his face was one of flat-out annoyance.

Arthur removed the silk handkerchief from his jacket pocket and dabbed at his forehead, while giving Dante the once over. "You must be the bodyguard." He gestured up at Dante with his handkerchief before stuffing it back into the pocket of his linen blazer. "Kerry sent me a text about you." He looked Dante up and down, nodding his approval. "Well, you certainly are big. Probably put the fear of God in people by looking at them." He sniffed. "You're also gorgeous," he said with a look Kerry had seen far too many times. "Do you ever do any modeling?"

"What? No," Dante sputtered.

Kerry covered her mouth to keep from laughing out loud.

A huge smile cracked Arthur's face as he did nothing to suppress his amusement at Dante's reaction. "What's your name, handsome?"

Dante narrowed his eyes. "Dante Coltari, President of Inferno Securities." His voice was quiet but carried strength behind it that no one would question.

"Arthur Lovegood." He offered a well-manicured hand to Dante. "Do you shake hands, or are you like our girl?"

Dante didn't move, and his features darkened. "Our girl?"

"Jesus." Kerry let out an exasperated sigh and went over to break things up before Dante beat the shit out of him. "Dante," she said, stepping between them. "This is my rep from my agency, Arthur. Arthur, this is Dante, er... I mean Mr. Coltari." She fumbled over her words like some love-struck teenager, and the laughter in Dante's eyes told her that he enjoyed it.

"Dante will do just fine," he said with a curt nod. He stepped aside and reluctantly allowed Arthur to make his way into the room. "Nice to meet you... *Artie*."

Arthur winced and cast Dante a lethal look that he usually saved for rival reps. "It's Arthur, but you can call me Mr. Lovegood," he snipped and without a second glance settled into one of the large armchairs as if he owned the place.

Dante closed the door with a bit more force than necessary. Kerry didn't need to touch either of the men in the room to figure out what they were thinking. Dante positioned himself in front of the door in his *Terminator* pose as Kerry made herself comfortable on the couch. She kicked off her shoes and tucked her legs up under her, shedding all formalities. This day, and her life, had gotten weirder by the second, and until today she hadn't thought that was possible.

"So, Arthur, to what do I owe this pleasure?" She tried to keep her voice light, but despite her best efforts it still belied her weariness.

"There's been a change of plans, darling. We're shooting at a different house tomorrow. Here's the new location information." He pulled an envelope from the inside pocket of his jacket. Kerry reached out to take it but ended up with a fist full of air. Dante had beaten her to it.

Kerry made a scoffing noise. "Excuse me. That is for me unless you plan on standing around in your underwear tomorrow." While the comment was meant to be a jab at Dante, it backfired because all she could do now was picture *him* in his underwear. Great.

He shot her a skeptical look and opened the envelope.

"You're fast too." Arthur made a short sound of approval. "That is rather impressive. Most fellows as big as you don't move that swiftly." He pulled the handkerchief from his pocket and dabbed at his forehead again.

Dante didn't look up from the paper. "I need the location information," he said abruptly. "This isn't in the French Quarter or the Garden District." He looked up and cast an accusing look at Arthur. "I should've been given this information the moment it changed. Not the day before we have to be there."

"Don't get your boxers in a twist, handsome." He

waved his silk hankie in Dante's direction. "I just found out about the change myself. Apparently the client decided to use this location instead. It's really not a monumental problem." He sighed dramatically. "Relax. Have a seat and some civilized conversation." He motioned for him to sit, but Dante ignored him. He looked as though he wanted to squash Arthur with one hand, and if looks could kill, he would be six feet under.

Kerry frowned and fiddled with her earring. "Well, where is it then?" She couldn't squelch the anxiety that crawled up the back of her neck and absentmindedly touched it as though she could wipe away the feeling.

Dante folded the paper and placed it inside his jacket. "It's an old plantation house out on the bayou." He turned to her, and his features softened. "It will be fine. I'll call Peter and have him go check out the new site."

She looked away from him hastily, tucked her hair behind her ear, and turned her attention to Arthur. She could get lost in Dante's big amber eyes, which seemed far more dangerous than some house on the bayou.

"The bayou? Hold on a second." She put her hands up, silencing both men. "Do you mean like near swamps where there are alligators and bugs?" Her voice rose and bordered on hysterical. She knew she sounded irrational, but she couldn't help it. This entire situation had her off kilter and made her more uncomfortable with every passing second. "I hate nature. Talk about cooties." She stood up, brushed past them, and made a beeline for the bar in her bedroom. "I'm an indoor girl," she shouted, while wrestling the top off the miniature bottle of wine.

The sound of Arthur's condescending laughter taunted

her from the living room. "You'll be shooting at an old house, honey. No one's going to make you swim with swamp creatures." He looked at his watch, and with a huff, removed his frame gracefully from the chair. "I've got to get going. Don't forget. We're taking the clients to dinner tonight. Why don't you and your bodyguard here meet us downstairs in The Carousel Bar at seven o'clock?"

Dante's features darkened. "What dinner? There was no mention of dinner on the itinerary I was provided."

"Plans change. Try to keep up," he said with a snap of his fingers. "See you downstairs at seven sharp." Arthur sashayed over to the door, but before leaving he threw one last comment over his shoulder. "Remember. Bring Purell if you need to. You'll have to shake hands and make nice with the clients."

Swearing under her breath, she emptied the contents of the miniature bottle into a large glass. This whole trip was a mistake. She took this assignment because she had hoped for a few relaxing days in The Big Easy. She figured on a one-day shoot at an old mansion in the Garden District, maybe a ride on the riverboat, and if she really got lucky, a late-night swim in the Monteleone's rooftop pool.

Now she was going out in the middle of nowhere to be surrounded by alligators. Then, of course, there's the dinner with clients, which is a different danger altogether. Not to mention Dante, the handsome, telepathic enigma that had her head spinning. She squeezed her eyes shut and drained the contents of her glass.

"It'll be alright. You'll be perfectly safe. I promise." His voice, low and soothing, blanketed her. She turned to find him filling the doorway of her bedroom. He'd once again appeared silently next to her. Arthur had hit the nail on the head. Dante was fast, but he was also quiet.

Kerry let out a short laugh and cast a sidelong glance at Dante. "Yeah, right." Who would keep her safe from him? He moved toward her, but she put her hand up, stopping him from coming any closer. "Please don't," she said through a hitching breath. "I really need to be alone right now, and if possible, take a nap before this insipid dinner tonight."

She turned her back on him and busied herself, pulling various things out of her suitcase. She didn't trust herself to look into those big eyes because she may very well throw herself into his arms and ask him to make it all go away. How pathetic. She cringed at her own weakness. She needed to be alone and get her bearings back. She'd been alone her entire life, and solitude was her comfort zone. At the moment, Dante crowded her personal space in every possible sense.

He nodded curtly. "As you wish. No one will disturb you."

Kerry looked up just as the bedroom door clicked shut. He'd left her alone just like she'd wanted, but now she had the overwhelming urge to call him back. Kerry let out a sound of self-loathing and frustration at her erratic emotions. She dropped the clothing into her suitcase and shoved it to the other side of the enormous bed, leaving her ample room to curl up in the soft, white bedding. She crawled into the dark cocoon of the covers. Her mind and body were exhausted from the day's developments, and all she wanted to do was sleep.

Her thoughts wandered to the fox from her dreams

and her visions. She longed for the sense of peace that always seemed to accompany it. She saw the gorgeous animal in her dream when she touched Dante. Maybe the huge red fox represented him in her dreams? She had to admit, he was pretty damn foxy in the flesh. Kerry smiled, yawned deeply, and struggled to find the path back to that dream. As she drifted to sleep Dante's voice rang in her mind. *Sleep tight, princess.*

"Don't call me princess," she mumbled as the dream realm captured her and carried her away.

Chapter 5

THE PUNISHER WALKED DOWN THE DARK COBBLESTONE road, paying no attention to the occasional drunken revelers stumbling through the street. New Orleans, even outside of Bourbon Street, had drunks on almost every corner. The Punisher brushed past them with barely a glance in their direction. After several blocks, the desired destination, a tiny voodoo shop, appeared at the edge of the French Quarter.

The Punisher pulled open the old creaking door, and a bell tinkled loudly, alerting the shopkeeper of a new arrival. The Punisher stood silently in the midst of the shop, hands stuffed tightly in the pockets of the long trench coat. The shelves along the walls were lined with hundreds of colorful bottles, candles, statuettes, and crystals—each item tagged and holding the promise of love, money, or power.

Within a few moments, a tall, thin woman emerged from a curtained doorway. Her dark ebony skin stood out in contrast to the white robes she wore. She had a multicolored scarf wrapped around her hair, and long dreadlocks stuck out in various places. She smiled brightly, and her violet eyes twinkled with something that resembled mischief.

"Hello, *cher*." Her voice sounded different. She wasn't Cajun. She had an accent from the islands. "What can I do for ya, darlin'?"

Their customer stood silently for a moment, hoping the memorized words were correct. "From Bourbon to Royal the drinks are sweet, and only the foolish wander down those streets."

The woman smiled, flashing large white teeth. She reminded the Punisher of a shark. Wordlessly, she pulled back the curtain and gestured for the Punisher to follow. Once in the tiny room she pushed a panel on the back wall, and a hidden door revealed itself. The woman nodded silently and motioned for her patron to go through the door.

A cold, damp stone room lay beyond the doorway, empty except for an old black man that sat at a wooden table. On either side were shelves. Each held one glass bottle.

The old man gestured to the chair across from him.

"Sit down, my friend." His voice sounded raspy and matched his crusty appearance. "What do you want from Beaumont?"

The Punisher eyed the old man, whose eyes were clouded completely white. He was probably blind. His wizened arthritic hands were wrapped around an ancient ceramic coffee mug, and his clothes seemed as old and worn as he did.

"I have been told you have a binding spell."

The old man laughed. It was a dry sound, like fall leaves blowing along the sidewalk. "What, or who, do you wish to bind? Vampire? Shifter? Werewolf? There are many unique creatures that walk this earth." He leaned in and lowered his voice. "But you already know that, don't you?" He laughed again, and the old wooden chair creaked in protest.

"A shifter." The words came out harsher than

intended and echoed in the cavernous room, but that only served to elicit a bigger smile from Beaumont.

"Of course." Without looking, he reached behind him, grabbed the bottle from the second shelf, and held it out to the Punisher.

The smooth glass container, no larger than a perfume bottle, looked cool and smooth. The power held inside made the Punisher's heart pound with anticipation.

"Sprinkle this on the shifter, and you suspend all of their abilities for one moon's cycle. Get your shifter to ingest in a drink or their food this, and they will be bound in their animal form for all eternity."

The Punisher reached out for the magical powder, but Beaumont snatched it back. Interesting. Perhaps the old man wasn't as blind as he let on, the sneaky old bastard.

"There is the matter of payment." Beaumont's smile had faded. He uncurled his other hand, waiting for his money.

The Punisher took out a huge wad of cash and placed it firmly in his gnarled hand. Beaumont moved quickly and grabbed the Punisher by the wrist. He pulled his customer closer and lowered his voice to hushed tones.

"Remember," he cautioned. "All magic has a price. Use this dark magic, and be prepared to receive its opposite."

The Punisher tugged hard and got free of the old man's surprisingly strong grip. Leaving the room quickly with the expensive purchase tucked safely away, the Punisher uttered one last thing. "Don't worry about me, old man. That will mean good magic will come my way, and that sounds fine to me."

Chapter 6

DANTE STARED AT THE ADDRESS ON THE PAPER AND couldn't squash the sense of dread that continued to gnaw at him. He knew this property because it was the same address Malcolm had given him before they left. It was owned by a member of the Vasullus Family, Joseph Vasullus. They were the only human family, other than the Caedo, who knew about his people. The Vasullus worked with the Amoveo for centuries to help keep their existence a secret. Two members of the Vasullus family even served on the Council with a representative from each of the ten clans. Knowing the house was owned by a Vasullus should've made him feel better. However, it had exactly the opposite effect.

The revelation of the Purist Movement had changed everything. The Purists considered the hybrids an abomination of their race, and his father said there were others that felt as strongly as he did. The scar in Dante's chest burned at the memory of his father's betrayal, and he rubbed at it absentmindedly. He'd even been willing to sacrifice his own son when he'd gotten in the way. If there were Amoveo willing to kill their own people to keep the race pure, then there could easily be Vasullus who felt the same way.

Dante stared intently at the address on the paper. What were the odds that Kerry's shoot would just happen to be switched to a property owned by a Vasullus family member? Dante scoffed audibly and tossed the paper onto the table in front of him. He didn't believe in coincidences. This entire situation reeked of trouble, and it looked like he was going to need some help.

There were only a select few he could trust. Malcolm and Samantha were obviously at the top of his list, but he certainly didn't want to ruin their newlywed bliss with what could be a dangerous situation for Sam as well. Richard, their prince, was aware of the Purists, but Salinda was pregnant, and Dante didn't want to take him away from his wife at such a delicate time.

Only two other Amoveo could be trusted with the safety of his mate: Steven and William. Not only were they his two best friends since childhood, but they had also been enlisted to help Malcolm when Sam was at risk. Aside from Richard, Samantha, and Malcolm, they were the only two Amoveo who knew of the Purist threat and of his father's betrayal. They all agreed that was the only way to sniff out the other traitors in the Purist sect. They didn't know who else could be trusted.

Dante sat up in the chair, closed his eyes, and reached out to Kerry's mind. The soothing rhythm of sleep pulsed around her. He smiled, and his tense muscles relaxed. He needed to be sure she was sleeping soundly before he called to his friends. The last thing he needed was Kerry walking out to find two strange men in the living room of her suite.

Satisfied that she would remain sleeping for a while, he withdrew from her mind and refocused his attention on creating a mental link with Steven and William. He established the link much more quickly than he ever had before. Connecting with Kerry had increased the strength of his abilities significantly.

Within minutes the air in the room thickened, and electricity crackled briefly as his two friends materialized before him. Dante opened his eyes and stood to greet his friends. Steven's friendly face immediately cracked with a huge smile, and William nodded curtly in his usual formal manner. The two men couldn't have been more different.

Steven, a member of the Coyote Clan, was open and friendly. His shaggy, sandy blond hair was as rumpled as his Rolling Stones T-shirt and ripped jeans. Steven's open and accessible demeanor worked well for him as a healer.

William was stuffy and Old World. His long blond hair, streaked with brown, was pulled back in a low ponytail. His slicked back hair matched the fitted pinstripe suit he almost always wore. William was a member of the Falcon Clan, specifically, the Gyrfalcon Clan. Dante always thought William had been born at the wrong time. He reminded him much more of the elders, not a man in his twenties. The Eagle and Falcon Clan members had a certain air about them.

"Thank you for coming," Dante said, keeping his voice low. He shook hands with both men and nodded toward Kerry's bedroom door. "She's asleep, so we should keep our voices down. Please have a seat."

William sat stiffly in the oversized chair, and Steven flopped himself easily into the corner of the couch. Dante stood. Too wound up to sit, he began to pace the room as he relayed his concerns to the two men. They listened intently as Dante explained who and what Kerry was. When he was finally finished he stood silently in front of them, watching and waiting for their reactions. As he expected, William's face remained serious, while Steven let out a low whistle.

"Another hybrid?" Steven's eyebrows knitted together. "I don't get it? Why didn't we pick up on that when we were at the beach watching out for Samantha? I saw Kerry then, but I didn't pick that up. Did you, Willie?"

Dante stifled a chuckle at the look on William's face. He hated being called Willie, and Steven always did it just to get a rise out of him. He had since they were kids.

William shot him a look through narrowed eyes. "No. I did not," he said in a voice laden with irritation. He shifted in his seat and cleared his throat. William hated being wrong. Dante was tempted to let him squirm but decided to let him off the hook.

"She's a powerful psychic, William. She has built and maintained an incredibly strong shield around herself." He shrugged one shoulder. "I don't even think she knows she's doing it, but it's been very effective in keeping her hidden all these years."

"That must be one hell of a shield." Steven leaned forward and rested his elbows on his wide spread legs. "She's in pictures all over the world. I can't believe none of us picked up on it."

"Especially you, Dante." William nodded toward him. "If she's really your mate," he said offhandedly.

Dante's eyes shifted and flared brightly. His gaze landed harshly on William. "She *is* my mate." His voice stayed just barely above a whisper. "You would do well to remember that."

William cocked his head and raised one eyebrow.

"I am merely suggesting that it seems odd you didn't recognize her as your mate when you saw her pictures," he said with a wave of his hand. "Really, Dante, do get a hold of yourself." He sniffed.

Dante breathed deeply and willed his eyes back to their human state. He stuffed his hands into his pockets and stalked over to the window, embarrassed for losing his temper like that. They were here to help him, and he was snapping at them like some moody teenager. William had touched a nerve because he was absolutely right. Dante hadn't known her from her pictures. It wasn't until he saw her in the flesh that he knew who and what she was.

"Wait a minute," Steven said. "What about the dream realm? Didn't you see her there?"

"No." Dante shook his head and turned back to face the two men. "I could feel her there, but I could never see her. It was, as you can imagine, incredibly frustrating. I didn't figure it out until I saw her with Samantha that day on the beach," he said quietly. "I recognized her energy signature. It was the same as the one that has haunted my dreams."

His mouth set in a grim line as he looked at both of the men who were nodding solemnly. They understood his frustration better than anyone. Neither had found their mates yet, and since they were approaching thirty, their time was running out. If too much time passed without finding their mates, they'd lose their abilities and would slowly die. It was a lonely, torturous, and painful demise that Dante wouldn't wish on anyone.

"William, I'll need you to keep watch from the air. The house is out on the bayou in a pretty remote area. If anything—and I mean anything—seems out of whack, you tell me, and I'm getting her out of there." Dante crossed over to them slowly, hoping that they would be willing to help. "So, can I count on your help for the next few days?"

William nodded his acceptance, and the muscles in Dante's neck immediately loosened. He then turned his attention to Steven. "I would feel especially grateful to have one of our best healers nearby."

"Absolutely," Steven said, smiling, but the smile quickly faded. "You don't think it's a coincidence. The shoot location, I mean?"

Dante shook his head. "Kerry's a hybrid, and the shoot just happens to be taking place at a home owned by one of the Vasullus family members?" he said skeptically. "I'd say that's a little too much of a coincidence, wouldn't you?"

"The Vasullus live to serve and protect our people," William scoffed. "Why would they want to hurt one of us? Even a hybrid?"

"I don't know, William. But I do know that I'm not willing to be complacent and risk her safety. Until we know more about the Vasullus who owns that house, we stick close." Dante's face remained as serious as his voice.

Steven nodded in agreement. "Malcolm did tell you that one of them lived down here. He must know more about them. We also have Amoveo kin that live here. Pasha Zankoff. She went to college with my sister. She's a member of the Tiger Clan." He smiled and wiggled his eyebrows suggestively.

William made a sound of disgust. "She isn't your mate, Steven. Really, show some dignity."

"Whatever man, she's still a hottie." William rolled his eyes, but Steven ignored him and continued. "She and her twin brother Boris own a little bar down here in the French Quarter, The Den. We could ask them for help."

"No!" Dante said sharply. "We can't be certain that they can be trusted. We don't know who else was working with my father." Frustration edged his voice, and he swore softly.

"Dante, we don't have to tell them who Kerry is. But they live here, and my guess is she and Boris could be pretty helpful. They must know the scoop on the guy who owns the house. And one other thing, fellas. They haven't found their mates yet either," he said pointedly. "If you ask me, the only Amoveo we can trust are the ones who are unmated like Willie and I."

"Our uncouth friend has a point."

"Thanks, Willie," Steven said with a smile.

"Piss off," William shot back.

Dante smiled at their familiar banter and let out a sigh. "You're right. We should find out everything we can. But I don't want them to know about Kerry. Not yet."

His friends stood up and faced him. The three remained silent for a moment as an unspoken fear of the unknown flowed between them. Their race's existence stood at a crucial point, the future uncertain for all of them. Dante stretched his arm out with his palm facing down. Steven, and then William, reached out and joined their hands with his. They closed their eyes, and together they silently uttered the ancient language. *Iunctus*. Each man proclaimed loyalty to the other, each willing to lay down his life and ensure the future of their race.

After William and Steven left, Dante decided to

investigate the client. Kerry had been hired as the new
face of Le Fleur Designs. Le Fleur was a fairly new
company, and it surprised him that they would be able
to afford Kerry as their spokeswoman. It seemed odd
that such a young company would hire a model of her
caliber. The designer, Jacqueline Petite, was a native of
New Orleans. Dante figured she must have some major
investors onboard to score a model like Kerry.

Much to his dismay, they specialized in high-end
lingerie, and he shifted in his seat as anger and jealously
reared their ugly heads. She would be prancing around
in underwear in front of perfect strangers? Other men?
The very idea of it ignited the crushing urge to smash
every piece of furniture in the suite. The rational side
of Dante's brain reminded him that this was her liveli-
hood, and she'd been doing this for her entire adult life.
Something told him Kerry would not find jealousy an attractive attribute and would only confirm her suspicion
that he was indeed a Neanderthal.

Dante leaned back in the chair and ran both hands
over his face. Various images of Kerry floated over the
computer screen. He laced his hands behind his head
and let out sigh of defeat. He knew modeling was her
business, but it didn't mean he had to like it. The shrill
of his cell phone interrupted his private pity party. Dante
snatched the phone from his pocket but kept his eyes
fixed on Kerry's image.

"Hello?" he barked.

"Hey boss. It's Pete. You okay?" Pete's familiar
voice snapped him back to reality. As Kerry's bodyguard, it was his job to keep her safe, not beat the shit
out of any man who looked at her.

"What? Yes." He fumbled over his words, embarrassed by his poorly veiled irritation. "I was just having a problem with the computer," he lied, slamming the laptop shut. "So how is it?"

"Well, I took a look around the new location," he began. "It's a pretty rural spot, and the place is really rundown, but we should be able to get in and out without a problem. It's privately owned. Get this. The old guy who owns this place lives in a tiny shed on the edge of the property. How's that for weird? He lets this big old house sit empty and get completely run down—but lives in a little shed. Word has it he works as one of the tarot readers on Jackson Square."

"Thanks, Pete." He let out an audible sigh. "Pick us up tomorrow morning at seven. She's got an eight o'clock call time, so that should get her out there in plenty of time."

"You got it, boss. "He was silent for a moment. "I have one question."

"Sure," he said absentmindedly. "What's up?"

"Why would they do a fashion shoot at this place? Wait until you see it. It looks more like a horror movie set."

"Apparently, this designer is born and bred here in New Orleans, so perhaps she's got some kind of personal connection." He shrugged. "I'm not sure, but you can bet I'm going to find out." He glanced at his watch and then to the closed door of her bedroom. "Kerry has dinner in about an hour with the clients and that obnoxious rep of hers. I better go wake her up."

Pete delivered a catcall whistle into the phone as if he knew exactly what Dante was thinking. "Nice. You get to go into Kerry Smithson's bedroom and wake her up, while I scout out the boondocks. It's good to be the boss."

"Very funny, you smart ass." He smiled in spite of himself. Pete could dish it out pretty well. "I'll see you tomorrow morning." Dante hung up to the teasing sound of Pete's laughter.

Dante slipped the phone into his pocket and went to Kerry's bedroom door. His fist was poised to knock but stopped at the sound of the shower running. Images of her naked, soapy body blasted into his mind. Dante placed both hands on the door and closed his eyes in an effort to gain some kind of control and rein in his raging hormones, but it did no good whatsoever. It only made it worse.

His eyes shifted, a low growl rumbled in his throat, and he pushed himself away from the door. His desire for her had the animal inside clamoring to get out. This entire experience with Kerry was uncharted territory. He always thought that when he found his mate everything would fall into place, smoothly and easily. That was the way it had always been for all of his people, but she was not like all Amoveo. Kerry being both human and Amoveo had changed the rules. Boy, had he been off base.

He ran a hand over his face and let out a low sound of frustration. In fact, it had been nothing but an uphill battle. Dante stood at the heavily draped window staring out over the city streets below. He wanted to sleep when she did and connect with her in the dream realm again, but he knew that would have been selfish. She specifically asked him to be alone, and connecting with her in the dream would not exactly be doing as she'd requested. They were making some progress, but the biggest hurdles still lay ahead.

He'd seen her pictures in magazines and on billboards but never made the connection. After all, he thought she was human, and according to his people's history it was impossible to mate with a human. He didn't know until he saw her in person and felt her energy call to his. The moment he'd clapped eyes on her at the beach he knew she was his mate. He also knew she was a hybrid.

Dante snorted and shook his head. *Lie*. Everything they'd been raised to believe had been a lie. The existence of Kerry and Samantha proved that Amoveo and humans could mate. Obviously cross-mating did not happen often, but it did happen. For years his people were under the impression that Samantha's parents had been killed by the Caedo family. It had been easy enough to believe. Over the last several generations the Caedo had hunted his people to the brink of extinction. But it hadn't been the Caedo that killed Sam's parents. It had been something far more sinister.

The Purists were infuriated over the pairing of Samantha's parents—an Amoveo man and a human woman. They felt human blood would muddy their ancient heritage and weaken the race. They were willing to kill their own people in order to keep the race pure.

Samantha had stayed hidden until she connected with Malcolm. Prior to connecting with him, all of her abilities lay dormant—but now they were strong, very strong. Kerry had a powerful psychic gift and had managed to keep her heritage a secret, but once they were mated her secret would be out. What then? It was the unknown, the uncertainty of their future that clawed and nagged at him mercilessly.

Prior to this the enemy had always been clear and the

lines between friend and enemy distinct—the Caedo—
but not anymore. Now the enemy hid among them. His
father had been killed before they could discover who
the other Purists were. It had been a betrayal of enormous proportions, and he never thought he would fear
his own people.

The soft click of Kerry's bedroom door opening drew
Dante out of his trance. When he turned around, the
image before him, quite literally, caused him to catch
his breath. Her long jet black hair fell loosely around
her creamy bare shoulders. Her voluptuous body was
draped deliciously in a strapless sapphire blue dress,
which hugged her full breasts and was short enough to
give ample view of her long lovely legs.

One look at her sent an electric shock right to his crotch
and hardened every inch of him. He wanted to devour
and discover every bit of her. He drank in the sight and
allowed his gaze to wander leisurely over her spectacular
form, savoring every delectable curve.

The twinkle in her eyes, a combination of lust and
trepidation, let him know she knew exactly what kind
of effect she had on him. He held her gaze and bit by
bit closed the distance between them. Her heart rate
increased as he invaded her space. Her energy waves
pulsed wildly through him, and it made him want her
even more. The stiletto heels made her just over six feet
tall, but she still had to tilt her head up a bit to look him
in the eye. Dante smiled. He imagined that there weren't
many men who had her looking up.

"You look stunning, Ms. Smithson." He didn't take
his eyes off of her, watching for any sign of discomfort.
Dante took her hand and raised it to his lips. Her large

eyes remained locked with his as a breathy sigh slipped from that luscious mouth.

God, how he wanted her. He wanted to taste, nibble, and lick at every delectable inch of that porcelain skin, to be buried deep inside and have her body writhing beneath his. Gazes locked, he brushed his thumb over hers. Her breath hitched, and he reveled in the pulsing energy waves that flooded off of her.

He was in big trouble.

It took an enormous amount of restraint to keep from taking her right then, but he knew it was too soon. He knew she wanted him, but he had to remind himself that he needed to take it slow. She may look like a sex vixen, but he knew better than anyone that looks were deceiving.

"If I may say, you are even more beautiful in person," he murmured softly against her fingers and placed the lightest of kisses on her soft, warm skin. All the while he held her gaze.

"Thank you," she said, her voice just barely above a whisper. "Please, call me Kerry."

"As you wish." Dante smiled. He released her hand and gestured toward the door. "Shall we go? It's almost seven, and something tells me Arthur doesn't like to be kept waiting."

Kerry laughed softly and shook her head. "No, he doesn't." Dante's heart squeezed at the sound of her laughter. He led the way to the elevator and prayed for the strength to keep her safe.

They walked into The Carousel Bar and found Arthur waiting impatiently at a table for four along the wall. His unpleasant energy rippled distinctly through the bar, and although he didn't realize it, distinguished him from the rest of its patrons. The Carousel Bar was exactly that—a carousel. The bartender moved confidently at the center of it all as he served drinks to people sitting on the circus-themed bar stools. The back of each chair flashed hand-painted images of circus animals. Zebras, lions, and elephants frozen in time circled slowly around the mahogany center. The entire bar spun bit by bit in the center of the room and Dante had to admit it was one of the most interesting bars he'd been in.

Arthur held a gin and tonic in his hand and a look of displeasure on his face. Kerry waved at him and was rewarded with a curt get-your-ass-over-here gesture. Dante reminded himself to ask Kerry exactly how she hooked up with a jerk like this. He had all the sleaze of Hollywood and the slippery slickness of New York. To make matters worse, there was no sign of the client anywhere.

"Time to make nice," she sang through a painted-on smile.

"I'll be right here if you need me," he said discreetly, touching her lower back and sending her subtle waves of reassurance.

Kerry cast him glance of gratitude and went over to play the game with Arthur. He did his best not to grin like an idiot. She was, slowly but surely, becoming more accepting of him and no longer flinched or withdrew from his touch, but seemed to welcome it.

Kerry settled herself into a chair across the table from Arthur as Dante positioned himself against the wall by the door for the perfect vantage point. He could see Kerry and every angle that someone could approach her.

They drank and chatted quietly at the table, which gave Dante ample time to scan the crowd. There was a businessman contemplating cheating on his wife with the woman he'd met at a meeting. The two old college friends who'd escaped for a weekend of fun without their husbands. When he scanned their minds he found nothing out of the ordinary.

The couple celebrating their anniversary and another pair trying to hang onto something that had died a long time ago piqued his curiosity. He shook his head and scoffed audibly at the idea of divorce. Amoveo did not divorce. All of their matings were predestined, and how could anyone argue with fate? For generations their race had been struggling to endure, and mates had become so few and far between, the idea of divorce seemed ludicrous. The last two generations, in particular, had such challenges finding their mates that Dante couldn't imagine throwing away such a hard-won gift.

His eyes finally settled on Kerry. Her long legs were crossed demurely, and she leaned back comfortably in her chair. She nodded and smiled tightly as Arthur rambled on about all the big plans he had for her future. Dante scanned his mind and found it flooded with greed. Nothing would ever be enough for him. He looked every bit the polished LA type, perfectly manicured from head to toe—all style and zero substance. He was a man who was not used to being kept waiting. Entitlement oozed from him, and his energy buzzed like an annoying bug that needed to get swatted. He wasn't dangerous, but he was a dirtbag. He cared about Kerry, but he cared about his bottom line more. Dante had to squelch the urge to pound the little worm into the ground.

Stop glowering, you're going to scare the customers. Her voice slipped into his mind unexpectedly. His startled eyes flew to her face, which held a satisfied smirk.

What the fuck? He whispered teasingly. *Why, you little minx.* A lopsided grin cracked his face.

Kerry tore her gaze from his and looked down at her martini with a satisfied smile. She stirred the crystalline liquid slowly with an olive-laden toothpick. *I guess you could say I'm not a stranger to unusual gifts.*

Arthur's insistent voice interrupted their silent conversation. "Hey, are you listening to me?"

"Of course I am." She smiled sweetly and bit a martini-drenched olive off the toothpick.

"Good. We've got some outstanding opportunities ahead of us. You've got several offers on the table, but they have conflicting dates. Our sister agency in LA is interested in submitting you for some film roles." He took a sip from his drink.

Kerry shook her head adamantly. "No movies, Arthur. I absolutely do not want to do any film or television." She put her hand up to silence the argument he was about to start. "No."

He laughed heartily and waved off her refusal. "Oh stop. You and I both know that you could make the leap to the big screen. You're the flavor of the month and have to strike while the iron is hot."

Kerry hated the idea of disappointing Arthur or the agency. They'd been good to her and certainly secured her some coveted jobs. Hell, they put her on the map in the fashion industry. She had become the poster girl, literally, for sexy, curvy bodies. She really did owe it all to Arthur. He pushed harder for her than any other rep in the agency.

Kerry knew that she was the only client he represented that really made any major money. The more seasoned reps at the agency had been trying to woo her away from him for years, but she liked only having to deal with one guy. Not all of the guys in the agency. Besides he never once tried to get in her pants. As snotty as he could be, Arthur had been good to her. She didn't look forward to telling him she was quitting the business, and this would be her last shoot. Looking into his face with the perfectly waxed eyebrows, Kerry sighed heavily and looked down at her drink. "Look Arthur, I—"

He cut her off abruptly. "The client's here," he said quickly. The wooden chair screeched over the floor in protest as he got up quicker than a snake.

Kerry looked up at Dante for some reassurance. Irrational as it may have been, she had developed some kind of bizarre connection with this man she barely knew. After all, there weren't exactly lots of people she connected with telepathically—hell, there weren't lots of people she connected with at all. She stifled the hysterical giggle that threatened to bubble up and reveal her for the conflicted mess she'd become.

Kerry drained the rest of her martini and glanced up at Dante. His face was etched into a mask of calm detachment, but she sensed something dark rumbling beneath the surface. She followed his gaze and saw what had captured his attention so intently.

The client had finally arrived.

Jacqueline Petite was one of the hottest new young

designers on the scene. She designed edgy French-inspired lingerie, but one look at her and you'd think she worked as one of the street artists down at Jackson Square. Her blonde hair, streaked with bright blue strands woven throughout, was piled high on her head. Heavy black eye makeup framed her blue eyes, and bright red lips puckered up as she gave air kisses to an ass-kissing Artie. A burgundy velvet cape fell loosely over her narrow shoulders, and a silky black dress covered her from neck to toe. Who the hell wears a cape in this climate?

Her oddest accessory, however, had to be the black cat that she cradled with one arm. She stroked its head softly with her free hand, and its bright yellow eyes were fixed on Kerry. She could hear it purring from across the room. The sight of her reminded Kerry of a witch, not a high-end designer. Calling this woman eccentric would be the understatement of the year. Who brings a cat to a bar?

I hope she's not wearing one of her own designs.

Kerry tried not to smile at Dante's comment and intentionally avoided his gaze, afraid she'd burst out laughing. The teasing tone of his voice actually tickled her mind. Speaking with him telepathically, their secret conversation, felt incredibly decadent and intensely intimate.

Be nice. Fashion is subjective. Kerry tried to scold him, but truthfully she couldn't have agreed with him more. Their private dialogue was interrupted by a very animated Arthur.

"Jacqueline Petite. This is—"

"She needs no introduction." Jacqueline bowed her head dramatically and dipped in a delicate curtsy. "*Bonjour*, Mademoiselle Smithson. I am honored that you have agreed to be the new face of Le Fleur Designs."

Kerry stood to greet her, but the cat let out a loud *meow*. Startled, she quickly sat back down. Jacqueline motioned for her to stay seated and murmured something into the cat's ear, while she gave it some reassuring strokes. Kerry exchanged a look with Dante and shrugged.

Arthur relinquished his chair to Jacqueline and grabbed another from a neighboring table. She hadn't attempted the Hollywood kiss or a handshake. Kerry felt some of the tension ease from her shoulders. Maybe this wouldn't be so bad after all.

"Please. Don't get up. You'll have to pardon Jester. That's just his way of saying 'hello.'"

"No problem." Kerry waved her hand dismissively and smiled tightly. That creepy cat continued to stare at her with those bright yellow eyes.

"Please, let me get you another drink." She waved without even looking up, and the waitress appeared within moments. Jacqueline ordered another round for Kerry and Artie and a Stinger for herself. Kerry half expected her to order a saucer of milk for Jester.

"As you know, we have changed our location for tomorrow. We will be shooting at one of the old houses out on the East Bank near Braithwaite. My friend Joseph owns it and is letting us use it for the next couple of days. It took some doing, but I finally convinced him to allow us to use it."

As Jacqueline spoke she continued to stroke Jester, who purred like a car engine and didn't take his unyielding stare off of Kerry.

"A mansion? Well, that sounds fine. The boys were trying to scare me earlier with swamps and alligators."

Jacqueline's eyes twinkled with mischief. "Yes. I

don't think you have to worry about the swamps, *cher*,"
she said, the lilt of her voice painted with just a touch of
a Cajun accent.

Kerry narrowed her eyes and cocked her head warily.
"Okay," she began slowly. "What is it? Why do I feel
like there's more to it than just a mansion?"

Jacqueline threw her head back and let out a big loud
laugh. "Now that is why I chose you." Her laughter subsided. "You see more than what is on the surface." She
nodded with a knowing smile. "It's more like the ruins
of a mansion in the middle of what resembles a jungle."

Kerry leaned into the table as though she didn't quite
hear her correctly. "I'm sorry? Did you say ruins?"

"Yes, *cher*. You heard me correctly. Ruins. Once
upon a time Breezemont thrived with laughter, love,
and life. But now—" Her voice softened, and she placed
a kiss on top of Jester's head. "Now it is a shadow of
what it used to be. There is something beautiful about it
beneath the surface. Like my lingerie, *cher*."

Kerry cocked her head. "Your lingerie?"

She nodded. "Women of all shapes and sizes can wear
their business suits or their mommy jeans, but underneath they wear my lingerie. It is the beauty that they
keep secret. The beauty that lies beneath, you see? There
is another reason that I chose you, *cher*."

Kerry arched a dark eyebrow. "Oh really?"

"I could have had the traditional model, but I wanted
a real woman like you. My customers aren't super-
models, *cher*. They are the modern day woman who
worries about her lumps and bumps. Ah, but put on my
lingerie, and she feels sexy, beautiful, and strong."

"I think I understand." Kerry nodded slowly.

"Well, I don't! But hey, who cares?" Arthur's voice broke into their conversation abruptly, and both women looked at him as though they'd forgotten he was even there. "We're very excited about this shoot. Right, Kerry?"

"Yes, of course," Jacqueline said with poorly veiled irritation at Artie's crass response. "I'm sure Kerry will know what I mean when she sees the house tomorrow." Jacqueline's face broke into a broad smile as the waitress arrived with their drinks. "*Merci!* Put this on my account, Marie." The waitress nodded with a wink and cleared away the empty glasses.

"Thank you for the drinks, my dear," Arthur said in his usual haughty tone.

This chick is a little off. Dante's voice cut into her mind and caused her to jump in her seat. Arthur gave her one of those what-are-you-doing-looks, which had her crossing one leg over the other and adjusting herself in the chair. She brushed her long hair back over her shoulder and smiled as Dante's smooth voice slipped welcomingly back into her mind. *It goes beyond the outfit, the hair, and even that damn cat.*

She shot him a reprimanding look that was actually a poorly veiled smile, but his face remained a mask of stone. Suddenly, Jester hissed loudly, his ears flattened back against his skull. Kerry looked at the hissing feline; its huge yellow eyes were fixed on Dante.

It hissed louder.

"Shhh, be nice, Jester." Jacqueline continued to stroke him until he settled back down. She cast a glance over to Dante and eyed him warily. "I don't think he likes your bodyguard. You'll have to excuse Jester," she said, turning back to Kerry. "He has very poor manners, especially when he's tired." She sighed. "It is getting late."

"I'm sorry," Kerry stammered, embarrassed that she hadn't introduced Dante. "You're very perceptive. That *is* my bodyguard, Dante Coltari."

"No apologies necessary, *cher*." She turned to Kerry, and before she could move, placed one delicate hand on her arm.

Kerry froze, her breath caught in her throat as she braced herself for the onslaught. However, the mind-splitting pain she expected never came. Instead, quick sizzling shocks zapped through her hand and up her arm. The blurred image of a man running after her flashed into her mind. He chased her, calling her name. She couldn't see him clearly, but she could feel everything.

Blood.

Grief.

Hatred.

Fear.

She saw it all falling around her like a giant jigsaw puzzle that she couldn't quite put together. Kerry's eyes grew wide, and Jacqueline removed her hand as quickly it had come.

"Not as perceptive as you, *cher*," she whispered. Jacqueline stood up from the table, and her long cape fluttered around her like wings. "I will see you all tomorrow at Breezemont."

She gave a quick curtsy, nodded to Dante who'd moved in right behind her, and breezed silently out the door. Jester's yellow eyes peering over her shoulder were the last thing Kerry saw before the world went dark.

Chapter 7

SHE'D BEEN PASSED OUT FOR ALMOST HALF AN HOUR. He caught her when she'd fainted and didn't give Arthur or anyone else a chance to get near her. He got her out of there as quickly as possible and carried her up to her suite. Arthur wanted to call a doctor, but Dante convinced him they should keep it quiet in an effort to keep it out of the press. The very idea of any kind of publicity got the guy practically giddy.

Once Dante settled Kerry into her bed, Arthur left, claiming that he needed to do some damage control with the bar patrons. Dante assumed that meant he would be calling the press himself. At that point, Dante didn't care. He just wanted the smug bastard to leave.

He watched Kerry's chest rise and fall as she slept. Whatever she'd experienced when Jacqueline touched her sent her over the edge. Her mouth was set in a frown, and her brow knitted in what he could only assume was pain. He closed his eyes and reached out to her mind, but once again met an impenetrable wall.

He let out a sound of frustration and opened his eyes to look at his mate. "Beautiful" and "mysterious" were the two words that came to mind whenever he looked at her. He pulled the covers up gently and brushed her cheek gently with his thumb. She murmured something and sighed, but did not wake up. He needed a healer. He had to be absolutely certain she was alright.

He closed his eyes and reached out for Steven, the only doctor—human or Amoveo—Dante could trust with Kerry's life. After what felt like an eternity, Steven materialized in the room wearing a pair of green scrubs, looking relatively unkempt.

"What's up?" He let out a huge yawn and ran a hand through his shaggy hair. "I was catching a few winks after my shift at the clinic."

"I'm sorry to wake you, but I need you have a look at Kerry," he said, gesturing to his mate.

Steven's eyebrows shot up. "Whoa. She's even prettier up close."

"I didn't ask you here to ogle her." Dante knew he sounded like a jealous moron, and the smirk on Steven's face only confirmed it. He cleared his throat in an effort to maintain his composure. "She fainted and hasn't woken up since."

"I see," he said moving to the side of her bed. "What happened before she fainted?" He pulled a chair over and sat down next to her.

"She touched someone, or rather, someone touched her." His face grew dark at the memory. Dante could swear that woman had known exactly what her touch would do. He'd scanned her mind, but it was like stumbling upon a mess of wires that were all tangled up. He sensed a lot going on but couldn't decipher exactly what.

"Uh-huh. You mentioned earlier today that she has a psychic touch, correct? She receives images and so forth. Doesn't pain usually accompany these visions?"

"Yes." Dante nodded. "When she touches a human. But it's different when she touches another Amoveo.

She can touch us without pain, and from what I can tell so far, the only image she sees is our clan animal."

"No pain." He nodded and made a sound of understanding. "Well, I guess that's good news for you, isn't it?" He threw a teasing glance to Dante and then looked back down at his still unconscious patient. "Does she normally pass out like this?"

Dante shook his head. "No. At least I don't think so. Besides, when Jacqueline touched her, I don't believe she felt pain. Her energy waves increased in their intensity, but it wasn't pain. It felt more like fear or confusion."

Her suffering weighed heavily on him. Dante cursed softly and sat in the other chair on the opposite side of her bed. Helplessness washed over him as he watched Steven examine Kerry. He placed one hand on her forehead and the other on her hands, which were folded on her stomach. He closed his eyes and his face became a mask of concentration.

The energy in the room hummed as Steven joined his energy signature with Kerry's. His energy flowed through her body the way a car would travel a highway, taking note of the electrical impulses of her brain and the steady pumping of her heart. He didn't move a muscle for close to twenty minutes, and if Dante didn't know better, he might think Steven had fallen asleep. Dante watched intensely. His hands grasped the arms of the chair, turning his knuckles white. Why wasn't she waking up? Steven's voice gratefully broke the silence.

"Relax, big guy," Steven said with a crooked smile. He opened his eyes, his connection to Kerry now broken. "She's going to be fine."

"Thank God." Dante let out a sigh of relief.

"Whatever caused her to faint wasn't a physical problem." He sat back in his chair while keeping his eyes on Kerry. "It's as though she's shut herself down." He continued with caution. "Whatever she saw, it upset her so much she's withdrawn into the dream realm." He looked up at Dante, his face filled with concern. "She's in deep too. I don't think she'll come out on her own. Have you connected with her in the dream realm yet? I mean really connected to the point where she's actually seen you."

"Yes," Dante said softly. "Only in the form of my fox, but we have connected there."

Steven stood up and adjusted the covers over Kerry. "You have to connect with her tonight and reveal yourself to her in your human form. It's the only way she's going to come out of it. Whatever she saw frightened her, and she's hiding in the dream. I doubt she even realizes she's doing it."

Dante nodded his understanding and stood up. "Thank you, Steven."

"Don't thank me yet," he cautioned. "Let's make sure this idea works before you buy me a drink. Which, by the way, you'll be doing, right? Because you did interrupt my nap."

Dante laughed softly and shook Steven's extended hand. "You got it."

"Do you want me to stay while you're in the dream realm with Kerry? Make sure you both come out alright?"

"No. I'll contact you again if I can't get her to come out with me. I can count on you tomorrow if I need your help?"

Steven nodded his acceptance. "Absolutely." He whispered the ancient language, "*Verto*," and vanished.

Dante turned out the lights and went over to the bed. He removed both his jacket and tie and laid them across the chair. He unbuttoned the top few buttons of his shirt, and as gently as possible, lay down on the bed next to Kerry. Dante stretched out, folded his hands on his stomach, closed his eyes, and focused on his breathing.

His focus didn't come easily. The weight and warmth of her body next to his provided more distraction than he thought possible. Dante shook his head and sharpened his focus. Deep focused breathing was the quickest way to fall asleep and get to the dream realm. He concentrated on Kerry. Her scent, her energy, the sound of her breathing, all of it brought him closer to her. He drifted, softly and gratefully, into the cradling arms of sleep.

The darkness soon gave way to dense lavender mist that swirled madly around him. She was here. Her soft sobs whisked past him, and he could feel her anxiety within the mist that enveloped him, but he still couldn't see her. Her psychic shield held strong and continued to keep her hidden. Dante redoubled his efforts and called out to Kerry. She had to be willing to let him in.

Kerry, can you hear me? *He kept his voice quiet and did his best to keep his own fear at bay. The mist, thick and stormy, began to change, and darkness was soon replaced by pale lavender dappled with pink streaks of light. It was working. She heard him.* Come on, princess, you can't hide from me all night. Let me in.

Don't call me princess. *The irritation in her voice cut through the mist, parting it like a curtain leading him straight to her. Bingo.*

The mist dissipated, and the dream realm she'd

created revealed itself. Dante had to admit it wasn't what he'd expected. He thought for sure it would be the beach or some other natural surroundings, but it couldn't have been more different. They were in the midst of a rooftop garden overlooking New York City. The jet black sky glinted thickly with stars like diamonds. Warm winds blew softly, and the lights of the city twinkled brightly around them. The most significant difference that separated it from the real world was the glaring absence of noise. There were no honking horns, no sirens in the distance, no noise of any kind, but there was music. A song he couldn't quite identify drifted around him and blanketed the realm she'd designed.

Kerry sat in the center of it all on top of huge rock, arms hugging her legs with her back to Dante. Her long black hair hung loosely down her back and blew gently in the wind. Her cheek rested on the top of her knees. Barefoot and clad in a simple white tank top and pants, she seemed to glow in the middle of the darkness. She reminded Dante of a fairy, and he thought for a moment she might just sprout wings and fly away from him before he could reach her.

He moved toward her cautiously, knowing that she controlled the environment of this dream and could leave him alone in the mist once again. He heard her sniffle softly, and the winds gusted briefly in response. Dante walked up to Kerry and looked out over the city, silently beside her. They stayed there side by side for what seemed like an eternity before she finally spoke.

I'm so tired, Dante. *Sadness edged her voice and cut through him like a knife. She sighed softly.* I like it here. It's peaceful. I don't have to touch anyone or worry about anyone touching me. No visions. No pain. Just… peace.

You can have that in the material world too, *he said.*

She shook her head and rubbed her chin on her knees. Do you have any idea what happens when I touch people? *She looked up at him, her tear-filled eyes searching his pleadingly.* I see everything. Their innermost thoughts, deepest desires, buried secrets, and it hurts like hell. *She let out a shuddering breath. She looked away from him and rubbed her upper arms as if trying to get warm.*

Dante turned to her and anything he wanted to say evaporated. He found himself speechless and completely lost in the sight of her. She looked up at him, her deep brown eyes swimming with tears.

I see frightening things, *she whispered softly.* But not when I touch you. When I touch you… it's the fox. *Her lips trembled as though she had finally gathered the courage to say what she'd been thinking.* I see the fox when I touch you.

Dante reached out and brushed one large tear away with his thumb. Kerry's eyes remained locked on his, searching them for answers to her unspoken questions. She closed her eyes and leaned into him, nuzzling her soft cheek tantalizingly against the palm of his hand. The winds blew harder and hotter around them.

Is that all? *His voice sounded gruff and strained. Keeping his desire for her at bay grew increasingly difficult.*

No, *she whispered and shook her head softly.* When you touch me it feels absolutely marvelous… and that scares the hell out of me. *She took his hand in hers and turned it over, stroking his palm gently with the tip of her finger. She traced the deep lines in his hand as if committing every crease to memory. Dante kept his own needs in check and allowed her the freedom to explore and maintain all of the control.*

Touching people usually feels like acid is being poured in my brain and over my skin, but not with you. *She looked up at him, her large brown eyes peeking out seductively beneath long dark lashes. She uncrossed her legs and rose off the rock to face him.* Your touch is like honey, sweet and thick. Why, Dante? *She took both of his hands, and holding them to her heart, she moved her soft body up against him. Her full lips hovered temptingly inches from his.* Why can you touch me like this?

The last of Dante's resolve slipped away. He leaned in and captured her mouth with his. She moaned softly as he took her head in his hands and deepened the kiss. Her lips parted as his tongue demanded entrance and delved deeper into the velvety warmth of her mouth. If it felt this good to kiss her in the dream realm, he could only imagine how sweet it would be in the physical plane.

She wrapped her arms around his neck and pulled her to him, her full breasts crushed tantalizingly against his chest. Bit by bit she opened up to him and broadened their connection on every level. She kissed him back with passionate fervor and allowed their energies to mix and mingle, deepening their connection moment by moment. The winds howled around them, and the music grew louder. He suckled on her bottom lip and pulled back from her reluctantly. Her face was flushed and her lips swollen from his kiss. They stood there for a moment, their breath heaving in unison, and he knew now was his chance.

It's time to wake up, princess.

The fog of sleep lifted, and Kerry slowly became aware of her surroundings. She was in bed, and she wasn't alone. Her eyes flew open, and she found herself looking up into Dante's big reddish brown eyes. She grabbed the sheet and pulled it up to her chin, mentally taking note of the fact that she still wore her dress from their evening at the bar. She looked to the window and saw that it was still dark out. How long had she been here?

Dante's long muscular body was laid out next to hers. He laid there on his side, propped up on his elbow, with a satisfied smile, acting like lying in her bed was the most normal thing in the world for him to do. He still wore his suit pants and shirt, but he'd discarded the jacket and tie.

His thick auburn hair stuck up in several directions like a little boy with bed head. Kerry had to fight the urge to reach out and run her fingers through it. Memories of kissing him in her dream flooded her mind, and her face burned with embarrassment. She clamored for a witty comment about how he didn't belong in her bed, but her mouth and brain couldn't seem to cooperate and form a sentence.

"Nice to have you back in the land of the living." The amusement in his voice made her want to smack him.

"What the hell are you doing in my bed?" she bit out. Then she looked down at herself. "What the hell am *I* doing in my bed?" she said a bit more quietly.

He said nothing, but his eyes spoke volumes as his

gaze wandered slowly down the length of her body. Her heart thundered loudly in her ears, she held her breath, and suddenly it felt unbearably hot underneath the covers. Her skin felt too tight for her body and burned under the touch of his hot stare. She propped herself on her elbows in an effort to bring his attention back to her face, which she suspected glowed bright red.

His eyes locked with hers. "You fainted, and I carried you up here," he said with an all too sexy edge. His face remained a mask of calm arrogance.

Kerry's eyes narrowed, and she eyed him suspiciously. "And that's all?"

"That's all that happened." A crooked smile cracked his handsome face. "At least that's all that happened here," he said with a wave of his hand.

Dread crept up her belly, and she swallowed hard. "What do you mean *here*?"

"Well, the dream realm," he breathed. "Now that's a different story entirely. I quite enjoyed the oasis you created in the middle of New York City. It was incredibly beautiful and seductive." He reached up and traced his finger along her quivering lower lip. "Just like you."

Kerry froze, and all the blood drained from her face. "What?" The word came out in a rush as every bit of air left her lungs.

"Kerry," he whispered her name seductively, took her face in his hand, and kept his eyes locked on hers. Warmth flooded her body, and desire coiled tightly deep inside of her. "Please let me in." He leaned in and trailed delicate kisses along her jaw and down her neck. Kerry's breathing came quickly, and she wasn't sure if it was from fear or lust. "Tell me," he murmured against her throat between butterfly kisses. "Tell me again. What do you see when I touch you?"

Her mind raced frantically, unable to process the overwhelming pleasure and be logical at the same time. How could he know about her curse? She had told him in her dream. But that was just a dream, wasn't it?

She knew that she should get up and run out of this room and never look back. From the second she met him, her life had gotten more bizarre with every passing hour. But she was tired of being alone and keeping so much of herself a secret. Hope glimmered cruelly—all of that could be behind her.

She closed her eyes and sank into the delicious sensation of his lips, soft and fluttering along her skin. He placed one last kiss at the corner of her mouth.

"Tell me. What do you see when I touch you?" he asked in a voice gruff with desire. "Kerry, look at me."

Gathering her courage, Kerry opened her eyes and found herself looking into a pair of familiar glowing embers. They burned brightly, like fiery stars in a night sky. They were the very same eyes as the fox from her dream.

"Your eyes," she breathed softly as he held her gaze. Tears spilled freely down her cheeks. "The fox," she said with a mixture of relief and wonder. "I see the fox."

Before she could say more his mouth crashed down on hers with a savage intensity that sent bolts of pleasure throughout her body. The fox image burst into her mind, and years of pent up passion bubbled inside and boiled over. She opened up to him and reveled in the feel of his lips melding with hers.

Kerry wrapped her arms around his neck and pulled

him to her, relishing the weight of his hard masculine body on top of her. It felt so good to touch and be touched. A delicious tingling spread across her skin, and heat pooled low in her belly. She moaned softly as he kissed her with devilishly talented lips.

Kerry felt more alive in these last few moments than she had her entire life. She loved the way his muscles moved in his back—rippling, raw power pulsed beneath her fingertips. He shifted and settled his rock-hard body between her legs. Kerry wrapped one long leg around his in an effort to get even closer. He kissed her thoroughly, his tongue sweeping velvet strokes along the roof of her mouth. She responded feverishly, exploring his lips with hers, and thought she might lose herself in the pleasure. His hands tangled in her hair; his fingers massaged her scalp. Instinctively, she moved her hips against him, the evidence of his arousal pressed insistently against her feminine core. Sizzling, carnal pleasure shot through her and stole the breath from her lungs.

One hand wandered downward and ran along her rib cage, leaving trails of honeyed warmth on every spot he touched. His knuckles grazed the underside of her breast through the silk of her dress, and all the while he paid thorough attention to her mouth. Gently, he pulled down the blue material and filled his hand with one full breast. Her nipples tingled and peaked in response to his touch. Her heart beat a mile a minute, and her breath came in ragged gasps.

Too fast. This was all going too fast.

Her head spun, and her body burned out of control. Her brain, the voice of reason, started screaming at her to put on the brakes. She reached out to him with her mind, hoping he would hear her. *I've never done this before. I'm sorry.*

Dante's body stilled, and his touch became softer. Gently, tenderly, he suckled on her bottom lip and placed a chaste kiss at the tip of her nose. He closed his eyes, let out low growl, and rested his forehead against hers. They stayed there for several minutes, bodies intertwined, clothes askew, and his mouth hovering temptingly just above hers.

"You're everything I imagined," he whispered between ragged breaths.

Kerry's lips curved into a smile. "Funny. You're *nothing* that I imagined. I didn't dare imagine that anyone was out there for me," she said breathlessly.

Dante shifted his body and stretched out next to her. He leaned on his elbow and looked down at her solemnly, while he played with a long strand of raven hair. "Haven't you ever wondered where your gift came from?"

Kerry's blood went cold.

"Gift?" She made a scoffing sound and sat up in the bed, holding the sheet to cover her bare breast. "You think what I've got is a gift? Are you fucking kidding me?" Furious that he could be so completely dense, she scrambled out of bed and stormed into the bathroom, slamming the door solidly behind her.

Kerry cursed. Great. She'd managed to get close to him and push him away all in less than one day. That must be some kind of sick, twisted record, she thought wryly. Kerry stripped off her rumpled dress and wrapped her heated body in a soft robe. She closed her eyes and leaned against the bathroom door, determined to get up the guts to go back out and speak to him. It had taken all of her life to find this dazzlingly unique man, and she seemed to be doing just about everything to sabotage it.

Kerry took a deep breath, swung the door open, and came face-to-face with Dante. His eyes flashed with desire. She knew how much he wanted her because she wanted him just as much. Right now, however, her head had to get control over her body. She tilted her chin upward in gritty defiance. She had gone this long without sex—she could go a little longer.

If he was so stupid and blind to think that her visions were a gift, how could she possibly be with him? Clad in slacks and a rumpled shirt that remained only partly buttoned, he looked undeniably sexy. His full lips were set in a determined line, and she had to fight the urge to jump his bones right there in the doorway.

"So—" she began, curtly placing her arms tightly across her chest. "You think this *thing* I can do is a gift. Is that right?"

Dante stepped aside and gestured for her to come back into the room. Kerry nodded with a tight smile and moved past him to the bar to pour a glass of water. She could feel his gaze on her.

"Yes," he said quietly. "I think you have a gift."

She turned to face him. He'd settled himself into the armchair across the room from her. Her hand trembled as she took a sip. She willed her body to settle and leaned back against the edge of the bar. She stared at him over the rim of her glass. Her robe had fallen away, exposing her bare legs, and she couldn't help but notice the way he stole a glimpse.

"Hey, Tarzan, my face is up here." She snapped her

fingers and immediately drew his unabashed gaze back to hers.

The confident, unapologetic look on his face told her he wouldn't feel badly about admiring her. "Yes." His lips curved into a lopsided grin. "I'm aware of that."

He adjusted his position in the chair, those long strong legs of his splayed in an unspoken invitation. Before she could stop herself, her eyes darted to the obvious evidence of his arousal, which he did nothing to hide.

Whoa.

She threw back the last bit of water in her glass, wishing she'd poured whiskey instead.

"Listen, lover boy." She placed the empty glass back on the bar behind her. "Let me clue you in on a little something. Experiencing mind-numbing pain and seeing horrifying visions is not exactly a *gift*." Her voice rose, and she slowly moved closer to him as she spoke. "Never being able to hold someone who's hurting and offer them comfort, never having anyone there to hold you when you're scared or lonely. Childhood? Oh, that was fun! Do you have any idea how isolated I've been?"

She knew she sounded irrational, and quite possibly, completely hysterical, but she didn't care. All the things she'd carried inside and harbored alone were finally coming out. He'd cracked the dam and now would have to suffer the consequences and endure the emotional flood. Tears stung at the back of her eyes, and her throat tightened. "My mother could barely stand the sight of me by the time I turned four. Do you have any idea how it feels to know that your own parents are afraid of you? I've spent almost my entire life alone."

Kerry stood over him with her hands placed firmly on her hips as though she were daring him to call her crazy. Her throat was raspy and raw, her vision blurred by tears, but she could still see the look on his face. Then, even more clearly, she heard his voice in her head. *You are not alone*.

She squeezed her eyes shut and sat on the edge of the bed. "Stop that," she said with a hitching breath. "Why can you do that?"

You don't find it enjoyable to speak with me this way? His voice was seductive, and the extra emphasis he gave to "enjoyable" was laden with innuendo. She shot him a look of reprimand, but her body's reaction completely contradicted it. When he spoke with her telepathically it tickled her inside and out. It felt intimate, inviting, and deliciously seductive.

"You are not alone, and you are certainly not the only one. I'm sure if you think about it you'll realize that. There has always been one person you have had a connection with, and now there are two." His voice remained calm, and the sound of it seemed to soothe her to the very core.

Samantha. She knew he was talking about Sam. It was true. She'd always been able to touch Sam. There had never been pain, and the only vision had been of a wolf. Dread crept up her belly as she realized what he was suggesting.

"That's not exactly an answer," she bit out. She wiped her face with the back of her hand, loathing the way she'd let her emotions get the best of her. "Tell me what is going on. Why can I touch Samantha? Why you? You are obviously not..." She trailed off, not sure what to say. She didn't know what he was or even what he wasn't.

He raised his eyebrows and looked at her expectantly, waiting for her to complete her thought. "Not what?"

"Not normal." She licked her lips nervously. "Not human," she said in barely audible tones.

Kerry expected him to scoff at her for even suggesting that he wasn't human. To stand up and tell her she was crazy, but he did neither. Dante eyed her carefully, and leaning in, he rested his elbows on his knees. As he held her gaze, she couldn't help but note the way his hair curled temptingly against his shirt collar. The hard, masculine plane of his forehead, his perfect nose, high cheekbones, and firm lips all came together to form the most handsome face she'd ever laid eyes on.

She'd always been attracted to him, but this very moment he looked dangerous, mysterious, and sexier than ever. She nibbled on her bottom lip nervously, waiting for him to deny it and tell her he was human and perfectly normal. However, something deep inside of her knew that wouldn't be happening.

Silence stretched out between them as she waited for him to confirm or deny his humanity. Finally, after what seemed like an eternity, he rose from the chair. Kerry's heart raced, and she couldn't escape the sound of her blood pumping through her veins as it thundered relentlessly in her ears. He loomed largely before her, and she didn't know whether to run, cry, or jump him. Abruptly his eyes shifted into the eyes of the fox and remained locked on hers. Kerry sucked in her breath, and her body stilled. Those two burning embers seemed to bore right through her and sparked every fiber of her being to life.

"No," he whispered. "I am not human."

Before Kerry could open her mouth to protest, he closed his eyes, stretched his arms open wide, and whispered, "*Verto*."

The air in the room thickened, and he shimmered as if she were looking at him underwater. Seconds later Dante had vanished, and the enormous red fox from her dreams and her visions stood before her larger than life. It looked at her with those same glowing amber eyes, and a large bushy tail swished hypnotically behind it.

I am Amoveo—a member of the Fox Clan—as you can see. Kerry held her breath as Dante's voice wafted into her mind like a sudden caress. She stared at him with wide eyes, and her mouth moved, but no sound came out. She noted that the rich auburn color of the animal's coat was an exact match to Dante's thick hair. He seemed much larger than a regular fox would be and had a muscular body that radiated raw power. His face was mostly red and brown, but he had a bright white mask around his eyes. His large ears were trimmed in a dark brown, as were the white socks of his feet and the tip of that bushy tail. He was... magnificent.

She could barely process what she saw or form any coherent thought before he shimmered and shifted back to his human form. He stood once again as the tall and devastatingly handsome man he'd always been. With impressive speed he leaned in and placed one hand on either side of her on the bed, trapping her there between his massive, muscular arms. They stayed in that position for what seemed like eons, face-to-face, his mouth suspended just a breath away from hers. Very gently Dante brushed his firm, warm lips along hers and placed a featherlight kiss on the corner of her mouth. Hot, honeyed bliss blanketed her skin from head to toe, and every inch of her tingled.

"I am Amoveo," he whispered. "And so, my beautiful princess, are you." Then without another word he stood up and walked out of her room, closing the door silently behind him.

Kerry let out a shuddering breath and tried to settle her quaking limbs, while she stared after him at the closed door. Her mind swam with a million questions, and her eyes swam with tears. She clutched the top of her robe closed and squeezed her eyes shut in an effort to find some kind of stability. Her body, mind, life, and emotions were raging completely out of control. She stood on unsteady legs and made her way over to the bar. Right now, a drink sounded like a very good idea. With trembling hands Kerry threw ice cubes in a glass and doused them in the caramel-colored liquid.

"Telepathy, weird dreams," she said through shaky breaths. Muttering to no one in particular, she walked over to the windows and looked out over the New Orleans night. "He's some kind of shapeshifter, and apparently, so am I." Her voice sounded hysterical again. When did she turn into such a girl? "I'm even talking to myself. Fabulous—as if I don't have enough issues already."

Shapeshifter—or what did he call it? Amoveo?

Samantha. She needed her friend now more than ever. She wished like hell that she was here. Dante was right about Sam being different. Deep down, Kerry had always known that Sam wasn't like everyone else. Her thoughts wandered to Malcolm. She never touched him, but his energy had always seemed unusual. Was he one of these Amoveo animal people too?

"Lord, have mercy. I'm losing it." Kerry sighed audibly, threw the drink back, and squeezed her eyes shut, relishing the fiery liquid as it splashed down her throat. She hoped it might burn off the effect of Dante's touch. Even with the turmoil raging inside of her, the memory of his touch alone made her wet.

She held the cool glass to the heated skin of her throat, and the air slipped from her lungs in a heavy rush. She knew that she would never escape him. No matter where she went, he would be right there, deep inside of her, and under her skin. It's as if he had marked her somehow, and that terrified her even more than the fact that'd he'd just turned into a fox.

She laughed out loud at the ridiculousness of her situation and let out a sigh of frustration. Kerry reached up to pull the drapes closed and froze when she caught sight of herself in the window. The glass slipped from limp fingers and bounced on the thick carpet. Slowly, as if in a dream, she reached out to touch her reflection. Her eyes gleamed bright yellow, just like Jester's. She found herself staring into the eyes of a cat.

Chapter 8

THE NEXT MORNING DANTE WAITED RATHER IMPATIENTLY for Kerry to emerge from her bedroom. He hadn't slept well, and unfortunately, she'd shut him out of the dream realm again. A sleepless and dreamless night left him grouchy and short tempered. She had closed her mind to him as well. Hell, he half expected her to barricade the door and never come out. After all he'd revealed to her the night before, he wouldn't blame her. Nerves and self-doubt began to get the better of him. What if she refused to believe what he told her? What if she refused him? So much was still so uncertain.

His internal pity party was interrupted by Kerry as she finally came out of her bedroom. Clad in a simple sundress and sandals, her hair gathered up in a clip, and a face void of makeup, she still took his breath away. She avoided his gaze and made her way over to the telephone on the side table. She threw a large bag on the couch before picking up the phone.

"I suggest you get in the shower, and get yourself together. We have to be at the location in just over an hour. Hurry up. I don't want to be late," she barked.

His stomach tightened in hard knots, and he felt his patience slipping away bit by bit. She wanted him to hurry up? Well, no problem. With a wave of his hand, using his visualization abilities, he divested himself of all his clothing. He stood casually with only a white towel now tied around his waist.

"Well, we wouldn't want you to be late, princess."

Kerry whipped around to face him, to no doubt give him a piece of her mind. Instead, her mouth fell open, and she was rendered speechless. The shocked look was instantly matched by rippling energy waves flowing from her body. He stayed completely still, his attention focused on her stunned face as her eyes darted up and locked with his.

"What—what happened to your clothes? How did you…?" she stammered.

He closed the distance between them, knowing he was crowding her space. He wanted her to feel how much he needed her, how his body and soul cried out for hers.

"Visualization is just one of our gifts. Perhaps tonight, after your shoot, you'll let me show you more." Her body radiated heat, and her pulse beat wildly in her throat, which sparked an overwhelming desire to lick and nibble at that fluttering spot.

"I think I've seen enough for now," she breathed. "You should get in the shower. Please. I don't want to be late." She cleared her throat and turned away from him.

"Whatever you say, princess," he smiled and did as she requested.

Dante showered as quickly as possible and emerged in fresh clothing. He opted for jeans and a T-shirt since they would be out in the bayou. The idea of sweating it out in a suit again definitely did not appeal to him. When he walked into the living room, Kerry looked him up and down. She shook her head and gave him a quizzical look.

"So where did you get those clothes? You didn't have a bag anywhere." She put up her hand to stop him before he could respond. "And don't tell me you conjured them out of thin air."

Dante smiled and walked over to the door. "As you wish... princess."

Kerry folded her arms and didn't move from her spot next to the couch. "So you're not going to tell me? Fine," she huffed. Kerry scooped up her bag and moved past him, attempting to open the door. She grabbed the handle, but Dante leaned casually against the door, preventing her from opening it. "Get out of my way." She kept her voice low and avoided his gaze.

Dante folded his arms and continued to lean back against the door. "You asked me not to tell you that I conjured them up. I was merely granting your request." His voice remained irritatingly calm. "The truth is I used the visualization skills of our people. Amoveo have many unique talents. My friend Steven uses it for healing." He reached out and tucked a long strand of hair behind her ear. "As a member of our race, you have many unique talents, and I look forward to exploring them with you."

Her energy waves increased and pulsed through him in the most tantalizing manner. She looked up at him, her face etched in gritty defiance, and his heart almost stopped. Her eyes had shifted. She stared back at him with bright yellow cat's eyes. He'd been right on the money. She was a member of one of the Cat Clans.

"Your eyes," he whispered softly, as his lips curved into a knowing smile. "These are the eyes of your clan."

A look of horror and shock came over her. She

dropped her bag and covered her eyes with both hands. "Oh shit! That happened last night. I half convinced myself that I dreamed the whole thing. What the fuck is going on?"

His heart broke for her. Her pain and confusion washed over him in dark waves, and the idea that he was contributing to her discomfort just about killed him. Gently, he took her hands in his and uncovered her face. She kept her eyes squeezed shut, refusing to open them.

"It's common for our eyes to shift when we experience intense emotions." He kept his voice soft and sent reassuring energy waves to help her cope. "Keep your eyes closed, and breathe with me. Deep, calming breaths, and focus on your heartbeat."

He held her hands against his chest and breathed in unison. Her breasts pushed softly against his hands as their chests rose and fell in rhythmic breathing. Desire rocked him to the core as her thighs brushed temptingly against him. He silently prayed he'd be able to keep his own eyes from shifting as his need for her clawed at him relentlessly. After several deep breaths her energy waves slowed, and her heart rate decreased, more in line with his. Finally, she opened her eyes, and he happily noted they had returned to their human state.

He gave her a big smile. "There. You did it."

"Great," she said sarcastically, rolling her eyes. "My clan eyes are all gone. Whoopee for me. Let's go."

She attempted to pull away from him, but he held her hands firmly in his. His face grew serious. "Kerry. Today, after your shoot, we have to talk about this. It's not going to go away. You are Amoveo, and you need to learn the ways of our people."

Kerry's face had turned into a mask, a calm detachment. "Fine. You win. Whatever. Can we go now, please?" She tugged at her hands, and reluctantly he released her from his grip. Kerry stepped back and moved to pick up her bag, but Dante beat her to it. She smiled tightly. "I'm sure Pete is waiting for us downstairs and wondering where we are. I really don't want to be late for this job. At this point, I'd like to get it over with and get the hell out of New Orleans."

When they walked into the lobby, Kerry almost got ambushed by Brent, the nervous and sweaty hotel clerk. The poor kid ended up running face first into Dante, who with lightning fast speed had put himself in front of Kerry. Brent stumbled backward and would've fallen on his backside if Dante hadn't grabbed him by the arm. The kid went white as a sheet and stammered in an effort to get out his reason for coming over to them.

"What can I do for you?" Dante growled.

Kerry grabbed Dante by the shoulder and pulled him away from the overzealous concierge. "Easy there, killer." She rolled her eyes, and shaking her head, directed her attention to a very sweaty Brent. "Hi. Brent, right? Don't mind Mr. Coltari here," she said with a nod toward Dante. "He's all bark and no bite."

Or is it howl? Her sarcastic jibe shot into Dante's mind with all the sass she'd surely intended. He shot her a skeptical look. *Wolves howl. I am a fox.* She laughed softly. *Yes, you are. Now stop scaring this poor kid. He's just doing his job.*

The sexy purr of her voice sent an electric shock directly to his crotch. She winked at him, and he wanted nothing more than to pick her up, take her upstairs, and ravage her.

The boy squirmed uselessly in his grip. Dante had practically forgotten the kid was there. Straightening his back, he turned his full attention back to Brent.

The pale young man nodded and licked his lips nervously. "Yes, ma'am." He looked up at Dante, immediately took a step backward, and stuck his hand out. "This came for you this morning," he said, referring to the large red envelope in his shaking hands. Keeping his wide eyes on Dante, he waved it over in Kerry's direction.

Kerry took the envelope and laughed softly while opening it. "You know, Brent, he's very bossy and kind of pushy…" Her voice trailed off as her energy waves fired in rapid succession. Dante barely noticed Brent as he babbled an incoherent apology and scurried off. All of the color had drained from Kerry's face, and she looked up at Dante with fear and confusion.

"What is it?" He snatched the note from her hand, and white-hot anger boiled through him as he read the words in front of him in bold black marker.

YOU'RE GOING TO DIE. JUST LIKE YOUR
WHORE MOTHER.
—THE PUNISHER IS COMING—

"My mother? You don't think this could be true, do you? Oh my God, Dante. I have to call my mother," she said through a shaking breath. "Who the hell is the 'Punisher'?"

Dante stuffed the note in his back pocket and pulled her to him as she frantically searched for her phone in the massive bag. He held her there in the shelter of his body and scanned the lobby for Brent as he whisked her to the front entrance of the hotel.

Brent was nowhere in sight.

"I'm getting you to the car with Pete. You'll be safe there. Wait until you're in the car to call your mother." He kept his voice low and calm.

Dante walked her outside and was relieved to find Pete leaning casually against the car, waiting for them as planned. He smiled when he saw them, but it faded once he saw the look on Dante's face. He opened the back door without Dante having to say a word. Kerry settled into the backseat, and the moment the door slammed shut Pete turned to face a very angry Dante.

"You keep her in there. No one—and I mean no one—gets near her except for you or me. You got that?"

Pete nodded solemnly. "You got it, boss."

"I'll be right back. Stay here."

Dante stalked back into the hotel lobby and immediately went to the concierge desk. His fists repeatedly clenched and unclenched at his side. The very idea that someone would threaten his mate sent him to a dark and dangerous place he didn't even know existed. He pushed right past the four people waiting in line. One look from him silenced any objections they'd been about to voice.

"Where is Brent?" He bit the words out and struggled to keep his eyes from shifting.

The stunned young woman behind the counter stared up at him with wide eyes. "He's in the back." She pointed to an office behind the counter. "But you can't go in there!"

Amid her insistent protests Dante placed both hands

on the marble counter and hopped effortlessly over the front desk. He gave a curt nod to the shocked girl and let himself into the back office. As the door shut firmly behind him, he found a very shocked Brent sitting at a computer. Dante walked over and leaned onto the desk. Brent sat back in his chair, attempting to get as far away as he could go. Little beads of sweat formed on his pale skin, his face etched in absolute terror. Dante scanned his mind and found it filled with bright red fear.

"Who gave you that note for Ms. Smithson?" His voice, low and deadly, came out not much louder than a whisper.

"I don't know. It was sitting on the concierge desk when I came in this morning. The other girl, Maddy, didn't see who put it there either. I'm sorry, Mr. Coltari. Please don't beat me up." Brent babbled and answered with such speed that Dante thought the kid might pass out. "Why? Was it bad? The note I mean? What happened? Is Ms. Smithson okay? I would never do anything to upset her. We pride ourselves on excellent service, and lots of famous people have stayed here without any problems."

Dante narrowed his eyes and pushed himself off the desk. Brent let out visible sigh of relief as Dante increased the distance between them.

"Here's the deal," he began quietly with his glare trained on the kid. "No one else is to know about the note. Do you understand?" Brent nodded wordlessly, and his throat worked as he swallowed hard. "If you get any other notes or messages for Ms. Smithson, you be sure to call me right away." He removed his business card from his wallet. "If anyone asks about her or inquires as to her whereabouts, you will tell them that you don't know who she is, and you've never seen her before in your life. Are we clear?"

"Yes, sir." Brent nodded furiously and repeated that over and over. Brent watched with wide eyes as Dante walked out of the office and left him gratefully alone. The moment the door shut, he promptly grabbed the nearest wastebasket and vomited.

Dante made his way back outside and found Pete and Kerry exactly where he'd left them. Fear for her safety and a sense of dread nagged at him relentlessly. After scanning Brent's mind, he knew that the kid had nothing to do with writing the note. He wasn't Caedo. He heard the poor kid puking after he walked out. He had merely been the unsuspecting messenger. His mind raced with the frightening possibilities. Whoever sent the note had signed it "The Punisher"—it had to be a Caedo, a Purist, or possibly both. Her heritage was, obviously, no longer a secret.

He scanned the hotel lobby and found nothing. Stepping into the damp Louisiana air, he reached out in search of any clue as to who had left the note. Nothing. Whoever left it was long gone. Walking up to the car, his heart broke at the sight of her face in the window. Fear and confusion hung over her like a shroud. It flowed thick and dense like the New Orleans air. Pete, as promised, stood guard next to the car. Dante had to admit Pete was a formidable man, even for a human.

"What happened in there?" Pete asked with a nod toward the hotel.

"Nothing," Dante lied. "Just an eager fan hoping to get her autograph." He gave Pete a slap on the shoulder and forced a smile. "Let's get going. If we don't step on it, she's going to be late."

Pete made a sound of agreement and walked around to get into the car. Dante had surprised himself by lying to Pete. Pete didn't know about the Amoveo people, and Dante could've easily passed the note off as some run of the mill note from a kook. He'd always trusted Pete, but unfortunately the rules had changed, and he had to be suspicious of everyone. His father had recently taught him that very painful lesson.

Dante opened the back door of the car, and he couldn't help but grin as Kerry slid over to make room for him. Shutting the door, he did his best to ignore the inquisitive look from Pete.

"Did you get a chance to make that call?" he asked Kerry as innocently as possible.

Kerry narrowed her eyes. "Yes, actually. Everything's fine. I guess it was nothing."

Dante nodded and looked out the window. He reached out to her with his mind, longing for that intimate connection, needing to have her touch his mind with hers and feel her energy tangled with his. *Your mother is alright?*

Yes. She's fine. Seemed more annoyed that I had interrupted her day at the Elizabeth Arden Spa to be honest. Her voice, sweet and soothing, filled his head as their minds connected. *I guess it was just someone's idea of a sick joke.*

They rode in comfortable silence for a while, and he enjoyed the way her energy mingled with his. He reached over and took her hand in his, not caring whether Pete saw it. He needed to touch her, to feel her warm, soft skin against him. Dante's lips curved in a satisfied smile as she gently rubbed her thumb along his, accepting his touch and reciprocating it.

She never should've adopted me. The sadness in her voice pulled at him from the inside out, and then the realization hit him. He gripped her hand tighter and turned to her, capturing her gaze with his.

Adopted? Oh no. Slowly, Kerry's eyes grew wide as the real meaning of the note dawned on her as well. *Oh my God. That note wasn't referring to her, was it? Whoever wrote that was talking about my birth mother. Weren't they? Dante, what on earth is going on?*

"Hey, you two sure are quiet back there." Pete's voice snapped them both back to reality. "Hope everything's okay because we're almost there."

Kerry eyed Dante suspiciously. *You're not telling me everything, are you?*

It will be alright. I promise. He gave her hand a reassuring squeeze and prayed he could keep that promise. The truth was that he didn't know. For all he knew they could be walking directly into a trap. The fact that the house they were driving to was owned by a Vasullus weighed heavily on his mind. *Are you sure you want to work? We can turn back to the hotel. Perhaps it would be best if you got some rest.*

She looked back at him and tilted her chin in defiance. *My job is about the only normal thing I've got left. I'm not losing that too. I need some kind of normalcy. I need to work. Don't push it.*

Dante gave a brief nod of acceptance as she withdrew her hand. He had barely noticed that they'd left the city limits and were now in the rural area of

Braithwaite. Route 39 had flown by in one monotonous blur. They turned down a long, winding dirt road. It was so narrow that two cars could not pass at the same time. Someone would end up having to back up. Thick with brambles and sprawling cypress trees, it gave the impression of driving through a tunnel. For those few moments, it seemed as if they were the only people left on the planet.

They rounded the corner, and the old house came into view. It became glaringly clear why Pete had questioned this shoot location. Their car pulled up to a stop, and the tires crunched in what was left of a circular gravel driveway. The three sat in silence for a moment, taking in the timeworn sight before them.

A massive old plantation house loomed largely before their eyes. The white paint had long since chipped away on most spots of the wooden siding. The once black shutters, now a pale gray, hung sadly and sporadically on several of the windows. The large front porch, which at one time was undoubtedly welcoming, looked forlorn, and the columns that framed it seemed to weep under the weight of the sad old house.

Most of the windows were either cracked or broken and looked miserably over the unkempt landscape. The large driveway circled around an ancient stone fountain with a dancing cherub; its water had dried up long ago. It sat strangled beneath gnarled, overgrown thorny vines and jumbled brambles.

The photographer, Arthur, and Jacqueline had obviously arrived earlier in the morning and set everything up. Kerry consistently requested a closed set. A shiny white trailer trimmed in chrome sat parked to the right along with their various cars. Lights and camera equipment sat waiting at the foot of the steps, which led up to the massive porch. To the right of the old house sat a rundown little cottage, and it brought Dante right back to reality. He knew that Joseph Vasullus lived there.

Dante, his eyes fixed on the little hut, got out of the car and scanned the area with his mind. No danger lurked nearby, but one question nagged at him mercilessly. Could he trust anyone?

Well, you could start by trusting the two of us. Really. Dante, how insulting. William's terse voice caught Dante by surprise. He looked to his right and saw him sitting in a massive oak tree. His bright white feathers spotted with brown glowed amid the green leaves. His sharp black eyes were fixed on Dante. Even in his Falcon form he looked stiff. Dante stole a glance at Kerry, but she seemed too entranced by the old house to notice the rather unusual bird.

Sorry. Is Steven here too?

I'm back here to the left of the house. Relax brother. I see you got her out of the dream realm.

Dante put on his sunglasses and scanned the area for Steven. Sure enough, he saw him hunkered down in the overgrown grasses. *Yes, I did. We have a problem.*

And this is news? Steven chuckled.

As Dante relayed the latest developments and told them about the note and his suspicions, he watched Kerry as she moved easily amid the unusual surroundings. Her long body moved with sinewy and graceful fluidity. She climbed the one or two steps and opened the door of her trailer. Suddenly, she stopped in the middle of the open doorway. Dante watched, fascinated, as she looked around the property surrounding the house. He could see she was looking for something specific.

Within a few minutes her gaze landed on William, who sat up in the oak tree in the form of his falcon. Slowly, her attention turned to Dante, and even from this distance he could feel the intensity of her anger. Her voice slammed into him with the strength of a physical blow. *Holy shit! Is that one of your animal friends?*

Dante cringed. He should've known she would pick up on their communication. Based on how angry she looked, he also should've told her there would be other Amoveo in the area. *That is William, and he's here to help us.*

Before he could finish his thought, she dropped her mental shield and shut him out. With one last look of disdain, she went into the trailer and slammed the door. As he stood in the driveway helplessly staring after her, Steven's teasing voice whisked into his head. *Man you suck at this.*

Chapter 9

KERRY HADN'T BEEN THIS ANGRY IN A VERY LONG time. She had heard the expression—make your blood boil—but she never really understood it until just now. First he dumps a ridiculous amount of outrageous information in her lap, and then he has the audacity to spy on her with more of *his people*. As she worked on her hair, she could swear she saw actual steam rising from her head. When she had walked up to the trailer to get ready, she had detected an odd buzzing sound in the air around her, but it had been even more than that. The sound resonated and vibrated through her body and around it.

When she stopped to listen more closely, she heard voices within the buzzing. As if phone lines got crossed. She heard Dante's voice, or felt it; she wasn't really sure which. As soon as she spotted that weird bird she knew. Part of the energy she felt and heard came directly from that enormous bird in the tree. The second she laid eyes on it she knew it wasn't a regular bird. First of all, it was massive. Secondly, it was far too exotic to be in this far-flung area. It looked like it belonged in the Arctic or something. Either way, it definitely wasn't a normal bird.

Truthfully, she didn't know what she was more upset about. That he secretly brought in more of these Amoveo guys or that he'd been speaking to someone else telepathically. She had stupidly assumed it was something just the two of them shared.

Annoyed at her girlish jealousy, she furiously coiffed her hair into a sixties-inspired, bouffant hairdo and applied the dark dramatic makeup that Jacqueline had requested. Kerry always did her own hair and makeup for reasons that were obvious only to her. She'd become skilled enough at it that most clients let her do it herself. In the beginning of her career, it saved the clients money, since they didn't have to pay the additional expense of hair and makeup staff. Once she'd established herself, people took it as a unique quirk. On the rare occasion a client refused, Kerry would simply pass on the job. This usually led to them giving in and letting her do it herself.

Satisfied that she'd achieved the desired effect, Kerry turned to the rack of lingerie for the shoot. She eyed the hanging pieces carefully and found that Jacqueline had tagged each one with a number. To her surprise, number one also included a black satin trench coat, in addition to the lingerie. She removed the first garment, and a slow smile spread over her face. She remembered what Jacqueline had said at dinner—*the beauty that lies beneath*. Her smile faded as darkness crept into her mind. The images from touching Jacqueline flashed through her memory. That man in the vision was so angry and completely focused on getting to Kerry. She shuddered and shook her head, refusing to allow the memory to surface.

Without wasting more time she removed her dressing robe and quickly donned the satin and lace ensemble. The black satin bra and panties were paired with a lace garter belt and black silk stockings. Kerry slipped on the patent leather stilettos and took one final look in the mirror. Her alabaster skin seemed even whiter than normal today as she pulled on the jet black trench and tied it tightly around her waist. She couldn't wait to see the look on Dante's face when she walked out in this getup. She may struggle in several areas of her life, but no one could work a camera like she could.

Kerry stepped out of her trailer and found Dante standing guard just outside the door. He looked at her with that sexy smile. He practically devoured her with his eyes as he offered her his hand. Mustering up all of her self-control, she refused it.

"I'm still annoyed with you," she said. "It's going to take more than flashing me those sexy eyes." Even though that look melted her to the core, she certainly couldn't let him know that. "You're not off the hook yet. Later, after this is over, you're telling me everything. Got it?"

Keeping his eyes locked with hers, he nodded in agreement and extended his hand to her again. She held his gaze for a moment before she placed her fingers in his. Kerry reveled in the sensation of flesh against flesh. The thought of it used to terrify her, but Dante had changed all of that. Her lips curved, and her body burned under his hot stare as images of their naked bodies filled her mind in rapid succession. Her eyes grew wide with surprise, and he raised her hand to his lips.

"Careful, princess," he murmured. "It's not polite to look so surprised." He smiled wickedly. "I thought you might need some inspiration while you're working today."

He placed a hot, sweet kiss along her knuckles, which

promptly sent delicious waves of pleasure all the way
down to her toes. Heat crept up her cheeks, and she
glanced at the others to see if they'd noticed, but they
were all too busy getting ready. Her gaze flicked back
to Dante, and he winked. Kerry quickly snatched her
hand away and without a word went over to the shoot
setup. The gravel crunched under her heels, and the hot
Louisiana air clung to her.

The air seemed thick enough to swim through, and
just when she thought she couldn't stand it for another
second, a gentle breeze lifted her hair off her neck,
providing a welcome respite. Kerry let out a sigh of relief and reveled in the momentary break from the heat.
However, every second of the walk over to the house
she could feel Dante's eyes on her, which only served
to raise her temperature further. The man's effect on her
was nothing short of carnal. Hot, tempting, and intense.

Kerry walked to the steps of the house and waited
for Jacqueline and the photographer. The two were in
deep negotiations about how and where to shoot. The
photographer, Layla Nickelsen, hailed straight out of
New York, but looked more like a gritty, documentary
filmmaker than a fashion photographer. Her bright red
hair was tied up in a messy bun, and her fashion choice
consisted of khaki shorts and a white tank top. She had
not a stitch of makeup on her freckled face, and her serious green eyes were locked on Jacqueline.

"Look, I'm just saying that we're going to need more
than one day. It's already close to ten," she said with a
quick glance at her watch. "My assistant bailed on me
at the last minute, and the lighting here is going to go to
shit in about three hours." She threw Kerry a nod and a

wave. "Hey. I'm Layla—the photog. Good to be working with you."

"You too," Kerry said. Although she got the distinct impression that Layla didn't mean a word of it.

Jacqueline cradled Jester in one arm and waved dismissively with the other. "No problem, *cher*. Joseph assured me we could use the property for the week if we need it, and I booked Kerry for three days just in case. Didn't I?" she asked the cat, not Kerry. Jester meowed his acknowledgement loudly.

Kerry nodded politely and squirmed under Jester's unwavering yellow-eyed stare, which now looked all too familiar. He continued to meow after her as she made her way up the steps of house. "Yes, you did, and three days is all you're getting out of me."

She turned to the two women, but they were once again deep in conversation. The only one giving her full attention was Jester. Eyes locked on the cat, Kerry reached out to it with her mind. *What are you looking at pussycat?* Jester meowed even louder and purred like a car engine. Jacqueline didn't seem to notice as she and Layla continued to discuss their opinions on where the best spot to shoot was.

Kerry stood on the old creaky porch and leaned against one of the large pillars. Interesting. The cat seemed to hear her. She was just grateful it didn't talk back. Kerry shook her head and smiled at the insanity of what she had done. She looked out over the rambling property, and something inside of her had the overwhelming urge to run. Not run away. Just run. Freedom. She longed for freedom.

The sound of a twig snapping caught her attention.

She looked down to find that Dante had followed her. She walked slowly along the length of the porch, trailing her fingers along the rough railing. She kept her eyes locked with his as he shadowed her every move. Their seductive dance became instantly enhanced when his mind touched hers.

I see you're using your abilities more. He threw a glance toward the cat. *Given the nature of our race, it shouldn't surprise you that animals are sensitive to our telepathic abilities.*

Kerry arched one eyebrow. *You heard me?*

Yes. He smiled. *You're new at this. You're a strong psychic and are quite capable of keeping people out of your thoughts. You'll get the hang of it the more you use it. You kept me shut out for a long time whether or not you knew it. As you become more comfortable with your abilities, you'll have more conscious control.*

They stood there silently for several seconds, until Layla called her back to business. The moment Layla flipped some music on and the camera started clicking, Kerry came to life. The trench coat opened immediately and before long came off completely. Every pose she struck, every seductive look she cast, all were meant for Dante. The hardest part of the shoot had been keeping her eye on the camera and not on him. For the next three hours and through three states of undress, Kerry worked. She pushed her body to the limit and reveled in the intensity of the environment.

The location gave off an amazing energy that seemed to recharge her mental and physical batteries. She usually hated working in natural settings, but the energy of this house made her feel right at home. Working always made her feel powerful and grounded, and for those three hours there was no telepathy, and there were no visions. Layla would shout direction periodically and stop occasionally to chat with Jacqueline. Arthur sat in a director's chair mopping sweat from his forehead, while he texted everyone in the free world.

All in all, it felt like a normal shoot, and Kerry loved that.

"That's it," Layla shouted. She covered her eyes and looked up at the trees. "This light is gonna suck for the rest of the afternoon. All these goddamned trees," she grumbled. "Let's pick it up tomorrow morning at eight. Please be on time, so we can get the best early morning light."

"You got it. Thanks Layla," Kerry said with a wave.

Layla nodded her acknowledgement and began to pack up her equipment swiftly and efficiently. Clad in the miniscule lacy teddy and panties, Kerry made her way past the three of them without incident. She waved at Peter, who sat on the hood of their car and waved back with that big friendly smile. Dante stood in front of her trailer door in his Terminator pose, mirrored sunglasses and all. He didn't look pleased.

"Kerry," Arthur called after her.

He walked over as fast as his body would allow. Kerry had a feeling he never ran anywhere because he figured that the world could wait for him. The poor bastard was sweating profusely by the time he reached the trailer. Kerry actually felt sorry for him.

"Hey Arthur, what's up?" she asked as patiently as possible.

"I have to go out to the coast," he sputtered between

heavy breaths. "It seems that Natasha got busted snorting coke in one of the bathrooms while she was on location. That girl is a hot mess," he muttered. "I've got to go out there and do some serious damage control, or she's never going to get any damn work ever again. This is like the tenth time she's been busted on the set. Think you can handle the rest of the shoot without me?"

"Sure, you do what you have to do." She swallowed the lump that had formed in her throat and glanced at Dante. They would, for all intents and purposes, be alone together. She still wasn't sure if that was good or bad.

"Thanks for understanding." His phone beeped, signifying a new message. He made a loud sound of disgust and looked down at his cell phone. "Sweet Jesus, *and* a sex tape is apparently about to be released. For the love of God, what is wrong with this girl?" He texted something to someone, started walking back to his car, and blew her a kiss without even looking up. "Okay, I'm outta here. I'll call you after everything settles down and give you the four-one-one. Good luck with the rest of the shoot," he shouted as he got into his car.

Before driving off he yelled one last thing to Dante. "Be sure you take good care of her!"

Kerry waved and watched silently as he drove around the corner and down the narrow dirt road. A large cloud of dust filled the air, and when it was gone so was Arthur.

She turned to find Dante holding the door of her trailer open for her. This was it. She was actually alone with Dante. She'd been physically alone with him before, but somehow knowing Arthur was in town had given her a

weird sense of security. The charade that she'd allowed
herself to believe had come to a screeching halt.

The last shred of normalcy in her life left with Arthur.

She climbed the stairs and stepped inside, relishing the
cool air-conditioned trailer. Dante closed the door behind
her, and before he could touch her, she put her hand up
to stop him. She pulled on the silk robe and tied it tightly
around her waist. The last thing in the world she needed
was to be half-naked with Dante in a confined space.

She grabbed bottled water from the tiny fridge next
to the dressing table and sat down on the love seat. She
took a long drink from the bottle, while keeping her eyes
fixed on Dante. He'd removed his sunglasses and tossed
them onto the counter to his left. He looked even larger
in the limited space of the trailer, but something about
him, something above and beyond his size, filled any
space he was in.

"So... what's next?" she asked quietly. "Your friend
out there is a bird of some kind."

Dante nodded. "Yes. William is a member of the
Falcon Clan. He is a gyrfalcon."

"So you can turn into any animal or just your..." She
snapped her fingers, while searching for the right word.

"Clan," he finished for her. "There are ten animal
clans among our race. We have been here as long as
humans have. Longer perhaps." He shrugged. "And yes,
we can only shift into our specific clan animal."

"I see." She nodded slowly and looked at him through
narrowed eyes. "And you think I'm some kind of cat?"

"Not *think*. I know," he said with irritating confidence. "I'm just not certain which cat. There are four.
Lion, Tiger, Cheetah, and Panther Clans."

He crossed his arms over his massive chest. Kerry couldn't help but notice how well the white T-shirt hugged all the muscles in his torso. Her eyes began to wander toward the bulge in his pants, but she stopped herself and looked back up to his smiling eyes. Her face flushed with embarrassment. His smile told her he knew exactly what she had on her dirty little mind.

"Oh really?" Kerry adjusted her position in her seat, attempting to keep calm and try to wrap her brain around the crazy world she was now living in. "How do you know so much about me?"

Silence hung thickly in the air for several moments before he finally spoke.

"You are my mate," he said in hushed, almost reverent tones.

Kerry stood up and laughed. "Yeah. Right." She rolled her eyes and walked past him to the tiny bedroom to change her clothes. What a load of horse hockey. "Your mate."

She opened the door to the bedroom and let out a huge shriek when she came face-to-face with Dante. She whipped around and looked behind her to the now empty spot where he had been just seconds ago. She backed up slowly, shaking her head in disbelief, and kept going until she backed right onto the love seat. She sat there staring up at him with wide eyes. Her heart beat rapidly in her throat and threatened to burst right out of her body.

"What are you?" she whispered. "No more of this telling me little bits at a time. Just tell me, for Christ's sake. Rip off the Band-Aid. I can't take it anymore."

He stood before her with his eyes glowing bright amber. He looked sexy, menacing, dangerous, and wild.

He'd stalked her all the way over to the couch, and she thought he might devour her. To her surprise, he squatted down and rested on his heels in front of her. He blinked, and his eyes shifted back to normal. The serious look etched in his face softened.

"I'm sorry. I know that this is a lot for you to take in, but you have to understand my impatience. I have searched for you my entire life. Our people only have one predestined soul mate. We can only have children with our mate. If we don't connect with our mate and complete the mating rite by our thirtieth birthday, we lose all of our abilities and die." The lines in his face deepened. "And from what I'm told, it is a slow and painful death."

She searched his face for some sign of deception. Something to tell her that this was all some kind of sick joke, but she saw only honesty and a deep need to have her believe him. It was a desperation she hadn't seen in anyone other than herself. Kerry took a deep breath and nodded her understanding and willingness to hear more.

"No mate. No kids. Not easy to keep your race going, I guess." She did her best to keep her voice even and act like this was a normal conversation. "Keep going."

"We are dream walkers and telepathic, and we can travel at the speed of thought. As you now know," he said with that devastating smile. "Actually, that is part of our visualization skills."

With incredible tenderness he took her hands in his. She closed her eyes as the vision of the fox wafted across her mind. She smiled wistfully. She didn't know if she'd ever get used to the remarkable sensations his touch gave her. Her smile faded as gently as it came. Would she ever get used to the idea of turning into some

kind of huge cat? Kerry opened her eyes, and the pleading look etched in his features made her heart pound
in her chest. She swallowed hard. "Go on," she said
through a shaky breath.

"Until very recently we thought that we could only
mate with another Amoveo. However..." He took a
deep breath and tightened his grip on her hands. "The
existence of hybrids proves that to be a lie."

Kerry's face grew somber, and she looked down at
their intertwined fingers. "I'm a hybrid?" She spoke
slowly, trying to wrap her brain around all of it. "I'm
half Amoveo and half human?" Awareness, awe, and a
touch of fear laced her voice.

"Yes." He nodded. "You are... but you are not the
only one."

Kerry's head snapped up, and her eyes locked with
his. "Samantha," she breathed her name in relief and
wonder. Tears filled her eyes, and her throat tightened.
"Oh my God! Sam. That's why I could touch her without
feeling any pain." Kerry stood up and laughed through
the tears that now flowed freely down her cheeks. "She's
a wolf, isn't she?"

Dante nodded, stood next to her, and smiled, placing
his hands on her shoulders. "Yes. She is of the Gray
Wolf Clan and was the very first hybrid we discovered.
You, my beautiful princess, are the second."

Kerry looked at him with relief, genuine excitement,
and tears of pure joy. Looking into his eyes filled with
desire, she warmed rapidly. The smile slowly faded
from her face as she became acutely aware of his body
next to hers. She closed her eyes and breathed in his
scent—raw, spicy, and male.

Had she dreamed him into existence?

He stood there with his large, warm hands on her shoulders, as real as can be. How could someone so real be so completely unreal? Mystical and magical didn't even cover it. Lights flickered behind her eyes as his hands seared deliciously along her arms. Kerry allowed herself to float in the honeyed silk of his touch.

"I hate that you suffered alone and had to endure such pain." He spoke softly. His voice floated over her as he ran his hands down her arms and up again. "But there is one thing I am grateful for." He leaned down, captured one breast, and whispered wickedly against her ear, "No other man has touched you like this."

Kerry moaned softly in response and sank into him. Dante cradled her head in his hands and devoured her mouth with his. She opened to him and swept her tongue along his with newfound bravery. Heat flared and engulfed her body with wild speed. It flashed over her skin, and her eyes tingled almost to the point of pain. She knew they'd shifted to those bright yellow cat's eyes, and oddly enough, she didn't care. All she cared about was ravishing the man in her arms. She grasped his massive shoulders and hung on for dear life. Desire clawed at her as if she couldn't get close enough. He reached between them and loosened her robe, allowing him greater access to her ample breasts.

He kissed her thoroughly and removed her robe with experienced hands. With lips mating and tongues dancing in hot velvety strokes, his eager hands explored the ample curve of her hip, the roundness of her bottom. Her breath came in ragged gasps as the fire built inside of her. Her body ached and throbbed deliciously with every stroke of his fingers and brush of his lips. She wrapped her arms around his neck and deepened their kiss. Kerry tangled her fingers in his thick wavy hair like she'd wanted to do so many times and pressed her body tightly against his massive frame.

His mouth moved down her throat in a delicate, but intensely erotic way. It was as if his lips were committing every inch of her skin to memory. Kerry arched her back, allowing him better access to her neck. She moaned with pleasure and clung to him as he nibbled at her sensitive flesh. So many luscious sensations swamped her at once. His hand kneaded her satin-covered backside, and she wrapped one long leg around his, needing to get closer. Kerry grabbed fistfuls of his hair and pulled him up so she could look him in the eyes. She needed to see.

They stood there, gazes locked, bodies pressed tightly to one another, and their breath came in jagged gasps. As she suspected, his eyes gleamed amber, and she knew hers glowed yellow.

"You see, princess," he whispered against her lips. "We are made for each other."

He held her gaze and reached down to the hot juncture between her legs. Her lips parted, and a soft gasp of pleasure rushed out as his experienced fingers slipped under the damp satin panties and found her most delicate spot. She closed her eyes and allowed the rush of pleasure to wash over her as he massaged torturous circles on the sensitive nub. Kerry moaned softly as searing waves of carnal decadence flooded her. With each tiny stroke, the passion coiled tighter and drove her to the peak.

Just when she thought she couldn't take much more,

he sunk two fingers into her hot, wet channel. Kerry cried out as the orgasm burst through her body and streaks of white-hot bliss flooded her mind. She grasped his large muscular back as wave after wave stole her breath from her.

She stayed there, clinging to him as the delicious aftershocks rippled through her spent body, which only made her hold him even closer. Kerry buried her face in his neck and inhaled his earthy, wild scent. He was positively addictive. Sweet Jesus, would she ever get enough of this man?

Dante's hand ran delicately along her thigh as he placed featherlight kisses against her neck. Evidence of his unresolved need, still hot and demanding, pressed insistently against her hip. Kerry struggled to catch her breath and finally opened her eyes. His face remained stamped with desire, and just one look from him made her wet all over again.

"Dante," she breathed his name softly. Her leg slid slowly down the length of his. He held onto her as she swayed on unsteady legs and found her balance. Looking into his glowing amber eyes, she knew she was his. Something primal and wild inside of her had been dormant until she met him. He literally and figuratively woke up the animal inside of her. Every bit of her body and soul cried out for his, and that alarmed her more than anything else.

That cocky, lopsided grin spread slowly across his face. Dante leaned in to kiss her, but a loud knock at the door stopped him dead in his tracks. He cursed quietly and rested his forehead against hers. "Haven't they heard the phrase?"

"What phrase," she asked softly as she fiddled with the waistband of his jeans.

"If the trailer's a rockin' don't come a knockin'!"

The two of them burst out laughing. His eyes had shifted back to human form, but she adored them just as much. His big brown eyes were especially beautiful when he laughed. She liked his laugh, deep and rich. The sound of it made her heart skip a beat.

Without taking his eyes off of hers, he helped her put the robe back on and tenderly tied the sash. "Who is it?"

"Just wanted to tell you everyone else is gone, boss." It was Pete's muffled voice on the other side of the door. "I'm ready whenever you are. This place gives me the creeps."

"We'll be right out." Dante turned back to Kerry and brushed her long dark hair off of her face. His features had softened, and he looked at her with something that resembled love. Her stomach flip-flopped, and she swallowed the lump that had formed in her throat. "As much as I would love to stay here and continue what we started…" His words trailed off, and he smiled wickedly.

Kerry nodded her agreement. "Well, why don't you go outside, and let me get dressed? Something tells me that you might slow down the process."

"Something tells me you're right." Dante laughed and kissed her quickly before he let himself out of the trailer.

Chapter 10

WHILE DANTE WAITED FOR KERRY TO CHANGE, HE decided to take a walk around the property to make certain there wasn't anything he had overlooked. Peter seemed perfectly content to wait in the air-conditioned car and leave the exploring to him. He also needed to see if William or Steven had found anything out of the ordinary. He made his way over to the far left side of the house, and a splashing sound caught his attention. He looked over and saw an enormous alligator slipping into the murky swamp water from the neighboring grasses.

I've been avoiding that big bastard all morning long. Steven's irritated voice slid into Dante's mind. He looked around and caught sight of him behind the house. His thick sandy fur blended nicely in the dry, overgrown grasses. Dante walked back to greet his friend.

Looks like you managed to avoid becoming gator bait, Dante teased good-naturedly.

Steven sat up and scratched furiously at the back of his ear with his hind leg. *Man this grass is itchy.*

Dante looked over his shoulder, making sure they were still alone. *Did you or William find anything out of the ordinary?*

Nope. William flew out of here a little while ago without more than a couple of words. He said he'd meet up with us tonight, but that he had other business to take care of.

Dante's face grew serious. *Other business?*

Yeah. You know Willie. He's not much of a talker.

Dante nodded and forced a tight smile, but couldn't squelch the feeling of dread that crept up his spine. *I'm sure you're right.*

Look, I gotta get out of here man. This grass is killin' me. Let's meet up tonight at the Zankoff's place. Remember, she and her brother have that little bar on the edge of the French Quarter, The Den. There's a private room upstairs.

Of course. Thank you again for your help. I'll see you tonight around eight o'clock.

Dante turned back to the house as Steven vanished into the wind. He walked around to the other side of the giant old home and came upon the owner's cottage. The guesthouse looked to be no larger than perhaps one room, and it too sat in a state of disrepair. The dilapidated condition of this property seemed to be in stark contrast to everything he knew about members of the Vasullus family.

He attempted to get a view inside the house, but the curtains were tightly drawn. Dante placed his hands on the front door and closed his eyes. He reached out with his mind to scan inside the house.

To his surprise, the door swung open, and Dante came face-to-face with Joseph Vasullus.

The man did not look pleased with Dante's presence. His dark gray eyes peered at him from under bushy white eyebrows. His long salt-and-pepper hair was tied in a loose ponytail. He stood practically eye to eye with Dante. He'd been strong in his youth, but age had robbed him of most of it.

"What would make you think it's acceptable to invade the privacy of my home? I am a member of the Vasullus family, and you should know better than that," he barked.

Dante looked at the man with shock. "My apologies, Joseph." He bowed his head in respect. "I am Dante Coltari. A member of the Fox Clan."

"I know exactly who you are. I live here alone for a reason. I don't like people—human or Amoveo. I agreed to let Jacqueline use this property for her fashion shoot under the strict condition that no one bothered me. She kept bugging me about it, and I finally gave in just so she'd leave me the hell alone. I did not agree to let you, or anyone else, invade my privacy."

Confused, Dante pressed him further. "I'm sorry, sir. I don't think you understand."

"Oh, I understand you just fine. The only people who were given permission to be on this property were those fashion people. *You* were not given permission to be here. I suggest you leave." He started to shut the door but stopped to deliver one last message. "By the way, not all of the Vasullus bow down and kiss the feet of the Amoveo. Some of us want a normal, quiet life and want to live out the rest of our lives in peace."

Without another word, he slammed the door in Dante's face.

Shaking his head, Dante walked back to the front of the main house. What in the hell was going on? He looked back over his shoulder at the old man's cottage and saw the drape move. He'd been watching. He'd probably been watching the entire time. Anger and suspicion reared their ugly heads, and Dante struggled to keep his temper under control. The Vasullus were supposed to work with his people and help them. This bastard wanted no part of anything or anyone.

Dante let out a frustrated sigh, but all the tension went out of his body the moment he saw Kerry. She stood next to the car, looking as fresh as a summer breeze in her red sundress. All that dreadful makeup had been removed, and her long dark hair flowed freely around her shoulders. Dante smiled, and the knots in his back loosened. He went to her and took her hand in his, enjoying how soft she felt. Smiling, she looked past him to the caretaker house.

"So, did you meet the weirdo who lives in there?" she asked with a nod.

"Yes. He's definitely," Dante paused as though searching for just the right words. "I guess you could say he's outside the box. He's not very social and doesn't seem particularly interested in us or the shoot. All he wants is his privacy. I'll tell you more about it tonight."

"Well, if anyone can understand being different, it's me." She popped up on her toes and placed a warm kiss on his lips. "Let's get out of here and give him his privacy."

They rode back into the city in silence. Dante sat in the backseat with Kerry. Much to his delight, she leaned against him and rested her head on his shoulder. He adored having the weight of her body pressed against his. The way her thigh brushed enticingly along his was enough to drive him mad with longing. He grappled with his desire for her and craved the taste of her. His body pulsed with need, and his jeans grew increasingly uncomfortable. Occasionally, he caught Pete's smiling eyes in the rearview mirror. He'd have been blind not to see what was going on, but to his credit, he said nothing.

They arrived back at the hotel and found Royal Street bustling with tourists. Before getting out of the car, Dante gave Pete the rest of the day off with strict instructions to pick them up in the morning for the second day of shooting. He helped Kerry from the car, and, holding her hand, walked into the lobby of the Monteleone.

Moments after they stepped inside the hotel Kerry let out a shriek and tore her hand from his. Startled, he looked up to see her jumping up and down in a joyful embrace with Samantha. Standing immediately behind the two women, who giggled like schoolgirls, stood a smiling Malcolm. He walked over to Dante, shook his hand, and pulled him into a warm embrace. He pulled back and squeezed his friend's shoulder.

"Now you knew that this was bound to happen, right?" Malcolm asked with a smile.

"I don't understand." Dante furrowed his brow in confusion. "What are you doing here? Aren't you two supposed to be on honeymoon somewhere?"

Malcolm sighed and threw a glance to his wife and Kerry. "There's one thing I've learned about my mate in the very short time we've been together. Nothing will come between her and her best girlfriend."

"Well, I had considered calling you both to help her with the transition, but I didn't want to intrude."

"You didn't have to." He looked at Kerry. "She did. She didn't realize it, but she reached out to Samantha telepathically. Sam kept telling me it was the equivalent of sending a 911 text message and she had to get here to help her." He opened his arms wide. "So, here we are. Besides New Orleans is a great spot for a honeymoon."

Kerry and Sam walked over to the elevator with their arms linked, smiling through tears and still giggling. "We have a suite on the same floor as you guys," Sam called over her shoulder. "Let's go upstairs to our rooms so we can stop causing a scene in the lobby."

Once upstairs, Kerry and Sam gave Malcolm and Dante their marching orders—go in the other suite and leave them alone. Girl talk meant no men allowed. The two women went into Kerry's suite and got comfortable. They kicked off their shoes, ordered wine and cheese from room service, and hunkered down on the couch for the biggest girl talk of their lives.

Kerry sipped the cool, tangy chardonnay and relished the brisk liquid as she drank it down and listened to Samantha tell her story. She went through everything— how Malcolm found her in the dream realm, the Amoveo, the Caedo, the Purists—and the real reason that AJ attacked her. Kerry listened intently, and tears stung at her eyes as Sam recounted that fateful night a couple of months ago.

"Dante tried to save you, Kerry. He almost died in the process. His own father was one of the traitors— a Purist."

Kerry nodded and wiped the tears away. "I guess he won't be bringing me home for dinner anytime soon." Her laughter faded, and her face grew serious. "Wait a minute. I got adopted into the Caedo family tree? Aren't they the ones that hunt the Amoveo? Holy crap! AJ was my cousin on my mother's side. Wow. She's Caedo? No wonder she hates me."

Sam shook her head. "All of our research so far shows that your mother doesn't know anything about the Amoveo. She barely had a relationship with her father before he died. As far as we can tell, AJ was the only one in your family who knew anything about us."

"This is all too weird." She threw back the rest of her wine. "I can't believe you don't hate me," she said quietly.

"What?" Sam reached out and took her hand, and the wolf image whisked into Kerry's mind in a comforting way. "Why on earth would I hate you?"

Kerry couldn't bring herself to look Sam in the face. She pulled her hand from Sam's. "I lied to you." She sniffed. "I told you that I didn't remember anything about that night, but I did. I remember how I let AJ force me into calling you and you almost died because of me," she shouted.

All the guilt and anger she'd been holding in bubbled up and boiled over. The tears flowed freely, and the words came out in halting sobs as she finally forced herself to look Samantha in the face.

"If I hadn't been so goddamned pathetic, if I'd touched that creepy little bastard just once—I would've seen what he was up to."

Samantha said nothing, but looked at Kerry through sympathetic eyes. Kerry wiped at the tears that stained her cheeks. She wouldn't blame Sam if she never wanted to speak to her again. Sam took both of their glasses, placed them on the coffee table, and immediately scooped her up in a loving embrace.

"I love you, Kerry." She whispered as she hugged her closely. Kerry squeezed her eyes shut and held her friend tighter. "The only people to blame for that are

AJ, the Caedo, and the Purists." She pulled back, held Kerry's face in both hands, and looked at her through serious eyes. "Don't you dare blame yourself for any of this," she said sternly. "Got it?"

Kerry nodded and sniffled. "Got it."

Thank God for best friends.

Sam released her friend with a sound of satisfaction and instantly poured them both another glass of wine. "Besides, who else are you going to talk about shapeshifting with," she said with a wink.

Kerry let out a short laugh as she took her fresh glass of wine. "Well, that is true. I guess the universe sent me the perfect best friend." She raised her glass. "Here's to us. A couple of furry friends." The two women giggled as they clinked glasses.

"So," Sam began. "You probably have about a million questions. I'm still new at this too, but I'll help you any way I can."

"That's the understatement of the year." Kerry tucked her legs up under her and sipped a little more wine from her glass. "Can we start with how did you know to come here? Did Dante call you?"

"No," Sam said through smiling sapphire eyes. "You did."

"I did?" Kerry cocked her head and looked at Sam quizzically. "No. I distinctly remember *not* making a phone call."

"You didn't use the phone, dummy. I heard you. You reached out to me with telepathy, but obviously not on purpose." She made a face. "I find that to be one of the hardest things to do. Block out other people and keep my own telepathy under control."

Kerry shook her head in disbelief. "This conversation is surreal."

"Wait a minute here. What about you?" She gave Kerry's leg a playful swat. "You never told me about your visions or anything." She looked down at her glass. "I feel badly that you didn't feel comfortable coming to me."

Kerry gave her a skeptical look. "Oh, no you don't! You're not pulling that shit with me, missy."

"What?" Sam asked all too innocently.

She narrowed her eyes. "Why didn't you tell me about your little discovery? Wolf Woman?"

Sam opened her mouth to protest but burst out laughing. "Touché! I guess we're even on that front."

"Seriously, Samantha. This is bizarre. We're both hybrids, right? I don't think I'll ever get used to saying that, by the way. And we just happen to grow up next door to each other." Her eyes narrowed, belying her suspicion. "What are the odds that's a coincidence? What are the odds that the universe *did* just happen to send me the perfect best friend?"

Sam nodded her agreement. "Malcolm and I have discussed that, and unfortunately, we don't know. The real question is: who are your birth parents? We know that you had a human parent and an Amoveo parent, but we don't even know which was which."

"I know." Kerry rolled her eyes. "I'm in some kind of cat clan. At least, according to Dante, I am." She let out a giggle that bordered on hysterical and took another sip of her wine.

"Kerry. Look at me."

Kerry did as Sam requested and found herself staring

into Sam's clan eyes. Sam's deep blue eyes had shifted into the pale blue eyes of a wolf.

"Okay," Kerry said through a shuddering breath. "That's really wild."

Sam blinked, and her eyes went back to normal. "Okay—come on. I showed you mine. Now you show me yours."

"Well, I'll try. I'm just getting the hang of controlling it." Kerry closed her eyes and focused on Dante—the memory of his scent, his strong arms, those devilishly talented lips that made her burn from the inside out. When her eyes tingled, she knew her goal had been achieved. Kerry sucked in a deep breath and opened her eyes, revealing the irises of her clan.

Sam smiled broadly and nodded her approval. "Those are some gorgeous cat eyes you've got." She leaned in to get a closer look. "Malcolm's are yellow too, but they're very different. It's the pupils. They're a completely different shape and color. Yours are a sunnier yellow than his."

"Okay, that's enough." She waved her hand at her friend. "Stop inspecting me like a lab experiment."

Sam twisted her blonde hair around one finger and got a faraway look in her eyes. "Now, I wonder which clan you're descended from?"

Kerry closed her eyes tightly, imagined them as her plain brown eyes, and they went back to normal. When she opened them, she looked at Sam and found it hard to believe she could turn into a wolf. She needed to see it. No, she *had* to see it.

"Let's go," she said with a wave of her hand. "Wolf it. Wolf out. Whatever. I have to see this with my own eyes to believe it. Otherwise, I'm going to start thinking this is some elaborate episode of *Scare Tactics*."

Sam wiggled her eyebrows and swatted Kerry's knee. "You got it." She drained the rest of her wine and stood. Standing in the center of the room, she opened her arms wide and closed her eyes. Within moments she shimmered and shifted into a massive gray wolf with bright blue eyes. Kerry stared openmouthed at the creature her friend had turned into.

What do you think? Sam's sweet voice wafted into Kerry's mind as the enormous gray wolf walked over to her.

"That is really freaking cool." Fascinated, Kerry reached out to touch the thick gray fur as if to be sure it was all really happening. "You didn't say that word. Dante... he said something before he shifted."

I know. I don't have to for some reason. It seems certain aspects of my abilities are a little different. We think that's part of what they're worried about. Samantha sat on her haunches and allowed her friend the freedom to explore. Her fur was soft and warm and very real.

"Whoa." Was about all Kerry could muster. "Okay, can you turn back into yourself now, please?"

Sam's laughter floated into Kerry's mind as she shifted, and much to Kerry's relief, stood again in her human form. "What? No applause?" Sam teased.

Tears flooded Kerry's eyes again. She wiped at them with the back of her hand and made a sound of disgust. "God. This is pathetic. I've cried more in the last forty-eight hours than I have my entire life."

Sam sat down next to her friend and gathered her in another comforting hug. The wolf burst into Kerry's mind. She squeezed her tightly, and before releasing her, placed a kiss on her cheek. Kerry leaned back to look at her friend. Sam seemed more confident than she ever had in her entire life, more comfortable in her own skin.

What had she said when she first met Malcolm? Awake. That was it. She said she felt "awake" for the first time in her life. Looking at her now, and thinking back on the last two days, Kerry knew exactly what she meant.

"I have an idea," Samantha said. "Tonight when you go to sleep, focus on your cat's eyes. Keep the image in your mind. You may be able to connect with the clan identity in the dream realm. That's where I first saw my wolf."

"Right." Kerry sighed. "Let's see if I've got this covered. Dream walking, telepathy, shapeshifting, visualizing shit out of nowhere, and blinking in and out places like some goddamned genie. Am I missing anything?" she asked in overly bright tones.

"Well, we can only visualize ourselves into places that we've imprinted on." Sam saw the confused look on Kerry's face and continued. "Basically, we must have a mental imprint on the energy of the location. For example, you can visualize yourself into any place you've physically already been in. Like, I could go back to Nonie's right now if I wanted to."

"No shit," Kerry breathed. She shook her head and took another large sip of wine. "I guess it saves on travel expenses." She knew it was a stupid joke, but quite frankly, she didn't know what else to say. Gratefully, Sam ignored her lame attempt at humor and kept explaining.

"Well, yeah, but Malcolm and I had never been

here, so we did actually fly. Neither of us could get a clear bead on your, or Dante's, energy signature. Malcolm thinks it's a combination of your psychic ability and Dante's fiercely protective nature," she added quickly. She snapped her fingers and pointed at Kerry. "Or you can create an imprint by linking with another person's energy. Like that time that Malcolm showed up in the diner and scared off Richard? Remember that?" Kerry nodded quickly. "Because he's my mate, he connected with my energy signature, and he immediately imprinted on the location of where I was."

"This all sounds like a freakin' love fest," Kerry said with a sweeping gesture. "However, let's not forget the best part. We are hated by humans and some Amoveo who think we're abominations of the two races and want us dead. Right?"

"Hey," Sam said, quickly changing the subject. "The upside is that once you're mated, you'll age really slowly and live a very long time." She smiled broadly.

Her optimistic outlook fell on deaf ears. "As a hunted freak," Kerry said somberly.

Sam let out a frustrated sigh. "I know it's a lot all at once. Believe me, I do. But this really is the missing piece to your puzzle, Kerry. *Think* about it. I know you avoid touching people like the plague, but haven't you noticed a difference lately if you do touch someone?"

Kerry's mind immediately went to Jacqueline. She straightened her back at the memory of the images. "No more pain. Well, shocks. Little zaps just under the skin, almost like static electricity, but no pain."

"I knew it!" Sam clapped her hands victoriously. "It's Dante. Don't you see? He's shielding you somehow or helping you process everything better. Something, I'm not sure exactly what, but it absolutely has to do with being his mate."

"That's another thing. Mate? Come on. Isn't that a little barbaric?"

Sam smiled wickedly. "Have you had sex yet?"

"No." Kerry smacked Sam's leg, and her face flushed. "Not exactly." She looked away. It was embarrassing to admit she was a thirty-year-old virgin. Even to her best friend.

"Well, what are you waiting for?" Sam stopped as awareness dawned on her. "Of course," she breathed. "You never have. Have you?" Kerry shook her head and shrugged as she fiddled with her glass stem. "What about that guy in college or the one from NYC this year? You mean you never...? I can't believe I didn't know you were a virgin!"

Kerry shot her a reprimanding look. "Well, I'm sorry, but it would've been a little awkward trying to explain why. And don't look at me like that. I never lied to you. I just let you assume certain things and never corrected you."

"Yeah, well, trust me. It'll have been worth the wait. There are lots of perks that go along with being Amoveo." Sam wiggled her eyebrows suggestively, and the two women burst into hysterical giggles.

"Girl, you are too twisted." Kerry said through her giggles.

Their laughter subsided, and Samantha took her friend's hand. "We'll figure it all out together. You, me, Malcolm, and Dante are all in the same boat—at least until we find out who else we can trust."

"Dante had some bird guy... um—" She snapped

her fingers searching for his name. "William. That's it. William. He was hanging out up in a tree today at the shoot."

"Yes." Sam nodded and sipped her wine. "William and Steven helped Malcolm and I as well. They know about you and I. Well, Malcolm and I are no secret anymore." She shrugged one shoulder. "Truthfully, most Amoveo that I've met have been very welcoming. William and Steven are the only other two who know about the Purist Network other than us. Oh, and Richard, of course."

"Who's Richard?"

"He's the Prince of the Amoveo people. He leads the Council." Kerry's face belied her confusion, and she motioned for further explanation from Sam. "The Council is their governing body," Sam explained. "Two members from every clan and two Vasullus family members work with Richard to keep the peace among the clans and keep an eye out for any Caedo activity."

"So this Council... they don't know about the Purists who want us dead?"

"No." Sam shook her head. "Dante's father was *on* the Council. How's that for betrayal? We know he wasn't working alone, but we don't know who with. They are working in a very effective underground network." Sam's eyes shimmered with tears. "They killed my parents, Kerry. That boating accident when I was a baby." She let out a slow breath. "Well, it was no accident. My mother was human, as you know, and my father was in the Gray Wolf Clan. She had some kind of psychic ability, which made her able to mate with an Amoveo." She sighed and shrugged her shoulders. "Apparently, some of the Amoveo didn't like it. All these years, my parents' murder was blamed on the Caedo."

Kerry grabbed her hand and squeezed it tightly. "Oh my God. Sam, I'm so sorry."

"They blamed the Caedo, of course, and no one had a reason to think otherwise. Don't you see? They're very dangerous, and what worries me more is that we don't know who else might be one of them. That note that you got today really scares me. Whoever sent that knows you're a hybrid."

"Yes, but it also sounds like they know something about who my real parents were. If we find the son of a bitch—this sicko the 'Punisher'—who wrote that note, maybe I can find out where I came from."

The two women sat in thoughtful silence for a few minutes. Kerry inherently knew deep down that she was in danger. Someone out there did want her dead, and right about now the only people she really trusted were Dante, Samantha, and Malcolm.

"Can we really trust these other guys, William and Steven? What if they're involved somehow?"

Sam shook her head. "There's no way they're involved. They haven't found their mates yet, and their time is running out. Both are acutely aware that their mate must be either a human or another hybrid that is under the radar like us. They have just as much at stake as we do. More maybe." She shrugged.

"Are you sure?"

"Yes. If their mate were another Amoveo, they would've connected in the dream realm a long time ago and completed their mating ceremony."

Kerry looked at Sam as if she had lost her mind.

"Mating ceremony? What the hell are you talking about now?"

Sam smiled and held her hands up in a motion of defeat. "Oh no." She laughed. "I'm leaving that all up to Dante to explain."

A knock at the door prevented Kerry from peppering Sam with a litany of questions. She threw her the evil eye before she opened the door. "Who is it?"

"It's us." Dante's voice washed over her deliciously.

Kerry smiled and opened the door, allowing the two men access to the suite. Malcolm wasted no time settling down next to Sam on the couch and gathering her into the crook of his arm. Dante walked past Kerry and delicately brushed one finger along her palm, which instantly sent lovely shivers up her spine. He sat in the large armchair and winked at her wickedly. Kerry swallowed hard and attempted to control the firestorm he ignited with one touch.

She closed the door and eyed him suspiciously. "What's the deal? If you can blink in and out of places, why walk over and knock? Why not just—you know, poof." She made a lavish swirling motion with her hand.

Malcolm laughed heartily. "My gorgeous mate had informed me that if I did that while the two of you were talking, I'd be in big trouble."

Kerry went over and sat on the arm of Dante's chair. He looked up at her with that disarming smile and wrapped his arm around her waist. She still couldn't get over how good it felt to be touched by him. Even the simple act of placing his arm around her waist seemed like a bit of a miracle.

"Well, you were smart to heed her advice," she said to Malcolm. "See, Dante." She looked into his handsome face. "This guy here has figured out the key to a happy marriage."

"Oh really," he replied quietly. His fingers softly stroked her waist, and his eyes remained locked on hers. They stared into one another's eyes as their energy mingled and crackled in the air between them. The sound of Malcolm clearing his throat brought them back to reality. Kerry's face reddened, and she quickly hopped up off the arm of Dante's chair.

"We need to freshen up and unpack before we meet up with the others tonight. I'm sure you two want to do the same... or something." He smiled and exchanged a knowing look with Samantha. They rose from the couch with their fingers intertwined. Sam turned to Kerry and smiled reassuringly. "We'll see you downstairs later on this evening."

Then Malcolm whispered the ancient language, and they vanished into thin air.

Kerry made a sound of disbelief and shook her head. "I don't think I'm ever going to get used to that."

Chapter 11

AFTER SAM AND MALCOLM BLINKED THEMSELVES OUT of the room, Kerry became highly aware that she was alone again with Dante. She stood there feeling awkward and unsure of what to do or say. Dante said nothing but stared at her intently.

She squirmed under his hot gaze as the energy in the room shifted and rippled around her. It reminded her of being underwater and getting swept up in the current, the kind that turns you upside down and has your head spinning. At the moment, it was all she could do to keep from getting swept up in a tidal wave named Dante.

"What is that I'm feeling in the air? Is that you?" The words came out sounding much huskier than she'd intended, and she swallowed hard, hoping to keep her body under some kind of control. What was the deal? She turned into a horny harlot with one look from him. Was it like this for all women, or were shapeshifters hornier than humans? Yet another question to add to the list for Samantha.

"Yes. We read energy, or emotions, in the air. Like sonar." His gaze stamped with desire remained fixed on her. "What you're feeling now," he whispered, "is my desire for you, Kerry. I want you."

Kerry sucked in a sharp breath as he stood up slowly from his chair, wanting to move, but her quivering body wouldn't cooperate. She was a walking contradiction.

Her mind told her to slow down, that she was taking things too fast and that she didn't know what she was doing. However, her body wanted her brain to shut the hell up. *Now*.

He closed the distance between them with slow, deliberate steps, and with extreme tenderness removed the wineglass from her hand, gently placing it on the table next to them. He turned back to her and tucked a long dark lock of hair behind her ear. His eyes slowly seared their way down the length of her trembling body and back up again. It was as if he branded her with his gaze, claiming every inch of her as his without actually touching her.

"I have been eager to finish what we started earlier today," he murmured softly and placed a deliciously erotic kiss on the edge of her ear. "I can't get you out of my mind." His breath blew hot and moist against the hollow of her throat.

Her eyes fluttered closed, and she allowed herself to float in the seductive sensation of his voice. She tilted her head and opened herself to him as he ran one finger along her jaw and down her throat. She shuddered, full of apprehension and a need that clamored to be satisfied, reveling in the erotic effect of his touch.

"I can still taste you." He placed a hot kiss on her collarbone and licked and nipped at the soft flesh. Dante trailed his fingers down the heated skin of her arm and brushed his thumb along the inside of her wrist. Jesus. Even that one featherlight brush of his thumb practically brought her to orgasm. Kerry's eyes tingled and shifted, hard and fast. Her body quaked with lust and anticipation.

"I want you, Kerry. I want to taste every last inch of

you," he said the words slowly as his fingers tangled with hers.

Kerry opened her eyes, locked her glowing gaze with his, swallowed hard, and licked her bottom lip. No one had ever looked at her with such intense emotion. His desire for her was stamped in the devastatingly handsome features of his face, the brilliance of his eyes, and the humming muscles of his rock-hard body.

Lust. Desire. Protection. Love?

She'd been ogled plenty of times for her beauty. She'd been criticized and picked apart for her size. She'd been inspected in every possible way, but no one had ever looked at her like Dante did. He looked at her as if he could see her soul. He was the first man who really saw *her*.

"I trust you," she whispered.

Gazes locked, he took her hand and placed it against the impressive evidence of his arousal. The air rushed from her lungs, and her heart raced. This was it. No more movies. No more fantasies. No more imagining. This was real. He rubbed her hand against the hot length of him and brushed his lips softly against hers. The material of his jeans felt rough, and hot friction burned enticingly under her fingertips.

"Do you want me?" he whispered into her ear through shuddering breaths. "If you're not sure, then tell me now, because if we take this any further I don't know if I'll be able to stop myself."

She leaned back, forcing him to look her in the eyes. His gaze burned brightly, desire stamped harshly into all of his features. She almost laughed out loud at the ridiculous nature of the question. Did she want him?

She'd never wanted anyone, or anything, more in her life. All she wanted was to be connected to him body, mind, and spirit. She knew that the years of loneliness and isolation were a thing of the past, and she owed it all to the discovery of this brilliantly unusual man.

"I want you," she breathed. "I've never been more certain of anything in my entire life." She squeezed him through his jeans and nipped his lower lip. "Now stop talking, and take me to bed."

A slow smile spread across his face as he scooped her up effortlessly into his arms. Impressive. She was no wilting lily, and there weren't a whole lot of men out there who could pick her up as if she weighed nothing at all. A smile quirked at her lips. Now *that* was a turn on.

For a split second, Kerry had the brief sensation of falling, like that feeling that sometimes happens when falling asleep. The next minute they were in the bedroom of her suite. He cocked one eyebrow, admiring his own cleverness. "Fast enough for you, princess?"

Kerry raised one eyebrow in return. "I hope that not everything will be this fast," she teased. "I'd hate to blink and miss it."

A growl rumbled deep in his throat. "I want to be buried inside of you so deep… you'll never forget how it feels when I touch you."

Kerry tangled his silky soft hair between her fingers and pulled his face to hers, bringing their lips barely an inch apart. "I thought I told you to stop talking."

She pulled him to her, capturing his mouth greedily with hers. He opened to her willingly and swept his tongue seductively along hers. Kerry moaned softly, enjoying the vibrations that fluttered along their fused lips. Still holding her cradled in his arms, he knelt on the large soft bed and with the greatest care laid her down.

He stayed there for a moment, keeping his eyes locked with hers. Kerry swallowed hard, and her heart fluttered wildly in her chest. The anticipation was killing her. Her body remained wound so tight that she could very well orgasm from just looking at him. No. She wanted this to last.

Dante pulled his T-shirt over his head in one swift movement and tossed it into the corner of the room. The sight of his broad muscled chest brought a rush of dampness between her legs, and at this particular moment, she was extremely glad the lights were on; she didn't want to miss a single beautiful inch of him.

Her eye was immediately drawn to the star-shaped scar on his chest, and her heart gave a funny little flutter She nibbled on her bottom lip nervously as she reached up and ran her fingers along the dime-sized area of puckered skin. She knew he'd gotten that the night AJ had attacked her. He almost died for her, and she knew that he'd do it again if he had to.

She murmured softly, placed a tender kiss on his marred flesh, and smiled when he shuddered under her gentle ministrations. There was something powerful about the fact that she could elicit that kind of a reaction from him, that she could make him quiver, shake, and whisper her name.

It was evident that he could drive her into a horny frenzy with practically just a look, so there was a certain level of satisfaction to find that she could evoke the same response from him. Lips curved in a satisfied smile, Kerry rained tender kisses on his chest and lay back again to take in the glorious sight of him perched above her.

Her fingers brushed over the dark hairs on his chest and wandered down his washboard abs. She loved the feel of rough and smooth beneath her fingertips, and he moaned softly as she continued her exploration. Her eyes widened at the sight of the impressive bulge in his pants. It felt enormous beneath her hand, and if it was possible, it looked even bigger.

Her hands fluttered to the button of his jeans, and she fumbled briefly before he took her hands gently in his. A smile curved his lips as he shook his head slowly, and with great care, pushed her back against the pillows. Kerry smiled, but as nervous as she was, she knew she could trust him.

She was his, and he was hers.

Dante reached down, and with great tenderness, peeled the thin sundress from her heated body. As he removed the garment from her hot skin, he trailed delicate kisses along every inch of newly exposed flesh. She kept her eyes closed and focused on the breathtaking pleasure that whipped through her from head to toe. She lay now only in her panties. Her breasts felt full, and her nipples tingled as he showered kisses along her soft belly.

When he stood up, a chill passed over her as the warmth of his body left hers. He tossed the dress aside and swiftly divested himself of the rest of his clothing. Dante looked down at her with stark need stamped in his features. Her eyes grew wide at the sight of his huge shaft, and she watched with fascination as he stroked it slowly. She wondered how on earth she would be able to accommodate his size. Kerry's tongue flicked nervously over her lips, but the moment her eyes locked with his, any apprehension she had melted away.

"You are spectacularly beautiful," he whispered. "And you are all mine."

Smiling, he leaned over her and covered her body with his. She sighed as his hot skin sizzled seductively along hers. He settled himself between her legs and paid thorough attention to her mouth once again. His strong hands tangled in her hair, teeth nibbled, and lips seared delightful kisses down her neck. Kerry's breath came quickly as he took her nipple into the warm, moist cavern of his mouth. She arched her chest against him and mewled soft sounds of pleasure as he suckled her breast and rolled her other nipple between his fingers. She writhed against him. She had to get closer, needed… more. Something to satisfy the desire that threatened to consume her.

The pleasure burned low in her belly, and her womb clenched. He moved lower and sprinkled wet kisses along her waist and the full curve of her hip. Kerry grabbed his thick hair in her hands as his head moved down between her legs. She quivered and moaned softly as he brushed delicate kisses on the inside of her thigh and opened her to him.

Her body tensed, and panic bubbled up through the passion. She wasn't quite ready for what she suspected he was about to do. Her fingers dug into his shoulders as she touched her mind to his. *Dante…*

Dante, sensing her fear and nervousness, murmured soothing words in hushed tones as he peeled the miniscule panties from her body. "Don't be scared, princess," he whispered between soft kisses on her hip. "We don't have to go there yet."

Relief washed over her as he kissed his way back up her body, placing soft, delicate butterfly kisses along her waist, over her breasts, and up to the hollow of her throat, ministrations that were so gentle they almost made her weep.

He *knew*. She didn't have to say "no" or reject him. He didn't make her feel like some prudish little girl. He simply knew that she wasn't ready for that and respected it.

Dante lay alongside her and slipped one arm underneath her back, cradling her against the shelter of his body. He brushed his talented, gentle fingers over her sensitive breasts, which sent her heart racing.

"Is this alright?" he whispered against her hair. Eyes closed, absorbing every sensation, Kerry shuddered with pleasure and writhed seductively in response to his delicate, seductive touch. His fingers wandered over the quivering flesh of her belly and stopped short of her most sensitive spot. "Do you want me to stop?" he asked as kissed her ear.

"Don't you dare," she whispered hoarsely as she ran her hand along his rock-hard thigh.

"Your wish is my command, princess," he said as he slipped those talented fingers of his between her folds.

Kerry gasped with pleasure as he sank two fingers deep into her, while his thumb paid thorough attention to the sweetest spot of all. She gripped the sheets, her hands clenching furiously, as he continued to massage her to the brink. Her breath came quickly, and her body shuddered as she teetered on the edge of this newly discovered carnal need. Pleasure shot through her in lightning fast streaks, and she cried out his name as he brought her higher and higher. White-hot lights burst behind her eyes, and her hips bucked against his hand. Her head thrashed back and forth as he took her to the very edge.

Kerry reached behind her, grabbed the headboard, and held on as his talented fingers continued to torture her in the most delicious way. She writhed wildly, but he held her there, anchored her to the bed as he relentlessly brought her to the brink of orgasm. Just when she thought she couldn't take anymore, as she was about to go tumbling over the precipice, he stopped, and his mouth captured hers eagerly, knowing that she was ready for more.

Kerry kissed him back with ardent fervor and wrapped her arms tightly around his firm body. Dante pulled back and locked his glowing eyes on hers. Their breath came in ragged gasps, both on the edge of an all-consuming lust and struggling for control. Their sweaty, heated bodies slid lusciously against one another.

"Are you ready?" he asked softly.

"Are you kidding?" she asked through a shaky breath.

The look on her face held nothing but trust. He tenderly captured her mouth with his and carefully positioned the head of his erection at the opening of her swollen, wet entrance. Slowly, inch by inch, he sank into her tight channel. Dante stayed there for a moment, giving her time to stretch and accommodate his massive size. She moved against him, impatiently urging him forward.

"Don't tease me." She dug her fingers into his flesh. "I want all of you inside of me."

"As you wish, princess." Dante sank into her with one deep stroke, breaking through her thin barrier. He kissed her deeply, swallowing her soft cry. Heat flashed brightly as their bodies joined. Desire crashed over them as he drove into her with slow, deep, penetrating strokes. Kerry thought she'd lose herself in the intense tidal waves of pleasure. Dante increased the tempo, and she raised her hips to meet him, needing to increase the delicious friction as he entered her. He rode her furiously, and Kerry cried his name as he arrowed into her time and again.

The white-hot bliss swelled relentlessly, and as the orgasm began to crest, his voice crashed into her mind. *Nos es unus. Materia pro totus vicis. Ago intertwined. Forever.*

They cried out in unison as the orgasm tore through them. Ripples of intense heat and raw passion flared as their minds and bodies joined. Colors burst around them in the air and swirled wildly behind her eyes. The explosive climax ebbed and pulsed, until only the tiny pleasurable aftershocks flickered through their exhausted bodies. They lay with their bodies intertwined, and Kerry didn't think she'd ever catch her breath.

"That," she said through huffing breaths against the hollow of his throat, "was well worth the wait."

Dante chuckled softly and kissed the tip of her nose. "I'm very glad you approve." He moved off of her and disengaged himself from the warmth of her body. Dante lay next to her and pulled the huge comforter over their sweaty nakedness. He wrapped her in his arms, and she rested her head against his chest. She noticed the way his heart beat exactly in time with hers.

"Now that we've completed the mating rite," he said with a big grin, "I guess you're stuck with me."

"What?" Kerry propped herself on her elbow and looked at him as though he'd lost his mind. "That's it?

We go at it like a couple of sex-starved teenagers, you mutter some kind of nonsense I don't understand, and we're mated."

"Yes," he said in that irritatingly calm manner. The one that made her want to punch him in the nose. "And it's not nonsense. It's Latin."

"I see." She narrowed her eyes. "Well, Tarzan, would you mind telling me what you said?"

He laid his head back and adjusted the mountain of pillows as he played with one long strand of her black hair. "Basically: 'We are one. Mates for all time. Lives intertwined. Forever.' I said it in Latin though, because that is the formal language of our people." He shrugged one shoulder. "We use it for our formal ceremonies."

Kerry nodded slowly and held the covers over her naked and still highly sensitized breasts. "Forever is a very long time. What if you get bored of me? Or I end up thinking you're a major asshole? Then what? Huh?"

Dante laughed loudly. "I'm sure I'll make mistakes from time to time and qualify for asshole status. But I promise I'll do my best to keep that to a minimum. My goal in life is to keep you safe and make you happy."

Kerry opened her mouth to respond, but before she could utter a word, he took her face in his large, warm hands and kissed her deeply. She wanted to protest and tell him this whole thing was ridiculous, but he kissed it right out of her. The scary truth was that somewhere along the way she had fallen in love with him. As Dante wrapped her in his arms and ran his talented hands over her eager body—*forever* sounded pretty good.

The Punisher walked along the creaky porch of the huge old house. This was the place. This would be where everything revealed itself and where the traitor would pay for his sins. First that traitor would watch the bitch die, and then his own private hell would begin. The Punisher went inside the house and took stock of the exact layout on the first floor. All rooms opened into each other in an almost circular layout.

Once the downstairs had been evaluated, the Punisher went up to the second floor and perused the various bedrooms. The door at the end of the long hallway led to a room that revealed much more than any of them would expect. A sick, twisted smile spread across the Punisher's face as the smooth glass bottle rolled between two gloved hands.

"Everything is going to go exactly as planned." The words came out in a hissing whisper. "Once I have him bound in his animal form—he'll be trapped there for eternity and mine to do with as I please."

"But what about the others?" a male voice asked quietly. "Is there enough binding power for all of them?"

The Punisher had practically forgotten that he was there. He was a means to an end. Nothing more. He would certainly be easy enough to dispose of once his purpose had been served. The Punisher turned quicker than a snake, grabbed him by the throat, and shoved him against the wall.

"Are you questioning me? Because you do realize that I could crush you like a bug. Just a bit more pressure and—snap—you're dead." The Punisher laughed as the stupid fool's eyes bugged out, and his face turned bright red while he attempted to shake his head and deny the accusation. The Punisher's fingers dug deeper into his neck, which elicited a wretched gurgling noise. "I didn't think so." The vice-like fingers loosened their grip and sent him to his knees. Gasping for air, he attempted to utter an apology.

"Silence!" The Punisher pinned him there with a piercing stare. "You can be certain that my end of the arrangements will be perfectly taken care of. You just worry about your job." The Punisher squatted down and took his chin in a gloved hand. "Do your job, and you will receive all that I promised you. Understand?" The man nodded wordlessly, and the Punisher helped him to his feet. "Now, run along, and prove to me that you're worthy of the rewards that you seek."

He bowed quickly and scurried out the door. The Punisher sighed and took one last look around the carefully arranged room. Tomorrow. Justice would be served tomorrow. The Punisher stuffed the bottle back into the pocket of the long trench coat and walked downstairs. Stepping into the dark Louisiana night, the heavy black boots crunched insistently along the gravel driveway. Even the creatures in the swamp seemed fearful and silenced themselves to avoid the Punisher's wrath.

Chapter 12

After a decadent afternoon of lovemaking, all Dante really wanted to do was sleep with Kerry's naked body wrapped tightly around his. However, their meeting that night could not be ignored. They met Sam and Malcolm downstairs as planned, and the four walked over to the Zankoff's bar.

The Louisiana air had cooled, and a warm, comfortable breeze seemed ever present. The moment they stepped outside, Dante sensed Kerry's energy shift as she eyed the various pedestrians nervously. He reached out and took her hand in his. She looked up at him with a mixture of gratitude and trepidation.

It will be alright. Remember to practice shielding your mind. It should help you shut out any unwanted visions.

She smiled and squeezed his hand, clearly grateful for his reassurance but still wary. Now that they had completed the mating rite, their connection held stronger than ever. Dante hoped it would help her manage her abilities, but the truth was he didn't know. He could only hope, and it was ridiculously frustrating to feel so helpless. All he wanted to do was to fix everything and make it all okay. The truth was that he was as uncertain about how this would play out as she was.

The two couples navigated the bustling French Quarter quickly and easily. Malcolm and Dante stayed particularly alert, scanning their surroundings periodically for any threat that might be hiding nearby. They walked all the way down Royal Street in order to avoid Bourbon Street for as long as possible. Royal Street was not quite as busy at night. Antique shops and art galleries dotted the narrow street, and it found more pedestrian traffic during the day. After several blocks, they turned left onto Ursulines and finally found their desired destination, The Den.

The Den sat at the corner of Ursulines and Dauphine. It was a tiny bar in one of the oldest buildings in the quarter. Dante couldn't help but notice that the bar's emblem was a snarling tiger. It made sense. They were both members of the Tiger Clan, and two more Amoveo who were hiding in plain sight among the humans.

They stepped inside the understated dark space and found it surprisingly empty. The walls were lined with old-fashioned muskets, paintings of pirate ships, anchors, and other seaworthy paraphernalia. Two crusty old men sat at the long wooden bar on stools that they likely frequented on a nightly basis. A few people peppered the tiny tables, but all in all, it was quiet compared to the rest of the quarter's watering holes.

Dante caught the young bartender's eye. He was Amoveo, and in all likelihood, Boris Zankoff. He motioned for them to meet him at the end of the bar. They approached him cautiously, and Dante sized him up more like a potential enemy than an ally. Boris had long dark hair, and like most Amoveo men, he stood well over six feet. Based on the size and strength of him, he hoped he wouldn't have to fight him. Tigers were known for incredible strength and skill in battle.

Boris smiled broadly and extended a hand. "Welcome

to The Den," he said as he shook hands with Dante and Malcolm. "It's a pleasure to meet you." He turned and delivered a devastating smile to the two women. "A great pleasure."

Dante cleared his throat and wrapped his arm possessively around Kerry. "Boris. I'd like you to meet my mate. Kerry Smithson." He put extra emphasis on "my mate." "This other lovely lady is Malcolm's mate. Samantha Drew."

The women smiled politely. Their uncertainty of Boris was glaringly clear. Their energy waves pulsed with nervousness.

Boris raised his eyebrows in surprise. "Really?" A huge smile spread across his face, and he leaned in so the other patrons wouldn't hear him. "You're *both* hybrids?" he whispered with genuine excitement. "Aren't you?"

Dante and Malcolm exchanged a look and pulled their women closer.

"This is wonderful news." He beamed. "Please go upstairs. We have the private room set aside. Steven and William are already up there. I will join you shortly."

They nodded their thanks and went to the wooden staircase at the back. As they passed the two drunks sitting at the bar, one of them grabbed Dante by the arm. "Be careful," he slurred through whiskey-tainted breath. "There's a tiger loose around here somewhere. I saw it, you know." He hiccupped loudly and almost fell off his stool.

Boris reached over the bar and grabbed the old man. Effortlessly, he hoisted him back on his seat before he landed on the floor. "Okay Bill. That's enough fish stories out of you. There's a tiger on our bar signage, big guy. Sit tight. I've got some coffee brewing now." Boris gave them an apologetic look. "I'll explain later. Please go on up. Make yourself at home."

As they walked up the creaking wooden stairs, Dante took note of the pictures that lined the wall. There were several shots of famous people who'd stopped in and taken photos with Boris or Pasha. They were remarkably similar, and both gorgeous. They looked to be in their midtwenties, which meant time was running out. It was disturbing that neither had connected with mates.

Dante sympathized with them. Not too long ago, he had been in their situation. No mate and an uncertain future. He shuddered at the memory and instinctively reached for Kerry's hand. He tangled his fingers in hers as she climbed the steps in front of him. He needed to touch her, to make sure she was actually there. He made a mental note to never take her for granted, to always remember how fortunate he was to have found her.

When they reached the landing, they found William and Steven at a table against the back wall. As they approached, Kerry gripped his hand tightly. *Are you sure we can trust them?*

Smiling, Steven stood up and gestured to the empty chairs. "You can trust us. I promise. Please. Have a seat."

Kerry flushed with embarrassment. "I'm sorry. I'm still getting used to things."

Steven laughed heartily as they all sat down. "No problem. Besides I can't blame you with Willie over here. He always looks that way. Don't worry. It's nothing personal."

William shot him a look of disdain and eyed his ripped jeans and heavy metal T-shirt. "Me? You're the one who looks like you just rolled out of bed. Perhaps these two beautiful women are disgusted at the sight of you." He straightened his tie and smoothed the lapels on his jacket. William then turned his serious dark eyes on Sam and Kerry. "I am at your service, ladies," he said with curt nod of his head.

The four sat at the table as Steven poured everyone a beer from the icy pitchers on the table. Dante drew a long sip and relished the cold crisp beer as it slid down his throat. Silence hung awkwardly in the air, and it became glaringly clear that no one quite knew where to start.

Dante cleared his throat and raised his glass. "I suppose I should begin with a toast to my beautiful mate Kerry, and the lovely Samantha. Without you two ladies, Malcolm and I would surely be lost."

Everyone raised their classes and amid the clinking came Boris's deep voice. "Here's to finding our mates as well and ensuring the future of our race."

Dante and Malcolm eyed him cautiously as he walked over with his glass raised. Boris immediately tapped his glass with everyone at the table before making himself comfortable next to William.

"I have to say, I am very happy to meet you all. You must understand that until recently, there had only been rumors about the existence of hybrids. It is truly a miracle for those of us that still haven't found our mates," he said, gesturing to William and Steven. "My sister and I have been unsuccessful in connecting with our mates. When you're in your teens, thirty seems so far away," he said wistfully. "But in your twenties… well, without a mate… it's too close for comfort."

"You do realize that not everyone in our race is as excited about this as you are, don't you, Boris?" Malcolm asked.

Dante could tell he was testing the waters with Boris, looking to see if he was as genuinely happy as he claimed to be. Dante couldn't detect any deception or darkness in his energy signature. So far, he seemed to be on the up and up. His gaze flicked to Kerry's tense face. She smiled briefly, but quickly turned her attention to the drink in her hand.

"What?" Boris cast a confused look back at him and scooped up some bar mix from the bowl on the table. "Why would you think that? If we can't find our mates, then we're in big trouble." He popped the snacks in his mouth.

"I realize that, but—" Malcolm exchanged a knowing look with Steven. "There are rumblings that some of our people look down upon the cross-mating with humans."

Boris scoffed and brushed some crumbs off his shirt. "That's ridiculous." He took a pull off his beer and leaned back in his chair. "We are at the point that if we don't mate with humans we're going to die out. Our entire race will disappear."

"True, Boris," William interrupted. "It's not as if we have a choice. Fate is fate, and we are at its mercy."

Dante felt Kerry's body shiver at the mention of fate. He couldn't blame her. It seemed as though none of them had very much control over their futures, but to hell with it. She was his future, he was hers, and no one had better try and get in the way of that.

He reached over, rubbed the back of her neck reassuringly, and connected his mind with hers. *Are you alright?* He glanced at her, and she nodded almost imperceptibly. She obviously didn't want to risk using her telepathy around the others.

"Does anyone know anything about Joseph Vasullus?" Malcolm asked.

"Yes." Boris nodded, and a hint of sadness lined his eyes. "He is Vasullus, but he's not like most of them."

Kerry raised her hand as if she was in school, and all eyes landed on her. "Excuse me? Can someone please take pity on the newbie over here?" she said, pointing at herself. "And please explain to me who or what a Vasullus is?"

"Nuts," Sam said with a snap of her fingers. "I'm sorry." She made an apologetic face. "I forgot to tell you about them in our chat today. They are the only humans other than the Caedo family who know all about our race. They're kind of like our protectors. Generations of them have helped to keep us hidden from the human world. They're on Team Amoveo basically," she said with a big smile. "I guess you could say it's their family legacy."

"Uh-huh," Kerry said slowly. "So, wait a second." She put her hands up as if she were stopping traffic and narrowed her eyes. "You mean to tell me that the location for my photo shoot, which is the whole reason I'm in New Orleans in the first place, just so happens to be at a house owned by one of these Vasullus guys." She turned to Dante. "You knew about this?" Realization came over her features. "No wonder you were acting so hinky."

Dante felt Kerry's apprehension rise. *I didn't want to overwhelm you with information. I'm sorry.*

Kerry rolled her eyes and crossed her arms. *Don't do that again. From now on, it's full disclosure. Got it?*

Dante nodded, took her hand in his, and squeezed it. *Got it, princess.*

The others eyed the two of them warily. The tension between them was palpable, and silence hung thickly in the air. William shifted uncomfortably in his seat and straightened his tie. They knew that the two of them were communicating telepathically, even if they couldn't hear what was being said. It was obvious Kerry was irked. Awkward.

Steven was the first to break the silence. "So Kerry's photo shoot just happens to be taking place at a house owned by a Vasullus?" He took a sip of his beer and looked expectantly at the rest of them. "That *does* seem to be too much a coincidence. Doesn't it?"

"Unfortunately, yes," Boris nodded somberly. "It wouldn't bother me if he was a traditional Vasullus family member, but as I was saying, he's not exactly one of the boys."

"How do you mean?" Malcolm asked quietly. "I've never heard of a Vasullus family member who was not devoted to our people."

"Well, he doesn't work within the fold, so to speak. He's made it perfectly clear to Pasha and I that he wants nothing do with us, or any other Amoveo, for that matter." He leaned his elbows on the dark wooden table and poured himself another beer. "That's fine with Pasha. She can't stand him."

"So you're saying he's *not* on 'Team Amoveo,'" Kerry said, making air quotes with her fingers. "Awesome."

"Do you know why he has chosen to reject his

calling?" Malcolm asked with genuine concern. "Why he's turned his back on our race?"

"When I asked him once, he babbled on about how he didn't choose to be in the Vasullus family and that he was sick and tired of fate forcing a future on him." Boris shrugged and placed his pilsner glass on the scarred table. "Destiny could kiss his ass and so on. Blah, blah, blah." He sighed, laced his fingers behind his head, and leaned back in his chair.

Malcolm turned to Samantha. "I should call Davis and see what he knows about Joseph. I didn't realize the extent of the situation."

Kerry almost spit out her beer. "Wait. Davis? The old caretaker guy? Nonie's boyfriend? Old Davis is one of these Vasullus people? You mean he knows about all this crazy shit?"

Samantha smiled at her friend's obvious surprise and nodded. "Yup. Davis Vasullus. Pretty cool, huh?"

"I don't think I can take any more surprises. Jeez." Kerry shook her head in disbelief. "Nonie knows all about this stuff too, doesn't she?"

Sam smiled and leaned her head onto Malcolm's shoulder. "She knew about this longer than I did. How's *that* for crazy?"

Do you think we can trust Boris? Malcolm's voice cut into Dante's mind. He glanced over at him and flicked a quick glance to their host.

I don't think we have much of a choice. He seems genuine enough. We have to tell him about the note at least. See if he's ever heard of the "Punisher." But we keep the Purist Conspiracy to ourselves.

Malcolm nodded as Dante removed the red note from

his pocket. He opened it up and slid it across the table for the other three men to see. "This was delivered to Kerry at the hotel this morning."

The three men leaned in and read the note in silence. Anger and frustration rippled off them in violent waves. The glasses and pitcher on the table vibrated and skittered in response to the volatile energy coming off the men. Kerry's eyes widened. She gripped Dante's hand and dug her fingernails into his palm. He had sensed her panic the instant their energy waves pulsed through the room. Dante reached out to her and reassuringly joined his mind with hers. *Focus on your breathing, and filter it out.* Her mouth set in a tight line, and she let out the breath she'd been holding. Slowly, her grip on his hand loosened, and her heart rate slowed down. She threw him a subtle glance of gratitude.

"Who the hell is the 'Punisher'?" Steven asked, breaking the tension. "It sounds like a bad comic book character." He scoffed, shoved the note away, and chugged the rest of his beer.

"We don't know, and that's part of our problem." Dante kept his voice low.

"Well, it's obviously one of the Caedo," Boris said. He turned his gaze to Samantha. "The story about the Caedo coming after you, Samantha, is quickly becoming legend. We've been very impressed by how quickly you have adapted to your abilities. We heard you gave that AJ character a run for his money." His smile faded when he turned his attention to Dante. "We were very sorry to hear about the loss of your father. We've all heard about how bravely he fought. At least he died in battle, the death of a true warrior.

You must be honored that he died in an effort to protect Malcolm's mate."

Boris didn't notice the look exchanged by William and Steven, who knew the true story of that night. Dante did his best to keep his feelings about his father's betrayal at bay. They didn't know if they could really trust Boris and Pasha yet, so for now, they would have to believe the lie. He wrestled with his conflicting emotions and struggled to keep his energy waves even.

"You'll never know how strongly I feel about what my father did," Dante said through a strained smile.

"Hey listen, on the way back to the hotel, why don't you swing by Jackson Square. Joseph works there as a palm reader for the tourists. Look, he might be willing to help you two." He shrugged. "Hey, who knows? Maybe he just has a thing against those of us in the Tiger Clan. It's worth a shot, right?" He paused for a second and then gave Kerry a quizzical look. "What clan are you from anyway?"

Kerry shrugged. "I have no idea." She nodded toward Dante. "He's convinced I'm from one of the cat clans."

Boris nodded as his intense gaze slid over her. Dante didn't like the way he seemed to be inspecting his mate and fought the urge to break his nose. Boris glanced at Dante and smiled. He shook his head and popped some more snack mix in his mouth.

"Shit," he said between crunches. "You are one jealous and protective guy. Relax, brother. I'm just trying to see if she's from our clan."

Dante shifted in his seat, embarrassed for being so bloody transparent. "Well?" Kerry squeezed his fingers reassuringly and winked at him playfully.

"You're a cat alright," he said to Kerry. "But not the Tiger Clan. I'd bet my hide on it. So, maybe you should give old Joseph a chance to help you out."

"I doubt it." Dante shook his head somberly. "I met the old goat today—out at the house in Braithwaite. He was less than welcoming. But he might respond differently to one of you," he said with a nod to Kerry, Malcolm, and Sam.

"You approached him at his place?" Boris let out a low whistle. "He's got a reputation throughout the city for being less than social. I'm surprised you didn't wind up with a shotgun blast up your ass." Boris scoffed, but then his face grew serious. "You've got to find out more about Joseph. But watch your back." He sat thoughtfully for a moment, and his brow furrowed. "I think we should talk to that designer, Jacqueline. From what I hear, she's the only one in town he will speak to with any civility."

Kerry let out a sigh, squeezed her eyes shut, and rubbed her temples. "This whole situation is getting more twisted by the second."

William glanced at his watch and stood abruptly. "I have other business to attend to. If you need me, do not hesitate to call on me."

"You've been disappearing quite a bit lately, William." Surprised by William's sudden departure, Dante looked at him through narrowed eyes. "Steven said you took off today at the shoot too. Is everything alright?"

"You are not the only one with pressing business, Dante, or with a mate to find," he shot back sharply. He turned to the others and bowed his head. "Good night." Then he whispered the ancient language and disappeared into the air.

Kerry shook her head. "I am never going to get used to that disappearing act."

Steven waved off her concern. "Ah, William's always been a bit of a loner. He keeps it close to the vest. Who knows? Maybe his favorite men's store got in more of those nifty suits he likes so much."

Steven's teasing comment had the desired effect and got them all laughing. The tension in the room dissipated, and he poured himself another beer. "Okay," he began. "So the game plan is the four of you are going to go down to Jackson Square and try to talk to the cranky old goat Joseph. Boris and I are going to see if we can sniff out more information from Jacqueline, and see what we can find out about this Punisher guy," he said.

Dante stood up from the table with Kerry's hand firmly in his. "That sounds about right. I can count on you tomorrow? We'll need extra eyes out at the shoot again."

Steven nodded. "Absolutely." Then he rose from the chair and elbowed Boris in the ribs. "First I'm gonna go downstairs and flirt with Pasha," he said with a cheeky grin.

"She's not your mate." Boris rolled his eyes and sighed. "You're wasting your time."

"I know," Steven said. "But dude, she's hot!"

Boris held up his hand and made a face of disgust. "Okay, enough. That's my sister we're talking about."

Steven laughed and slapped Boris on the shoulder on his way back downstairs. The others followed him down to the bar, which had gathered a few more patrons since they first went upstairs. Steven had, as promised, sidled up to the bar in an immediate attempt to lure Pasha into becoming his Miss Right Now. She smiled at them as they walked out and rolled her big green eyes as Steven began to flirt with her relentlessly. Boris, of course, went over in an effort to rescue his twin sister from her persistent suitor.

The two couples stepped into the warm night and began the walk over to Jackson Square. Dante enjoyed the feel of Kerry's hand in his as they made their way back up Ursulines Street. Malcolm and Samantha walked in front of them, their arms wrapped around one another as if they'd been together for years, as opposed to weeks. Fate may be a cruel bitch sometimes, but it sure did know what it was doing.

He stole a glance at Kerry and smiled as she moved in sync with him. Her long ebony hair blew off her face in the soft breeze, and he noted how perfectly chiseled her features were. Even her profile turned him on.

She turned and captured his eyes with her inquisitive brown ones. "What are you staring at?"

"You better get used to me staring at you. I plan on enjoying the sight of you for the rest of our lives." He brought her hand to his lips and placed a tender kiss on her fingers. Her flesh shivered under his touch, which only served to make him want her all the more. This woman had him completely bewitched.

They made the turn onto Chartres Street and walked the next couple of blocks to Jackson Square. Within a few minutes the narrow street opened into the lively, bustling square. St. Louis Cathedral loomed largely to the right, oozing with history and spectacular beauty. The square itself thrived with tourists and artists alike.

Beautiful, colorful artwork hung along the wrought-iron fence that lined the square, and each artist sat proudly and patiently as tourists wandered by inspecting the various treasures.

Malcolm turned to Dante, who stood completely still as he scanned the crowds. "Do you see him?"

"I do," Kerry whispered and pointed to the walkway on the left side of the square.

"How could you know? You didn't meet him," Dante said quietly.

"I'm not sure," she said softly. "I just know."

Kerry walked in the direction that she had pointed to. At the very end of the stone wall was an old man. He sat at a card table draped with brightly colored scarves. A red bandana was tied around his head, and a long gray ponytail was tied loosely at the nape of his neck. As they got closer, Dante saw that she was right. The man at the table was indeed Joseph Vasullus.

―――∿∿∿―――

Kerry saw the old man hunched over at the table, and something inside of her stirred. Mesmerized by the odd sense of familiarity, she moved toward him as if in a dream. He looked up, and as soon as he spotted them he began to pack up his table. As the four got closer to Joseph, his panic slammed into them with ferocious intensity.

Dante squeezed her hand more tightly than usual. *I don't like this. He's obviously upset that we're here.*

Kerry shot him an irritated look. *Well, wouldn't you be if four shapeshifters came charging at you all at once? We've already determined that he doesn't care for you*

very much. He's not going to help us if we bully him.
Dante nodded his reluctant agreement and asked Sam
and Malcolm to keep their distance for the time being.

Kerry knew that this old man was connected to her
somehow. Boldly, she sat down in the chair across from
him as if he weren't trying to run away, and she was just
another customer. Dante stood next to her protectively,
his face dark and serious. Kerry stayed there for several
seconds, while Joseph ignored her and continued to pack
up his wares. He averted his eyes, refusing to look at her.

"Excuse me?" she said in the sweetest voice she
could muster.

"I'm closing up for the night," he barked. "No
more readings."

"I think you should sit tight, old man, and show my
mate some respect." Dante's voice, low and deadly, cut
through the air mercilessly.

Joseph's gaze flicked briefly to Kerry. For a moment,
she could swear she saw something that resembled tenderness. However, it was quickly replaced with a mask
of stone. He looked at Dante, completely unfazed by his
thinly veiled intimidation tactics. He narrowed his pale
gray eyes and looked Dante up and down.

"I'm not afraid of you, boy. I told you earlier today
that I want nothing to do with any of you. I suggest you
go away and leave me alone like I said." He proceeded
to dismantle his table, forcing Kerry to get up from her
chair. He wordlessly placed the folded chairs and table
against the stone wall.

"Do you know anything about someone called the
'Punisher'?" Kerry asked.

He stilled for a moment, but said nothing and

continued packing up his bag. Kerry knew that she needed to touch him and see what secrets he held inside. Dante touched her back reassuringly. *Go ahead. You can do it. I'm right here if you need me.*

"Please, Joseph. We need your help." She reached out to touch his arm, but he picked up his bag and stepped back quicker than a snake.

"Don't touch me," he spat. "I suggest you leave here, young lady. Get out of New Orleans as fast as possible." He nodded toward Dante, fear and panic undulated off of him relentlessly. "If your young man here really cares for you, he'll take you away from this place tonight."

Before Kerry could say more, he shuffled away. They watched him scurry off, and Dante wrapped his arm around her waist, pulling her into the shelter of his body. When Joseph reached the end of the street, he turned around and shouted one last message.

"Don't trust anybody. You hear me? Nobody!" Then he rounded the corner and disappeared into the dark Louisiana night.

Chapter 13

THEY WALKED BACK TO THEIR HOTEL IN THOUGHTFUL silence. None of them understood why Joseph harbored such ill feelings toward the Amoveo. In fact, no one uttered a word until they reached their floor of the hotel. Dante finally broke the silence with unabashed anger and frustration.

"This doesn't make any goddamn sense," Dante seethed. "Why is he so dead set against us and so completely unwilling to help? He must be involved in all of this."

Samantha shrugged, and her voice stayed steady. "It's anybody's guess. But I agree with you. He definitely knows something."

Kerry nodded. "Absolutely, he's hiding something. I could feel it. He was terrified of us, but he also seemed fearful for us too. I don't think he's dangerous. At least, not for me." She made a loud sound of frustrated disgust. "I can't explain it." She sighed. "Lately, I don't have a logical explanation for anything."

"Let's get some sleep," Malcolm suggested. "Tomorrow while you're at the shoot, Samantha and I will reach out to Davis and some of the other Vasullus to see what we can find out about our friend Joseph. I'd rather not bother the prince with all of this nonsense, especially since Salinda is pregnant. I don't want to take him away from her in her delicate condition."

Kerry and Dante bid their friends good night before heading into their suite. The instant the door closed behind them, an ice cold ripple of dark energy streamed through Kerry's body. A wave of dizziness came over her, and she grabbed Dante's arm to keep from falling over. She looked up at him with wide, startled eyes.

"Someone's been in here," she whispered. Panic threatened to overtake her, and darkness started to close in. Someone had been in the suite when they were out. She could feel it. The energy they left in the room was thick and sticky, like molasses. "Oh my God. I feel like I'm going to pass out. Why is this happening?"

"Breathe with me," he coaxed. "Close your eyes, and filter it out. Your psychic abilities have intensified since our mating was completed."

They stood together, face-to-face, her hands clasped tightly to his thick, muscular arms. Slowly, the dark sick energy faded and was replaced by Dante's tender, soothing musings. Her breathing slowed, and her heart beat once again at a normal pace. Kerry let out a long slow breath and loosened her vice-like grip from Dante's arms.

"I'm okay now," she said slowly. Kerry looked up at him with gratitude. "It just took me by surprise, that's all. God, when did I become such a girl?"

Steady on her feet once again, she slowly surveyed the living room. It looked completely undisturbed. Nothing had been moved or seemed out of place, but an intruder had most definitely been in their suite.

"Someone was in here, Dante. I'm not crazy, and I'm not talking about housekeeping. Someone bad was here. They must've been." Kerry shivered and rubbed her arms in an effort to warm herself. "It's like they left some kind of residue." Her voice trembled with a mixture of awe and fear.

It fascinated her that her psychic abilities were now amplified after her mating with Dante, but it unnerved her as well. She had never felt so completely uncertain, and she began to feel like a surprise lurked around every corner. Kerry made her way into the bedroom, and her blood went cold at the sight before her.

A bright red envelope lay on the pillows of her bed. Looking at it, she couldn't help but conjure up images of blood. The twisted gift sat there, mocking her. She didn't have to read it to know there was nothing good going on inside that note. It had to be from the Punisher, which meant that the sick bastard had been in her room.

"Dante!" She'd meant to yell it, but it came out more like a squeak. She cringed for sounding as helpless as she felt.

Dante pushed past her, and his eyes shifted harshly when he saw the unwelcome surprise. Anger pulsed from him wildly, and Kerry sensed every muscle in his body go rigid. His breath hissed out in one massive rush as he snatched the envelope. It hurt her to see him so upset, but it was even deeper than that. His anger raced through her and around her, and her own fear was immediately replaced with an urgent need to soothe him. She knew his anger stemmed from his fear for her safety.

Kerry reached out and connected her mind with his. She eased in with a gentle, soothing touch to calm the raging fury that threatened to boil over. His body relaxed a bit, but his anger remained.

Dante ripped the offending envelope open and

withdrew the note inside. Side by side, her arms wrapped
around his waist, they read the ugly words that screamed
up at them from the page.

THE BITCH WILL DIE FIRST WHILE YOU WATCH.
THEN IT'S YOUR TURN—TRAITOR.
DEATH IS COMING FOR YOU.
—THE PUNISHER—

Dante shook with anger. Kerry shuddered and hugged
him tighter. She buried her face in the warm hollow of
his neck. She breathed in his distinctly male scent. He
threw the hateful message across the room and wrapped
his arms tightly around her. Dante kissed her hair and
rubbed her back reassuringly.

"He won't come near you. So help me God, Kerry. I
won't let anything happen to you." His voice, raw and
gruff, enveloped her in a blanket of security. He rocked
her softly and stroked her hair with exquisite tenderness.
Kerry closed her eyes and allowed herself to float in the
security of his embrace. The deep baritone of his voice
rumbled through his chest and along her cheek. "We need
to tell Samantha and Malcolm about this immediately."

Kerry convinced Dante that it would be far more appropriate to knock on their door like a couple of regular
people, opposed to just materializing in the middle of
their suite. Based on her experience with Dante, she
doubted they were over there playing Scrabble.

Sure enough, a surprisingly gracious Malcolm answered the door clad in the hotel bathrobe. "What's
going on?" Malcolm gestured for them to enter the suite
and ran a hand through his tousled hair.

Kerry stifled a smile. Oh yeah. No Scrabble playing over here.

"I'm sorry to bother you both," Dante apologized. "But when we got back to our suite tonight, we found this waiting for us on the bed." He held up the crumpled paper. "We thought you should know about it before you speak with Davis and the others."

He handed the note to Malcolm and immediately pulled Kerry into the hard shelter of his body. Her arm fit perfectly around him, and her other hand rested on his chest. His heartbeat thrummed strong and steady beneath her fingers. *Strong and steady*. Kerry smiled and hooked her thumb through the belt loop on his jeans. Those were two words that fit him perfectly, but he couldn't hide his feelings from her. He glanced down at her with a tight smile. She knew it was meant to reassure her, but there was no use trying to hide his concern. She could see it and feel it.

The bedroom door clicked open, and Samantha emerged, looking equally tousled. She went directly to Malcolm's side and read the note with him. Concern rippled from both of them, and the lines in their faces deepened.

"This was in your room?" Malcolm wrapped his arm around Sam's waist and handed the note back to Dante.

"Yes," he hissed.

"I knew something was wrong when we got into the suite," Kerry said quietly. She looked at Sam. "It was like they left behind some kind of residue. It was definitely an energy signature, but not like any that I've ever encountered." She made a sound of frustration. "It was thick and dark and very strong."

"Evil," Sam whispered.

Kerry nodded solemnly. "Definitely. But there was something else." She paused for a moment and closed her eyes in an effort to recapture the moment from earlier that night. "There was an extra layer to it," she said quietly. "The darkness, the ugly thickness of it, was blanketing something—no, someone else." Her eyes flew open, and she looked up at Dante. "There were two of them."

"Are you sure?" he asked gently.

Kerry nodded furiously. "Yes. That's it," she exclaimed. "There were two of them. That must be why it was so strong, so overwhelming!" Her smile faded, and her momentary pride at figuring it out was quickly replaced with the reality of their situation. "Well, shit. One person wanting to kill me is bad enough. But two? Well, that really sucks."

"As disturbing as all of this is," Malcolm began. "It is helpful. The person writing these notes is referring to a 'traitor.' This obviously means that we're dealing with a Purist." His somber gaze landed on Kerry. "Could you tell if they were both Amoveo?"

Kerry's face fell, and she shrugged one shoulder in defeat. "No. I'm sorry." Well, so much for feeling like she had figured anything out.

"Hey," Samantha said sternly. "Don't you dare start to feel badly about yourself or your abilities." Her eyes softened, and she looked at Kerry through loving eyes. "You're the one who confirmed that we're definitely not dealing with a single player."

"You should listen to your friend. She's a smart cookie," Dante said with a wink to their friends. The

levity in his voice quickly faded, and his face grew somber. "You two should watch your backs as well. If we're
dealing with more Purists, then none of us are safe."

Malcolm nodded his agreement. "We'll go back to
Westerly tomorrow and touch base with Nonie and
Davis. There must be something that can help us from
the experience with Sam's parents, and our own encounter with the Purists." He ran his hand through his hair
and looked lovingly down at Sam. "Maybe there was
something we overlooked. Some clue as to who else has
been involved in all of this." He turned to Dante with serious eyes. "Did you ever find anything in your father's
papers? After all, his job on the Council was to see if he
could identify other humans who might be able to mate
with our people."

Dante's jaw clenched, and his back straightened at
the mention of his father. "No," he said tightly. "My
mother and sister have been handling all of my father's
effects." His voice dropped to almost inaudible tones.
"They haven't had much contact with me since his
death. I'm afraid that they blame me for not being able
to save him." He cleared his throat, obviously struggling
to contain the raw emotions that still hovered beneath
his strong exterior. "It doesn't matter. To them, he'll
remain a hero. I don't ever want them to know that he
was a traitor."

Kerry's heart broke for him. He was clearly still
deeply wounded by his father's betrayal, and it was compounded by the fact that he couldn't even be honest with
his mother and sister. As the rest of them mulled over
the last few details about tomorrow, Kerry remained
focused on Dante. He was amazing. Not just because

of his devastatingly good looks or rock-hard body—which were unquestionably drool-worthy—but because of the man he was on the inside. He would rather let his mother and sister hate him than ruin their image of his late father.

Incredible, she mused. Who would've thought that the sexiest thing about this man would be his heart?

They said their good-byes and agreed to meet the next day to compare notes. Before Kerry could walk to the door and leave in a traditional way, Dante picked her up and through a wicked grin whispered, "*Verto*."

The odd sense of displacement was accompanied by Samantha's laughter as they vanished from the room. Within seconds he had visualized them back into the bedroom of their suite. He promptly placed her on unsteady legs and cradled her hips with his hands.

"Are you alright?" he asked and placed a soft kiss on the corner of her mouth.

Kerry let out a slow breath and nodded. "I have a bit of a head rush."

"You'll get used to it after a while," he said as he kissed his way down her neck. Kerry leaned her head to the left to allow him easier access to her sensitized skin. His hands slid down her rib cage, along the curve of her hips, and cupped her ass.

"That I'll get used to," she breathed. "But I hope I never, ever, get used to this." Kerry ran her hands along the muscles of his broad chest and slipped her arms around his back. She held him to her and floated in the cradle of his touch, his body, and his heart.

She sank into him and closed her eyes as the image of his fox filled her mind. The sweet honey of his soft ministrations chased away the fear and carried her in a cloud of warmth. *Safe*. She felt safe with him. Death threats, Purist Networks, Caedo, none of it mattered. She knew deep in her soul that he wouldn't let any harm come to her. The reality of her feelings for him hit her brutally.

She loved him.

Her heart ached with loving him, and *that* was terrifying.

Kerry took a deep breath and lifted her head to look him in the eyes. The instant she captured his gaze, her eyes shifted to the eyes of her clan. She licked her trembling lips nervously and searched for the courage to say three words. The three words she'd never even considered uttering to a man. They were just three little words. Right? Then why the hell couldn't she bring herself to say them to him?

He stared back intently, his warm amber eyes searching hers for answers. "What is it?"

Losing her nerve, she smiled and nuzzled his neck once again. "Nothing. I'm just glad you're here with me. You make me feel safe. I trust you, Dante."

She wanted to tell him, to scream at the top of her lungs how much she loved him. That she craved him and needed him with every fiber of her being. However, looking into those searing eyes and wrapped in the shelter of his arms, she still didn't have the courage to say it out loud. She wondered if she ever would.

Dante stroked her back softly and held her body tightly against his. Soon his gentle strokes became more insistent; her heart fluttered as his body hardened against hers. His desire for her pressed insistently against her. Hot, hard, and demanding. He trailed his fingers along her spine, leaving little licks of fire in its wake. Kerry moaned softly in response and placed a warm soft kiss against the base of his throat. She didn't think she'd ever get enough of him. She ran her hands up his strong arms and took his head in her hands. She locked her heavy-lidded eyes on his, and a slow smile spread across his face.

Dante grabbed her ass, held her tightly against him, and ever so slowly ground himself against her. She kept her gaze locked with his as she reached down between them and released him from the confines of his jeans. Feeling a new sense of bravery and confidence, she wrapped her fingers around the hot length of him. A low growl of pleasure rumbled in his throat. She watched with satisfaction as the sensations washed over him and became deeply etched in his face. He threw his head back as she stroked his hot shaft with surprising skill. She loved the power of being able to give him this kind of pleasure. She wanted to give him more, everything she possibly could.

Kerry dropped to her knees, placed her hands on his hips, and looked up at him with a nervous smile. *I'm new at this.* She nibbled her lower lip.

Dante reached down and held her face in one hand. *You don't have to do that. I don't want you to do anything you're not comfortable with.*

Would it please you? Kerry blew softly along the length of him.

He smiled, his body shuddered, and a low growl rumbled as he fought for control. Dante's eyes opened, and he looked down at her with desire and something that looked a lot like love. He stroked her cheek with his thumb. *Everything you do pleases me.*

"How about this?" she murmured wickedly. Kerry leaned in and licked the full length of his massive cock. His body quaked, he swore softly, and he gathered her hair in his hands. His voice floated into her mind, sounding as desperate and turned on as Kerry felt. *Woman you are killing me.* That was all the encouragement she needed.

Kerry held onto his narrow hips and lapped at the pearly drop that had appeared on the tip and wrapped her lips around him. Dante groaned loudly as she slowly took him deeper into the warm, dark cavern of her mouth. Tentatively at first, but soon her tempo increased, each time taking him further and deeper. He whispered soft words of pleasure and coaxed her along. She held the base and squeezed tightly as she suckled him to the very brink.

When she sensed him reaching the edge of his control, she brushed his shaft with one last long stroke of her tongue. Kerry kissed her way up his rock-hard abs, lifting his shirt as she went along. She pulled it over his head and ran her hands along his beautiful chest. His heart beat rapidly just under the surface in perfect time with hers.

"I have to be inside of you," he whispered gruffly. "Now."

He wrapped his arm around her waist and spun her so her back was pressed up against him. Kerry looked up and saw their reflections in the mirror. She reached up with both hands and threaded that silky soft hair of his between her fingers. She sighed with satisfaction as the cool strands surrounded her heated skin and sent her heart racing.

They stayed there for a moment, eyes locked on their

decadent reflection. He kissed her cheek, waved one hand, whispered the ancient language, and the rest of their clothes disappeared before her eyes. Kerry's eyes widened at the erotic sight of her naked body stretched out against his.

He reached around and took her full breasts in his strong hands. She arched her back, pressing herself deeper into his hold. He took one rosy nipple and tweaked it gently between his fingers. Kerry's breath came quickly, and his full erection seared against the sensitive skin of her lower back. She was mesmerized by the sight of them and almost didn't recognize the wanton lustful woman in the mirror.

That's you, my love. You are beautiful, sexy, and mine. Kerry sucked in her breath as one of his hands reached down and grabbed the hot juncture between her legs. She moaned softly as his talented fingers slipped into her slick folds and found her most sensitive spot. He worked the tiny nub furiously, and the pleasure crashed over her with relentless intensity. Hot and tight— building and burning almost to the point of pain—sweet torture that threatened to consume her.

He pulled her long hair to one side, kissed her neck, and gently bent her over the bed. His strong hands brushed over her ribs and settled at the dip of her waist. Kerry placed both hands on sheets that felt strikingly cool against her heated skin. She spread her legs apart, granting him access to her swollen entrance, which pulsed wildly with wanting him. He stood behind her, and she quivered with anticipation.

"Take me," she whispered.

Their gazes remained locked in the mirror, and with

one powerful stroke he drove himself deeply inside of her. Kerry cried out with undeniable pleasure as he filled and stretched her further than she thought possible. His hands gripped her hips, his fingers melded against the soft flesh, and with deep penetrating thrusts, he arrowed into her again and again. Sizzling streaks of pleasure shot through her, and they cried out in unison as the orgasm built quickly and pushed them both over the edge.

Breathless and spent, Dante leaned forward and placed a tender kiss on her shoulder. He held her to him and gently lay down on the bed, spooning her body with his. They stayed there curled up as if their bodies had been made perfectly for each other; perhaps they had. Kerry took one deep shuddering breath and snuggled further into his protective embrace. She smiled as she listened to the even rhythm of his breathing as he drifted into sleep.

As she remained tangled with him, she took note of every delicious spot where her body touched his. Gratitude flooded her heart; she never dreamed this kind of connection would be possible for her. Kerry let out a sigh of contentment, closed her eyes, and tried to sleep.

She thought about what Sam had said about the dream realm. Kerry had never consciously tried to go to the dream realm, but as her body lay entwined with Dante's, she figured now was as good a time as any to try. As the cloud of sleep carried her away, the last image that floated through her mind were the large yellow orbs of her cat.

The fog of the dream realm lifted, and the gravel crunched loudly beneath her paws as she trotted along the driveway of the old house. The warm night air enveloped her, and the nighttime sounds of the bayou swarmed around her. She picked up the pace and trotted over to the steps of the mansion. Kerry crouched low, and all the muscles in her long lean body bunched as she leapt up to the porch in one elegant motion. She landed with silent grace and padded to the entrance of the house.

The massive door stood open just a crack. Kerry reached up with one large black paw and pushed it open. She stuck her head in first and peered around the corner into the enormous entryway. Directly across from the front door, she caught sight of movement and stilled until she realized it was her own reflection. Moving cautiously, she approached the giant gilded mirror, and her heart almost stopped at the unbelievable sight before her. The reflection was not one she had ever seen before, and yet it seemed hauntingly familiar.

Dante was right; she was a cat.

She had shifted into a giant black panther with glowing yellow eyes that stared back at her. Kerry moved closer to the mirror and the mahogany table in front of it. She had to get a closer look. She stood on her hind legs and rested her front paws on the edge of the table. Her lips curled back and revealed a mouthful of sharp white teeth. I am one badass kitty cat.

Yes, you are, my dear. Dante's voice spilled over her, and she glanced up to find him standing next to her, looking as devilishly handsome as ever, sporting that rumpled bed head that curled her toes. He was barefoot in a pair of low slung jeans and a white button-down shirt. The man looked good enough to eat.

Make one pussy joke, and I'll kick your ass. *She let out a low snarl and hopped back down on all fours. She sat on her haunches and looked up into his handsome, smiling face.* So, I guess this is my clan, huh? Samantha suggested I try to connect with it in the dream realm. She'll love that she was right. *She held up one giant black paw and inspected it.* I'm a panther. *She wondered if she sounded as stunned as she felt.*

You are spectacularly beautiful… in either form. I'd love to join you, but since this is your first time in your clan form, I think it's best if I guide you in my human form.

Kerry cocked her head. That's a good idea. One weird experience at a time; sounds fine to me. *She stood and headed to the sweeping staircase that loomed largely next to the massive mirror. Her tail switched behind her, reflecting her curiosity.* So what do you suppose is upstairs?

Anything you want, I imagine. *He walked over to her and ran his hand along the tip of her tail.* This is your dream, and as a result, you control the environment. Why did you choose this house? I thought you would select an NYC landscape again.

I didn't. *She stopped and sat at the bottom of the steps.* Well, I didn't mean to. I'd never been here before the shoot yesterday, and even then I never went inside.

Hey, let's go for a run. *He tugged on her tail.* I wonder if you can outrun me. *The challenging tone in his voice was unmistakable, and Kerry couldn't help but notice that cocky smile on his face as he backed up toward the open front door.* There aren't many places we can run together with you in your clan form, at least not without causing a scene. *The dream realm is the only place we can run truly free. Come on. I'll even give you a head start. Ready, set*—*but before he said "go" Dante sprinted out the front door, laughing as he went.*

You cheater! Laughing, Kerry bounded after him into the inky black night. She found him waiting for her in the driveway, his amber eyes glowing brightly like a beacon calling her safely to him. She leapt down the steps and landed next to him with barely a sound.

They ran together in the bayou she had created. As they navigated the swamp and grasses, Kerry voiced her displeasure. Laughing at her haughty tone, Dante coached her on how to change the environment. He explained that all she had to do was envision what she wanted, and the realm would morph to accommodate her wishes.

She knew where she wanted to go first and pictured it in her mind's eye. She thought of Nonie and Sam. She remembered their long walks on the beach, which were usually accompanied by beautiful fits of laughter.

As the dream realm shifted, a thick fog rolled in and enveloped them. Panic rose as she lost sight of Dante. Just when she thought she'd scream with fear, his familiar voice touched her mind. I'm right here. Remember this isn't a physical plane, and now that we're mated I can find you as long as you keep your mind open to me. Keep the image of your destination at the forefront. I'm not leaving you.

Within moments the fog dissipated, and Kerry felt sand squishing under her paws. The waves crashed loudly, and salty mist sprayed over her. Relief flooded her spirit at the sight of Dante walking next to her; his thick auburn hair glistened with droplets of salt water. They stood side by side and looked up at the brilliant night sky. Now this is what I love most about being at the beach. The stars. There are millions of stars.

So are we going to have that race or what? *He squatted low in a runner's stance, and the mischievous look that she'd grown to love glinted back at her brightly. Kerry crouched low as though she were ready to pounce on him. She licked her lips and let out a low purr that sounded more like a car engine than a cat of any size.*

Catch me if you can, *he murmured with a wink. Then, with lightning fast speed, he took off down the beach, sand spitting up from his bare feet and the tails of his shirt fluttering behind him in the wind. She watched him for a moment, taking in the raw power that rippled from him. He was quite simply magnificent. Strong. Masculine. Sexy. And getting a major head start.*

With a sudden burst of speed, Kerry pursued her mate. It didn't take long for her to catch up; after all, she had four legs to his two. With smooth strides she raced up next to him with ease.

You may be fast, but I've got these. *Kerry reached out and swatted his leg playfully with one paw, tripping him, and sending him tumbling onto the sand in a laughing, breathless heap. Before he could get up, she pounced on him, pinning him onto his back. She pressed one paw on each arm and lay her furry body over his.*

Now who's the cheater, *he said, smiling through heavy breaths.*

She held him there and touched her mind to his. You're wearing far too many clothes. *She snarled softly, carefully took the buttons of his shirt between her razor-sharp teeth, and with one swift yank, tore the shirt wide open, revealing the beautifully crafted torso she'd come to crave.* That's much better.

Purring, she got off of him as he sat up and gave a cursory glance at his ripped shirt.

It's a good thing it's the dream realm. I really liked this shirt. *He removed the tattered garment and tossed it aside. He pulled his knees up and draped his strong arms over them casually as he gave her that sexy smile.* So, Ms. Smithson. What do you plan on doing with me now?

She crouched low, her bright yellow eyes stayed locked with his, and her tail switched behind her. Beating your ass to the jetty. *Her teasing tone touched his mind as she took off like a shot down the beach, laughing as she went. She glanced over her shoulder to see Dante scrambling to his feet and sprinting toward her. As she ran across the sand in her panther form, with the love of her life in hot pursuit, happiness filled her heart, because for the first time in her life she didn't feel alone.*

Chapter 14

KERRY AND DANTE WALKED OUT OF THE HOTEL INTO the bright morning sunlight with their arms linked comfortably around each other's waist. Neither missed the smirk on Pete's face as he opened the back door of the waiting Mercedes.

"Good morning, Pete," Kerry said sweetly as she slid into the backseat.

He raised his eyebrows and gave a knowing look to Dante. "So, whatever happened to our motto about not getting involved with the client?" he whispered quietly.

Dante turned to him, intending to remind him of his place as the employee, but the teasing grin on Pete's amused face diffused any irritation he felt. He opened his mouth, but no witty response came quickly enough.

Pete raised his hands in defeat and shrugged his shoulders. "Hey, you're the boss."

Dante cleared his throat and slipped on his aviators. "I won't argue with you there."

Pete chuckled softly and shut the car door after him. "Man, oh man, it's good to be the boss," he murmured with a smile.

As they drove out to the old house, Dante watched the scenery fly by, and his mind went over the possibilities. He couldn't get that vicious message out of his mind. They knew it had to be another Amoveo—a Purist. A Caedo would not have been able to slip in and out of their room unnoticed, and the energy signature left behind was far too powerful to have been left by a human. Although Kerry was convinced that two people had been there. The other person could very well have been a human.

He swore silently and rapped his knuckles lightly on the window. He hated feeling so helpless and in the dark. They had to figure out who else had been in league with his father. He made a mental note to himself to reach out to his twin sister, Marianna. Maybe she had found something that would be of use to them. It still remained to be seen whether or not she'd even speak to him.

He glanced at Kerry, and the tension in his neck immediately loosened. He'd done his best to keep his mood light and keep Kerry's mind off the Punisher and his sick intentions. Even last night in the dream realm, he'd kept things playful. His gaze slid leisurely over his mate. She was absolutely stunning—inside and out. It amazed him that she'd managed to remain so loving after growing up so isolated.

Her jet black hair hung loosely over her shoulders and gleamed almost blue in the morning sunlight. He reached over and rubbed a soft lock between his fingers. It was the same color as her fur when she was in her Panther form.

"Penny for your thoughts," she whispered softly. Her chocolate brown eyes looked back at him warmly. Her smooth skin with barely a line on it practically glowed. She was luminous.

He smiled and released the silky strands. "I'm just admiring your beauty."

"Boy, you are full of shit." Kerry scoffed audibly and smiled. *I can feel the uncertainty oozing off of you. It's one of the perks of being mated, right?*

Dante smirked and flicked a glance toward Pete in the front seat. "Whatever you say, princess."

Kerry made a sound of good-humored disgust. "Men are so difficult. Why are men so difficult?" she shouted to Peter.

"We're just a little thickheaded, Ms. Smithson." He winked at her in the rearview mirror. "We're not as evolved as the females of our species."

"Of any species," she mumbled quietly. She playfully stuck her tongue out at Dante before looking back out the window.

Dante chuckled softly. *You better not stick that tongue out at me unless you plan to use it.* He touched her mind with his easily and sent wicked images to her.

Kerry's face reddened visibly, but she kept her gaze fixed on the world outside the car window. *You really think you're charming, don't you?*

Dante adored the way the teasing notes of Kerry's voice floated effortlessly in his mind. He said nothing, but didn't take his eyes off of her. He still couldn't quite believe that he'd found her, and they were mated. There had been many times when he feared they'd never find one another and that he would die alone. He couldn't lose her. No one was going to take her from him.

The car turned into the long gravel driveway and traveled swiftly under the canopy of cypress trees. They pulled up in front of the old house, and Dante was relieved to see everything looked as it had yesterday when they left. The trailer sat waiting for Kerry's numerous clothing changes, camera equipment set up much like yesterday. Layla and Jacqueline were buzzing around, but somehow it felt different. There was an extra ripple of energy that hadn't been here yesterday.

Dante's eye was caught by movement near Layla's van. A young girl hopped out of the van, hustled eagerly over to Layla, and handed her what looked like a camera lens. She had long brown hair and fair skin. She was just a kid, couldn't have been more than twenty years old.

Suspicion reared its ugly head.

Hadn't Layla said that her assistant had bailed out on her? Shit. He hated surprises. This whole day was beginning to reek of trouble. So much for keeping the mood light. Dante also remembered that reliable Artie wasn't here as he'd been yesterday. That reminded him that he hadn't heard a word from or about the old boy since he'd left.

He turned to Kerry. "Have you heard from Arthur since he left yesterday?"

"No," she said with a quick shake of her head. "But that's not unusual when he's busy putting out one of Natasha's fires. I'm sure I'll get a text or voice mail from him at some point today." She looked at him through narrowed eyes. "What?"

"Nothing." He shrugged.

Before Dante could get out of the car, Kerry put a hand on his arm to stop him. She gave him a skeptical look. He couldn't hide anything from her, and he really didn't want to. He sighed and sat back in his seat. Dante had wanted to keep things as stress-free as possible today. Apparently, that wouldn't be happening.

"Pete, would you mind giving us a minute?" she asked without taking her sharp, dark eyes off Dante.

"You got it," he said as he got out and left them alone in the silence of the car. The air rippled subtly as Dante's concern for her flowed freely.

"I know you're worried about the Punisher, and don't get me wrong, I am too. But you can't honestly be thinking that Arthur has anything to do with all of this," she asked incredulously. "He doesn't even know about the Amoveo."

Dante leaned his elbow on the window and ran a hand over his face. "You're right," he said, relenting. "The likelihood of Arthur knowing about any of this is slim to none. But I, never in a million years, thought my own father would be a traitor. So you'll have to forgive me if I'm suspicious of… well, almost everyone."

Kerry's hand slid gently down his arm, and she took his hand in hers with crushing tenderness. "Dante," she began quietly. "When we're done with the shoot, we're going home." She stopped abruptly and shook her head. "By the way, that's a whole other discussion. I don't even know where you live. Where is your home?"

He captured her gaze with his. "I have an apartment in the city and a house in the Catskills, but we can live wherever you want. My home is with you." Her energy pulsed faster and matched that lovely fluttering spot in her neck that he loved so much. He knew she was doing her best to be brave, to be the tough-as-nails bitch that everyone thought she was. However, he knew better.

"Good," she licked her lips nervously. "But don't try and change the subject. The point is I refuse to live the rest of my life in fear. Don't you get it? Until I met you that was all I had—fear and pain. I will not go back to that," she said adamantly. "The Punisher, or whoever this crazy bastard is, can kiss my big white ass."

Dante laughed softly at her bravado. "Your ass is not big. It's perfect." He looked down at their fingers tangled together and stroked his thumb along hers. The velvety soft feel of her skin reminded him of butterfly wings. Delicate and beautiful. The resolve in her voice and the determined look on her face made it very clear that she meant every word she said.

"If it will make you feel better, I'll text Arthur right now and get an update. Okay?" Kerry pulled out her cell phone and texted a message with impressive speed. Within a few seconds the message was sent and the phone back in her bag. "It may not be telepathy, but it's the next best thing," she said, smiling as she placed a warm kiss on his cheek. "Come on, Tarzan." She looked out the window. Layla was tapping her watch impatiently and waved them to hurry. "The natives are getting restless out there. The quicker I finish this job, the quicker we get out of New Orleans."

When they got out of the car, Dante didn't feel any better. The unease he'd felt earlier only grew. He couldn't put his finger on it, but the energy of the bayou definitely had an extra thread in it that wasn't there yesterday. He watched the young assistant through narrowed eyes. Her energy signature was probably the change that he felt.

He scanned her mind and found it full of the need to please. She most likely just wanted to do a good job, so Layla would hire her again. Why didn't he feel any better? He scanned the area around them and caught sight of William perched in the exact same spot as yesterday. He sat perfectly still and had his sharp black eyes trained on the three women at the steps of the house. *Thank you for coming again today, William. Steven is here as well?*

William's curt voice shot back, but he didn't take his eyes off of Layla, the kid, and Jacqueline. *You're late, and no, Steven is not here. I haven't seen hide nor of hair of him since last evening. He's probably still trying to get Pasha to go to bed with him.* William puffed his white and brown speckled feathers and adjusted his position in the large tree.

No need to ruffle your feathers. Kerry teased. *I'm sure he'll turn up.*

William's head turned sharply at the sound of Kerry's voice interrupting their telepathic conversation. His feathered head bobbed down, and his razor-sharp gaze landed on Kerry. He let out a short squawk, and Dante had to struggle to keep from laughing. William was rarely taken by surprise and very rarely let it show. Dante turned to find her standing next to him and staring up at William. Smiling, she winked at him and took Dante's hand as she walked toward her trailer. He noticed she had used her telepathy with much more ease and exuded extra confidence. It made her sexier than ever.

Dante threw a glance back at the others as they prepared for the shoot. "I don't think I should come inside with you." His thumb brushed a soft stroke along the top of her hand, and he lowered his voice seductively. "I doubt you'd get much done with me in there. It's very unlikely I'd help you put clothes on."

"Chicken," she teased. Kerry opened the door and climbed the two steps into the doorway of the trailer. He kept her fingers tangled with his. "I'm going to need that hand." She laughed and pulled it from his grasp. "I trust you'll keep an eye on things out here and keep me safe." Kerry glanced at William. *Both of you.*

The moment the door closed, the smile faded from Dante's face. He stood at the bottom of the stairs and scanned the area around them once again. That same odd energy ripple he'd felt earlier still lingered. Dread nagged at him. Steven hadn't shown up. That wasn't like him. He was a joker and a free spirit, but he was also a warrior and a friend. He closed his eyes and reached out for Steven, but met only a void. He made several attempts, but each time he found nothing.

Dante cursed under his breath. Something was very wrong.

The sound of the door clicking open pulled him from his thoughts. He stepped aside to let Kerry pass by and his mouth went dry at the sight of her. A red satin negligee clung to every delicious curve of her body, and delicate lace was woven in an intricate pattern all over. The design snaked seductively around the curve of her hips. On anyone else it would be garish, but on her it screamed sex. His woman was the most beautiful woman on the planet, and he doubted anyone would disagree. Truthfully, he wouldn't care.

Dante let out a low whistle as she sashayed down the steps.

"You're going to help that woman sell a ton of lingerie," he murmured. When she whisked past him, he got a whiff of her distinctively spicy, feminine scent. Dante did his best to keep his desire in check, but being around her made that a near impossibility.

Kerry threw a wink over her shoulder as she walked toward the porch of the house. "That's why they pay me the big bucks, baby."

Dante's lips tilted as he watched her walk away. The mesmerizing sway of her hips silently called him to her, inviting him to follow. Boom-chica-boom-chica-boom. Damn. That confident strut told Dante that she knew exactly what kind of effect she had on him, and she loved it. Her comfort level with him made him happier than anything else. He found it remarkable that she could be at ease with him so quickly and with everything that had transpired over the past couple of days. He was amazed at her ability to just roll with it.

She may be half human, but her heart was all Amoveo.

"Great," Layla barked with a quick glance to Kerry. "You're ready. Let's get going while we still have some good light." She pushed her curly red hair off her face and waved the girl over. "Kerry, this is my new assistant Melissa. I fired that kid who didn't show up yesterday." She shook her head and adjusted the lighting umbrellas. "Freakin' guy begs and begs to work with me, like his 'effin life depends on it. He scouted the location with me and did all the prep work. But then, the day of the actual shoot, he doesn't show," she fumed. "What a dick."

The young girl waved sheepishly and gave Kerry a shy smile. "Hi. It's really nice to meet you, Ms. Smithson."

Dante felt sorry for the poor kid. Layla was definitely not a woman to mess with, and it was pretty clear that if this girl screwed up even a little, she'd be on the unemployment line. She didn't seem to be a threat. She was incredibly thin and timid. He was more curious about the guy that had been fired.

"Oh, *cher*," Jacqueline piped in sweetly. "You should give the boy another chance. Things can arise beyond our control." She sat in the director's chair and cradled Jester as usual.

"No second chances in this business," she said bluntly. "That kid cost all of us time and money." She glanced at her watch.

"I'm sure Melissa will be very reliable and helpful," she said in her typical singsong voice. "Won't you?"

"Yes, ma'am," she said quickly. She flicked a shy smile to Dante and Peter. "I'll do my best to make everyone happy."

Layla rolled her eyes at the girl's pathetic attempt at flirtation. "That big guy there is Kerry's bodyguard Dante, and the guy at the car is their driver, Pete." Both men nodded politely at Melissa. She gave them a shy smile and looked away quickly. "Okay." Layla grabbed the camera from Melissa and handed her the light meter. "Enough with the introductions. Let's get to work."

Layla switched on her iPod station, and the gritty sound of The Strike Nineteens filled the bayou. As if they'd been working together for years, the two women instantly stepped into action. Dante stood off to the side and watched intently as Kerry worked her magic in front of the camera. Both she and Layla had an admirable focus and intensity. For over an hour, Dante stood perfectly still with his arms crossed and didn't take his eyes off of Kerry. Jacqueline sat nearby in a director's chair with Jester cradled in her lap and watched the dance between the model and photographer.

An hour and several songs later, Jacqueline called for a change. "That's enough with that one." Jacqueline's Cajun lilt rose above the music. "Let's switch it up. Change into the white bridal negligee, would you please?"

"No problem," Kerry said. She started to walk down the steps, but stopped midway as a blank, glazed expression came over her face. Without a word and in a trance, she turned and went to the front door of the old house. The energy in the air thickened and rippled.

Something was terribly wrong. Dante launched into action and bounded up the steps with lightning speed. He pushed past a startled and more than annoyed Layla, practically knocking over her, Melissa, and all of the equipment.

Layla grabbed a large light just before it went toppling over. "Excuse you."

Dante ignored the less than flattering comments she muttered about him. Silently, he took his place at Kerry's side and tried to calm the suddenly undulating nervous energy that flowed from his mate. He placed one hand on her lower back and sent her subtle waves of reassurance.

"I have to go inside," she whispered and licked her lips nervously. Her eyes still held that odd faraway look. "I have to see it."

Dante, we've got a problem. William's unamused voice rang sharply in Dante's head as Kerry placed her hands on the massive brass handle.

Tell me something I don't know. Dante shot back without taking his eyes off of Kerry.

Fine, he replied in a matter of fact tone. *Joseph Vasullus is standing behind you with a gun*.

Dante's eyes shifted harshly, and a low growl erupted from his throat as he shielded Kerry's body with his.

"No!" The deep baritone voice of Joseph Vasullus rumbled through the bayou.

The sudden shout startled Kerry and brought her out of her trance. She pulled her hand away from the doorknob as though she'd been burned. She looked up at Dante through confused eyes. He spun around and pushed her behind him protectively as his deadly amber gaze landed on the old man. Joseph stood in the driveway with a large shotgun in his hands. Directly behind him stood Pete, who had his gun drawn and aimed right at Joseph.

"What the hell is going on? Where the hell did all these guys with guns come from?" Layla shouted to an equally startled Jacqueline. Melissa sat cowering on the ground, hiding behind one of the lighting umbrellas. "I thought we had permission to shoot here."

Jacqueline shot her a look of panic and nodded toward the gun.

"I meant shoot *pictures*," Layla rolled her eyes. "Jesus. Do something, Jacqueline. You're the one who knows this crazy old man."

"I'm not crazy," he barked. He didn't take his serious gray eyes off of Dante and Kerry, the gun still clutched in his wrinkled hands. "No one goes in that house. No one!"

"I know that, *cher*," Jacqueline murmured in soft soothing tones. "Come on now. It's going to be alright. Please put the gun down." Jacqueline moved cautiously toward him. Jester meowed loudly in her arms. She placed a reassuring hand on his shoulder. "No one is going inside, Joseph, not without your permission." Her eyes darted nervously at Kerry and Dante, then back to Joseph. Her voice stayed soft and soothing. "Please put the gun away. You're scaring our visitors, *cher*."

"They're not my visitors, goddamn it," he growled.

Dante noticed that he kept the gun low, and although he held it tightly in his hands, he wasn't pointing it at them anymore. His dark gray eyes glared back at Dante with a mixture of fear and anger. Kerry squeezed Dante's shoulders and gently tried to push him aside, but he held his ground.

Kerry cleared her throat softly and peered over Dante's shoulder. "I'm sorry, Joseph. I didn't realize that you didn't want us in the house. I just wanted to see what it was like on the inside." The lilt of her voice floated around them in the steamy air, soft and hypnotic. "I would imagine it's quite beautiful. It must have some incredible moldings and detailing."

Gentle waves of reassurance flowed in the air, and bit by bit, Dante saw the tension ease from Joseph's timeworn face. He slowly lowered the gun to his side; even Pete lowered his weapon. Kerry had successfully defused a very tense situation with her own calming energy. Dante's eyes had even shifted back to their human state, and he only hoped that had gone unnoticed amid the momentary chaos. Although right now, that would be the least of their problems.

Your mate is getting the hang of her abilities with surprising speed, Dante. William's tone seemed irritatingly calm. *However, if that old man takes one step closer to Layla and the two of you, I will kill him where he stands.*

Dante glanced up and saw William crouched stone still on the branch in the huge oak tree. He knew that within seconds William could be down on the ground in his human form and snap Joseph's neck like a twig. The last thing they needed was to reveal themselves to Layla, Melissa, Pete, and Jacqueline. That would be another mess he didn't need to deal with. *I don't think it will come to that*.

"You see, *cher*? She was just curious," Jacqueline murmured through a shaky voice as she linked her arm with Joseph's.

Joseph grunted and spat on the ground next to him. He didn't take his eyes off of Dante. "You all need to get off my property now. No more photo shoot. The deal is off, Jacqueline! You've all got fifteen minutes to clear out before I lose my patience." He yanked his arm away from Jacqueline abruptly and stalked back to his cottage.

"Fine with me," Layla said with her hands still raised in the air. "We've got enough shots. The worst case scenario is we can finish in the studio. No job is worth getting shot over," Layla muttered as she began to pack up her things. "God, I can't wait to get out of this crazy city."

"You and me both," Pete said as he shoved his gun back into his holster. He extended a hand and helped a horrified looking Melissa to her feet. Dante noticed Melissa looking at him with eyes as big as saucers. She must've seen his eyes shift. Crap.

"Everything's going to be alright," Peter said as he hoisted her to her feet.

She nodded and flicked a glance to Dante. "Do you

see stuff like this all the time?" Her voice dipped to a scared whisper.

He shrugged. "I was in the NYPD. I've seen it all."

"I don't give a shit if you were president of the United States. You get your asses out of here now," Joseph shouted. He was halfway to his cottage with the shotgun still clenched tightly in his fist. He may be old, but he still had some pretty good hearing.

Jacqueline stood weeping softly and clutching Jester. "She was just curious," she pleaded after him.

Joseph reached his cottage and threw open the door. He turned slowly, and his stormy gray eyes landed on Kerry. Dante bristled as the cold finger of dread tripped up his spine. He didn't want Joseph Vasullus so much as looking at his mate. Instinctively, he wrapped his arm tightly around Kerry's waist and pulled her to him, needing to feel her warm, soft body safely tucked up against his.

Before Joseph slammed the door, he shouted one last word of warning. "You know what they say, Ms. Smithson. Curiosity killed the cat!"

Layla and Melissa packed up their camera equipment in record time and took off in her van like bats out of hell. William had left as well, citing his own pressing business. Only Jacqueline and Peter remained. Peter, of course, kept an eye on Joseph's cottage just in case he decided to make another appearance. Jacqueline stood next to him, weeping quietly.

A cold shiver ran through Kerry's body as Joseph's last words rang through her head over and over.

Curiosity killed the cat. As she packed up her things in the trailer, she suspected that Joseph knew exactly how much his comment hit the mark. Kerry scooped up her bag and took one last look around the dressing trailer to be sure she hadn't missed anything. Dante stood looking out the window. He'd refused to let her go into the trailer alone. At the moment, she welcomed his protective instincts.

"He knows," she said quietly. "He knows who my parents are. I'm sure of it."

Dante turned and gathered her into his arms, whispering soft words of reassurance. He placed gentle kisses on the top of her head. Kerry dropped her bag and allowed herself to be swallowed up into his embrace. Yet even the warmth of his body couldn't chase away the chill that clung to her.

"He won't hurt you." Dante leaned back and took her head in his hands, forcing her to look into his glowing amber eyes. She smiled and placed her hands over his, relishing his honeyed touch and his protective bravado.

"That's just it. I don't think he wants to hurt me, Dante."

Dante dropped his hands and looked at her as though she were completely nuts. "Of course! Guns are often used as a form of affection. What was I thinking?" The sarcasm dripped harshly from every word.

Anger and frustration flared hotly. How could he dismiss her like that? "Hey. Don't talk to me like I'm stupid." Kerry took a step back and crossed her arms defensively over her breasts. "I know we're in the middle of a dangerous situation, okay. But when I was standing on that porch today, something called to me."

Dante opened his mouth to argue with her, but she put her hands up to silence him. If he knew what was good for him, he'd shut up before he dismissed her any further.

"I can't explain it." She rolled her eyes and let out an exasperated sigh. "Look, I am sure that Joseph and this old house are connected to me somehow. There's something here, Dante. Think about it," she continued passionately. "Last night, in the dream realm, we came to this place. I'm willing to bet you a million dollars that the inside of that house looks just like it did in my dream. I'm telling you that the answers to my past are here."

Dante cursed silently and looked back out the window as if he was trying to escape the cramped space of the trailer. He stood with his back to Kerry, and although it was only a few moments, it seemed to stretch out for eternity. When he finally spoke, he didn't turn around. "Malcolm and Samantha have gone back home to speak with Davis. I'd really rather not attempt more communication with Joseph until we hear what Davis has to say about him. Malcolm assured me they would be back in New Orleans later this evening."

The muscles in his shoulders bunched with tension, and he let out a frustrated sigh. She knew he was scared for her safety. Amoveo or human, no man liked to show fear in front of his woman. Finally, after what seemed like an eternity, he opened the door of the trailer, which was accompanied by a puff of damp Louisiana air, filling the trailer instantly.

"If Joseph won't help us," he said with gritty determination, "perhaps Jacqueline may have the answers we're looking for. Steven and Boris were supposed to talk to her, but I don't have the patience to wait and hear what they found out. I'm speaking to her myself."

Kerry's eyes widened, and a huge smile spread across her face. "Of course!" She placed a big kiss on Dante's unshaven cheek. "Good thinking, Tarzan."

They stepped out of the trailer and found Peter and Jacqueline chatting by their cars. Dante wrapped his arm protectively around Kerry's shoulders, and she knew he kept one eye on Joseph's cottage. Jacqueline rushed up to them with a tear-stained face and a mewling Jester still cradled in her arms.

"*Cher!* Please forgive me. I had no idea Joseph would do something like that." She sniffled loudly. "I should've warned you about the rule about not going inside. Since we were shooting only on the exterior, it must've slipped my mind."

Her pleading words fell on deaf ears with Dante. He said nothing, but his menacing look made his feelings about her oversight quite clear. Every muscle in his body tensed and rippled subtly against her. Kerry knew he was ready to attack if need be. She looked back at Jacqueline and couldn't help but feel sorry for her—and that poor cat. If she kept petting him like that, she was going to give the poor little bastard a bald spot.

"Jacqueline," Kerry began slowly. "I need you to answer a question for me."

"Anything, *cher*."

"How well do you know Joseph, and why in the world won't he let me into that house?"

Jacqueline squeezed Jester tighter and rubbed her cheek along his furry head. Her mascara-stained eyes darted nervously toward the cottage, and she lowered her shaking voice to a whisper. "I will tell you everything that you want to know, but we must go now. Meet me tonight at my home in the Quarter. I will tell you everything. I promise."

"Obviously, selecting Kerry and having the shoot here at Joseph's house—none of it is a coincidence," Dante bit out. "Is it?"

"No, it's not." Jacqueline shook her head solemnly.

"Who exactly are you, lady?" Dante's eyes narrowed, and his voice dropped low. "Why should we trust you?"

Jacqueline said nothing but extended one hand to Kerry. "If you do not trust me, perhaps you will trust her?"

Kerry licked her lips nervously and glanced at a concerned-looking Peter who had stayed by the car. She knew he must be wondering just what the hell was going on. Dante held her tighter, and his voice slipped into her mind. *I'm right here. You know I can get us out of here in seconds.*

Kerry nodded her acknowledgement and threw a glance of gratitude in his direction. She steeled herself, and in this particular moment, was very glad to have him next to her. Kerry sucked in a steadying breath and took Jacqueline's extended hand in hers.

No pain.

Her eyes closed, and her body jerked as electric shocks sizzled up her arm, and a bright new image filled her mind.

The material world around her fell away, and she saw Joseph as a young handsome man on the steps of the house. The house, like Joseph, gleamed with the energy of youth. He stood on the steps laughing and smiling. Love swamped her heart, and warmth flooded her body. A woman with long dark hair ran up the steps to greet him. She jumped into his arms, and her dazzling laughter jingled around them. Suddenly, without warning, a gunshot rang out, and the earth-shattering roar of a big cat rumbled around her. The keening wail of grief filled her mind, and everything went black.

Jacqueline removed her hand; the image vanished as the bright light of the bayou came back into focus. Kerry's spent body sagged against Dante, borrowing his strength on many levels. A large tear slid down her cheek, and her breath came rapidly. Dante held her tightly, and his soothing voice slipped inside of her. *I'm here, princess. It's over.*

She knew she was safe, but she couldn't stop shivering. The most unsettling part was that she didn't know if it was sparked by fear or grief, and she wasn't even certain if it was Joseph's or her own. It was as if she had absorbed all of the feelings from the vision as her own. Another first. Great.

"You see, *cher*," Jacqueline whispered through sympathetic eyes. "He wasn't always like this. Come tonight, to my home, and I will tell you everything."

Chapter 15

THE PUNISHER WAITED FOR THEM IN THEIR HOTEL room, knowing that it would be worth the wait. The large antique clock on the wall clicked loudly in the empty suite. The Punisher let out a sigh of contentment. Revenge would be sweet. How could these traitors be allowed to walk freely among their race? They were polluting the purity of their ancient bloodlines with humans. The Punisher cringed at the thought. Even worse were these mutations, the ones they called hybrids. The Punisher scoffed loudly at the very idea of a hybrid being equal to a pure-blooded Amoveo. Anger boiled, and the room swirled with the Punisher's dark energy.

A deep breath and some serious focus helped back the energy up and clear the space. The last thing the Punisher needed was to tip them off before they even got back to the room. The Punisher smiled as the smooth glass bottle rolled gently between two ice-cold hands. The cork came loose easily, and the Punisher poured some of the black powder onto a delicate crystal plate, taking great care not to touch any of it. Oh no, that would not be good. The last thing the Purists needed was one of their best advocates powerless for a month. With great care the bottle was sealed back up and put away for later. There was still plenty left to bind the others.

A subtle shift in the energy of the room captured the Punisher's full attention and warned of their impending arrival. Waiting. Patiently waiting. A second or two more, and they would be here. Yes! Static crackled in the air, and two of the traitors materialized in the room just a few feet away. The male realized it first. The confusion and surprise on his face was well worth the wait. Before he could utter a single word or realize what was happening, the Punisher smiled and stepped closer to the two lovers. With one large breath, black powder flew into their faces.

They sputtered and coughed, brushing away the powder that burned their eyes and nostrils. Initially it looked as though the powder wasn't working, but within seconds the two shimmered and shifted unwillingly into their animal forms. The surprised look on the wolf's face almost elicited a laugh from their captor. The eagle shrieked and flapped its massive wings furiously as the two beasts looked at one another through pathetic, helpless eyes.

With the wave of a gloved hand and whisperings of the ancient language, a large leather muzzle appeared over the wolf's mouth and a black leather hood over the head of the eagle. As they struggled against their new bindings, a long chain appeared, which only added to their fear and confusion, one end around the neck of the wolf, and the other bound to the eagle's leg.

The Punisher made soft sounds of reassurance and let out a maniacal laugh as the two of them stopped struggling. "Shhhh. There, there. No point in fighting it. Besides, I thought you two wanted to be together forever?" The Punisher's gloating laughter bounced off the walls. "Malcolm and Samantha, I'm sure you've realized by now that you have none of your gifts. No telepathy, no visualization, and no ability to shift."

The eagle screeched and attempted to fly, but the chain tied to its mate was far too short to allow any flight. The links pulled tightly on the makeshift choke collar around the wolf's neck. Samantha let out a whine and a low growl. Malcolm immediately stopped moving and settled on the floor blindly next to the massive wolf.

The Punisher laughed softly and made a scolding sound. "Careful Malcolm, or you'll choke the life right out of Samantha."

Samantha let out a low growl of warning. Her bright blue eyes glared at the Punisher through the leather muzzle that clung tightly to her furry face. Their captor stepped back and pulled out a sleek black handgun and pointed it directly at Malcolm.

"Now, now Samantha. If you don't behave, then I'll have to shoot a hole right through his bird brain. But what fun would that be?" They both stilled, likely weighing their limited options. "Malcolm, you may be blinded by your hood, but I know you can hear me. I have a gun pointed directly at you. It would make a pretty hole in you or your mate just as easily as in you. But don't worry… we have much bigger and better plans for you and your disgusting friends. Now, I'm going to take you someplace special, and later this evening your friends will be joining us."

The Punisher kept the gun pointed at Malcolm, carefully stepped over the chain, and stood between the prisoners. The Punisher, keeping a sharp eye on the wolf, picked up the chain that tied the two together. The whisper of one word from their captor, "*Verto*," and all three Amoveo vanished into the air.

Moments later they materialized in the room at

Breezemont that had been carefully prepared. The large bedroom in the old house stood just as it had been left the night before. Three of the massive steel cages sat empty, and the only occupied cage still had the black canvas cover securely over it. The beast beneath stirred restlessly. The sounds drew the attention of Samantha. Her ears pricked up, and her bright blue eyes flicked to the cage. A harsh yank on the chain elicited the desired whimper of pain from Samantha, and the sound of the gun cocking bounced through the room, silencing the wolf.

Her abductor opened one of the empty cages beside the crumbling fireplace and motioned for Samantha to go in. Reluctantly, she entered the cage, while emitting a low and deadly growl. Her glowing blue eyes locked with her jailor.

"Watch it, missy. No loud noises. I have a strong shield in place, which, so far, has kept our little surprise hidden. However, I don't want to run the risk of letting the cat out of the bag, so to speak."

The chain was quickly removed and the cage door slammed shut as the lock clicked into place and echoed throughout the room. With the chain clutched tightly in a gloved fist, the Punisher dragged Malcolm over and wrapped the other hand around his feathered neck.

"It would be so easy to snap your neck," his captor whispered softly as the eagle's massive wings flapped helplessly. Samantha growled, and her hackles went up, but their kidnapper merely laughed. "She's one protective bitch, isn't she Malcolm?" The Punisher released Malcolm and sighed loudly. "Alas, it's not quite time for that. No, we'd much rather make it a group event. So much more fun."

Their abductor lashed the chain tightly to a wooden perch, which stood next to Samantha's cage. After some resistance, Malcolm eventually settled onto the perch. He pulled at the chain tied to his leg, but that only got a bigger chuckle from their captor.

"Keep pulling on that chain, Malcolm. You'll rip your own leg off." The Punisher stepped back and admired the menagerie that had been collected so far. "Not that I really care," their enemy said with a rather dismissive wave and turned around to survey the room once more. "Very nice. You see everything is going as planned this time. The binding powder has worked as promised. It will keep you bound in your clan form without any of your abilities for a month—but you'll be dead long before it wears off."

The Punisher backed up slowly across the large room and sat in the worn wing chair against the far wall, with the gun still pointed at the helpless captives.

"I'm sure you're wondering what's next. Well… now, we wait. We wait for my partner to join us. He'll keep an eye on you, while I put the final pieces in place for our big finale this evening. I need to be sure we have all the players properly positioned." The Punisher glanced at the old mantel clock that was somehow still working after so many years abandoned. "We've waited all these years… what's a few more hours?"

Chapter 16

PETE DROVE DANTE AND KERRY BACK TO THE FRENCH Quarter in awkward silence. Kerry knew that Pete suspected something, but so far he hadn't uttered a word. Occasionally, she caught his eye in the rearview mirror, but she couldn't hold his gaze for long. He was very uncomfortable, not scared, but absolutely unsettled. His nervous energy rippled through the car and gave her a bit of a headache. She looked at Dante, who sat stone still next to her and hadn't taken his eyes off the passing scenery.

Peter cleared his throat and shifted in his seat. He flicked a glance to them in the backseat. "So, I'll drop you two at the front of the hotel?"

"Yes," Dante responded without looking up. "But I want you to meet us back here later and come with us to Jacqueline's house tonight."

"You got it, boss." Peter pulled the car to a stop in front of the Monteleone and turned around to face them. "Do you want me to take a look around Jacqueline's place? Get a feel for the layout and surrounding area?"

Dante's serious gaze locked with Pete's, and he nodded almost imperceptibly. "Absolutely. We'll meet you in the lobby at five o'clock and walk over together."

Kerry and Dante got out of the car and watched as Pete drove away. She adjusted the large black bag on her shoulder and linked her arm in his. She watched as the muscles clenched in his jaw, and his eyes scanned the street around them. Kerry's heart thudded in her chest. She'd never been the focus of such love, devotion, and fierce protection. As a model, she'd had total strangers fantasize about her and various buffoons try to get in her pants, but no one—no man—had ever really loved her. Even more importantly, *she* hadn't been in love before.

Kerry swallowed hard in an attempt to keep from crying like some ridiculous schoolgirl. "Hey, what do you say we try to go on a date?"

"What?" He looked at her as though she'd said she wanted to run down the street naked covered in chicken feathers. "Now?"

The shocked look on his face had her laughing out loud. She whirled to face him and took his scruffy jaw in her hands. "Yes, you big caveman. Now! I refuse to spend the rest of the day worrying." She stepped back and placed her hands on her hips, daring him to challenge her. "What else would you like to do? Sit around and watch the minutes tick by until the clock strikes five, and it's time to go to Jacqueline's?"

He raised one eyebrow and smiled at her suggestively. "I can think of a few things to help pass the time." Dante sidled closer and placed a tender kiss on the corner of her mouth.

Kerry giggled and kissed him on the cheek. "I'm sure you can." She laughed as his large hands slid down and cupped her ass. She gave him the most scolding look she could muster, and grabbing his hands, slipped out of his tempting embrace. "I'm hungry. Women cannot live on sex alone." She grinned. Kerry walked backwards and pulled her with him. "Malcolm and Samantha aren't going to be back until later. So let's just go have some fun. Put all of this craziness out of our minds and go on a date. You know… like normal people do." She eyed him skeptically and stopped dead in her tracks. "You do know what a date is… right?"

That slow, lopsided smile cracked his handsome face, and his amber eyes twinkled. He threw his head back and let out that deep, rich laugh that she loved, but only rarely heard. "Yes. Contrary to what you love to call me, I am *not* a Neanderthal." Slowly, he took her hand and brought it to his lips. He placed a warm kiss on her fingers and kept his smiling eyes on hers. "Your wish is my command."

His intense amber eyes locked on hers and practically devoured her. She had to admit he had the thickest, most spectacular lashes that she'd ever seen on a man.

"You bet your ass it is," she murmured. "Come on. Let's go do some sightseeing. Maybe grab some lunch?" She pulled his hand, encouraging him to walk with her. "I've been dying to try the coffee at the Café Du Monde, and I'd adore a ride on that riverboat."

Dante quickly wrapped his arm around her waist and pulled her to him. With great contentment, she noticed how easily they stepped in time with one another. She marveled at the way they seemed so perfectly in tune. That dopey line from that Tom Cruise movie kept running through her head—the whole "you complete me" thing. As scary and bizarre as her life had gotten, she wouldn't trade it for the world. For the first time in her life she did feel complete. Before Dante, she'd been broken and damaged. Alone and drowning in pain. Not anymore.

The dark memory of the letters seeped slowly into her mind and threatened her serenity, but Kerry quickly stuffed it back down. Not now. This minute, this hour, she was just a woman walking in the arms of the man she loved. No matter what happened in the future, she would at least have this—this day, with this man. Kerry smiled wistfully. Her man.

They made their way down Royal Street and turned the corner at St. Louis Cathedral. As they walked down St. Ann Street toward the river, a cool, delicious breeze picked up and washed over them, providing a brief respite from the muggy air. When they entered Jackson Square, the people and the colors seemed brighter. The square, littered with tourists and artists, had the added texture of jugglers and musicians. Kerry liked the organized chaos of the lively square. They walked along, admiring the various paintings, and Kerry couldn't help but look for Joseph.

"He works evenings. I'm not surprised he isn't here. Besides, I'm sure the old coot needs a rest after his little display with the gun," Dante said. His voice held an unmistakable edge of disdain.

She should've known he would see right through her. Kerry shrugged, but couldn't look at him. "I know. I guess I was just hoping… I don't know what I was hoping." She sighed.

They reached the edge of the square and crossed to the Café Du Monde for some of their world famous coffee and beignets. Sitting under the green-and-white-striped canopy, Kerry indulged in some fattening, but delicious, sugary goodness. The strong coffee complimented the fried dough perfectly. She licked her fingers and enjoyed every delectable morsel. However, the entire time Dante looked at her as if she were covered in sugar.

The winds picked up, and the sky darkened as storm clouds rolled in. Unfazed by the threat of rain, they remained safely under the canopy. For over two hours, they talked about everything under the sun. He spoke of his business, his family, and regaled her with stories of growing up on their ranch in Montana. She noticed the way his eyes softened as he spoke fondly of his sister, Marianna. Her heart broke when sadness crept into his voice at the mention of memories with his father. As lovely as those times had been, all of it was tarnished by his ultimate betrayal.

"What clan is your sister descended from? You're from the Fox Clan, like your mother," she said, hoping that she was keeping it all straight. "But your father was part of the Bear Clan, right?"

"Yes." Dante nodded solemnly. "So is Marianna. The Kodiak Bear Clan."

"Oh," Kerry said with a tight smile. She didn't know if that was a good thing or not.

"I don't know if she'll ever forgive me," he said quietly. "She thinks that I could've done more to save him." He shrugged. "Maybe she's right."

"She's your sister, Dante. Your twin sister. I don't have any siblings, but if I did, you can bet I wouldn't let anything come between us." Kerry blew on her coffee and took a much needed sip. "Don't you think that you should tell them the truth about what your father did?"

Dante made a sound of frustration and leaned back in the wrought-iron chair. "I don't want them involved in all of this," he said with deadly seriousness. "The less they're involved and the less they know, then the safer they'll be."

Kerry narrowed her eyes and looked at him with curiosity. "Don't you think they'll have a few questions when you tell them about me? You know… the fact that your mate is a hybrid like Samantha?" Dante looked away from her, and her heart sank. Something that looked a lot like shame came over his face. Kerry swallowed hard. "They don't know, do they?" she breathed.

Fear gripped her heart, and she mustered up the courage to ask the question that had been lurking in the back of her mind. Was he ashamed of her? Ashamed that his mate wasn't a pure-blooded Amoveo? If this thing between them was going to fall apart, better it happened now. Although the truth was she didn't think her heart could survive that.

She tilted her chin and straightened her back, preparing herself for the worst. "Are you ashamed of me?"

His jaw clenched, and his intense gaze immediately locked again with hers as anger and frustration rippled off of him. His eyes flickered and shifted briefly. "How on earth could you ask me that?" He leaned in and took her hands in his. His eyes softened as he stroked his fingers over hers. "I am not ashamed of you," he said definitively. "Yes, of course they know about you. You are my mate. *You* are my life now."

Realization dawned over her with sickening speed. "They're not happy about it, are they?"

"No," he said quietly. "Mother has been so caught up in the loss of my father, I'm not sure she's even registered what's going on. But Marianna—" He sighed, and his shoulders sagged with defeat. "She not only blames me, but she also blames Samantha."

"And me," Kerry said quietly.

Dante shook his head. "No. It's not your fault, Kerry—or Samantha's. None of it is. My father chose to be violent and hateful. He made his own fate." Dante leaned both elbows on the table and lowered his voice. "As far as Marianna is concerned, our father died trying to protect a hybrid. Her feeling is that if hybrids didn't exist, then our father would still be alive." He lifted her hand to his lips and kissed her fingers softly. "She's angry," he said softly. "She just needs some time."

"Dante," Kerry began slowly and kept her steady gaze on his. "I hate to ask you this, but do you think there's any chance that your sister could be involved with the Purists?"

He sat back slowly, but kept his dark eyes locked with hers. His face remained a mask of stone, and the lines in his forehead deepened. Kerry held her breath as the silence hung thickly between them. She knew it was a risky question to ask. He could flip out and tell her to go to hell for suggesting something like that. Truthfully, she wouldn't blame him. It was a ballsy thing to ask— but it had to be asked. She studied his face and waited for what felt like eons before he finally answered her.

"That thought has crossed my mind," he said. "But, no." He shook his head firmly with his mouth set in a grim line. "I don't think so. She's been very busy helping my mother through her grieving and getting all of my father's affairs in order. She is also next in line to take his place on the Council, and as you can imagine, she'll have a great deal to learn. Honestly, I doubt she's had time for much else." He looked at her through those loving brown eyes and smiled. "I'm sure that once they meet you, they'll be as enamored with you as I am."

Kerry nodded and gave Dante a tight smile. "Right." She nodded. She was glad he felt okay about his sister, but the cold, hard truth was that Kerry didn't. She didn't feel alright about her at all. Jeez. Talk about having issues with the in-laws.

The blast of the steamboat *Natchez* had them both jump in their chairs, which promptly caused them to burst out laughing. Dante glanced at his watch and threw some cash down on the table for the bill. "We better hurry up."

Dante grabbed her hand, and they raced to catch the boat. Within moments of leaving the safety of the canopy, the skies opened up, and the rain came pouring down. They got to the booth and purchased their tickets in the nick of time. She couldn't help but admire the rivulets of rainwater that traversed the ropy muscles of his arms, or how his black T-shirt had molded to every delicious inch of his broad back. He'd pushed the wet hair off his face, and it left her free to inspect his magnificent profile. If sex, desire, and lust could be molded into a man, then Dante would be it.

Soaking wet, clothing stuck on them like a second skin, and laughing like two little kids, they boarded the old-fashioned riverboat. Taking her hand, Dante led the way to the top level and to the bow of the boat. The rain had discouraged many passengers from taking the ride, and the ones who did decide to go, stayed inside the safety of the ship's cabin. However, the two of them stood at the railing in the rain and looked out over the choppy, indigo river.

Kerry pulled her long wet hair off her face and tied it back quickly with the ease of experience. She closed her eyes and opened her mouth. The pelting raindrops stung her lips, and the clean water bathed her tongue. Even with her eyes closed, she could feel Dante's gaze on her. His energy pulsed over her and mixed with the cool water as it ran down her body, creating an intensely erotic sensation.

Dante sidled up behind her and placed one hand on either side of Kerry on the railing. Gently, he pressed his massive body up against hers and placed a butterfly kiss along the edge of her ear. She made a soft sound of contentment and leaned into him.

"I just can't resist touching you," he murmured into her ear.

"Who's stopping you?" She sighed.

He covered her hands with his, and she relished the way the slick skin of his arms slid tantalizingly along hers. That delicious sensation of honeyed warmth coursed through her veins. Her skin tingled as the enchanting phenomenon curled through her body from head to toe. He nibbled on her earlobe, and she angled her head, giving him ample access to her sensitized neck. He trailed wispy kisses along her skin and lapped at droplets of rain as that devilishly talented tongue flicked at her pulse, which beat wildly under the surface. She moaned faintly and licked the rainwater from her lips. Kerry attempted to reach up and touch him, but Dante captured her hands in his and placed them on the slippery railing.

"Oh, no you don't," he whispered gruffly. "This is about you. I just want you to feel me touching you."

They stayed there in that position for the duration of the boat ride. That entire time he simply cradled her in the shelter of his body, periodically placing kisses along her cheek or trailing his fingertips up the inside of her forearm. His knee would brush tantalizingly against the back of her thigh as his fingertips memorized the curve of elbow. He licked the rainwater from the curve of her ear, along her jaw, and down the length of her neck. Delicate kisses, a lightning fast tongue, and talented fingers explored every inch of exposed flesh.

It wasn't sex, but it was the most erotic and intimate experience of her life.

The rain broke, and the *Natchez* made its lazy turn back to the dock. Dante placed a firm kiss on Kerry's cheek and wrapped his arms around her in a massive bear hug.

"Time to go back," he whispered.

Kerry said nothing. What could she say? They did have to go back and face everything. She held onto his forearms, pulling him tighter to her as she finally opened her eyes and squinted against the sunlight that had broken through the gray clouds. The ride and their afternoon escape were about to come to a screeching halt.

Dante rapped on the bathroom door softly. "Come on, princess. Hurry up, or we're going to be late."

"I'll be out in a minute, Tarzan."

Dante chuckled and shook his head at her nickname for him. Ironically, what had started as an insult had turned into a pet name. It dawned on him that he'd never had a nickname before. Before finding Kerry, the idea of someone calling him anything other than Dante or Mr. Coltari was less than appealing. He had a feeling she'd be getting away with just about anything she wanted. It was simple really. He wanted to make her happy, because that made him happy. It really was as simple as that.

His cell phone chirped loudly in his jacket pocket. He pulled it out and looked quizzically at the unfamiliar number. It was a local wireless caller. That's odd. Jacqueline or Boris maybe?

"Hello?" Dante walked over to the window and looked out at the setting sun.

"Mr. Coltari?" The man's voice sounded vaguely familiar, but he couldn't quite place it.

"Yes, this is Dante Coltari. Who is this?"

"This is Brent, sir, from the hotel. Remember how you asked me to tell you if anyone asked about Ms. Smithson?"

Cold dread crept up Dante's belly, and every fiber of his body tensed. "Yes," he said in a barely audible tone and threw a glance over his shoulder to the closed bathroom door.

"Well, there were these two girls. Kind of young, you know. They couldn't have been more than fifteen or sixteen. I'm pretty sure they didn't mean any harm, but they were snooping around here and asking all kinds of questions about Ms. Smithson," he babbled relentlessly.

Dante couldn't get a word in edgewise, and the boy's rambling was giving him a headache. He went on and on about the girls, what they wore, the time they came by, and so forth. After just the first sentence, Dante suspected that these girls were likely just overzealous fans. They couldn't have been Amoveo Purists, for they were far too young, and it was very unlikely they were Caedo. He thought for a moment it might've been that assistant of Layla's, Melissa, but Layla had made it painfully clear that they'd be working in the studio until late in the evening. Dante tried repeatedly to interject, but each time the eager young clerk cut him off.

The boy kept talking, and Dante looked at his watch. Kerry had been in there for a ridiculously long time. Brent continued to babble away, and Dante went over to the closed bathroom door. Just before he knocked, Brent finally took a breath, and Dante didn't squander the opening.

"Okay, kid. Thanks for your help. I'll check it out. Bye." He shut the phone off and stuffed it into the pocket of his dark slacks.

"Kerry?" He knocked, but was greeted only with silence. He called her name again and rapped harder, but still nothing. Dante grabbed the door handle and found it locked. Fear crawled up his spine. "Kerry! Answer me now, or I'm breaking down the damn door," he shouted and banged harder.

Met only with silence, he threw his weight into the door and broke it open. Dark energy flooded out of the bathroom. A tsunami of evil slammed into him and stole the breath from his lungs. Gasping for air, gripping the doorjamb for support, he looked frantically around the empty bathroom. Kerry was nowhere to be found. Questions raced through his mind, and then everything stopped. A bright red envelope lay on the white marble countertop.

Dante's eyes shifted, and a low growl ripped from his throat. His body shook with rage, and sweat beaded on his forehead. Seething with rage, he snatched up the envelope and ripped it open. He'd barely pulled the note out before the words on the page shrieked at him.

GO TO BREEZEMONT
AND WATCH THE FREAKS DIE.
YOUR BITCH IS FIRST!
—THE PUNISHER—

Dante crushed the note in his fist and pounded the counter repeatedly. The marble cracked, and the mirror rippled as his energy waves thundered through the room. He looked at his own reflection in the mirror and stilled. His amber eyes glowed brighter than ever, and veins stuck out in his neck. He looked as insane as he felt. Focus. He needed to focus. Freaking out and trashing the suite was not going to get his mate back. He had to find her. Nothing would matter, none of it, if he lost her.

Dante pushed himself away from the counter and stalked into the living room of the suite. Where was she? Someone took her. Someone—one of his own people—had materialized in there and taken her right under his fucking nose. His mind raced, frantic, searching for an answer. He had to find her, connect with her. He closed his eyes and focused on connecting with Kerry, his anger fueled by helpless frustration. Each time he tried to connect with her, he was met with nothingness. A black, empty void was all that he found. That had only happened once before.

His eyes flew open. Steven. The same thing had happened today when he'd tried to connect with Steven.

He took the note out of his pocket and smoothed it on the dining table. He had to calm down and figure this out. She needed him. Dante focused on his breathing and did his best to keep the beast within him at bay. Hands splayed on either side of the wrinkled paper, he read it again, and the magnitude of the situation dawned on him.

WATCH THE FREAKS DIE

Freaks. The Punisher had others—Samantha and Malcolm? Praying he was wrong, Dante closed his eyes and desperately tried to connect with Malcolm and Samantha. However, in both cases, he found the same sinister void. He struggled to rationalize and reconcile what was happening. Maybe they were next door and just didn't want to be interrupted. He had to check.

He whispered the ancient language, "*Verto*," and within seconds he stood in Malcolm and Samantha's hotel suite. The same dark energy signature that had swamped him in the bathroom lingered here as well. It wasn't as strong, but it still slithered through the room. Dante's stomach rolled, and he grit his teeth against the sinister tentacle of energy.

"Malcolm? Samantha?" He called their names and quickly checked every room in the suite, but as he feared, they weren't there. All of their things were there, and the room was relatively undisturbed, but his two friends were nowhere to be found. Maybe they weren't back from Westerly yet?

Whoever took Kerry had been in here too. He

had to find them and warn them. Just before he left, something on the floor caught his eye. Feathers. He crouched down and picked up two brown feathers with a golden hue. Dante's heart sank. He knew they were Malcolm's. There was no question in his mind any longer. Whoever took Kerry had taken Samantha and Malcolm too.

Her captor had appeared behind her out of thin air, like something out of a childhood nightmare, or the embodiment of the grim reaper. She knew, even in that brief instant, that this black-clad intruder was the person who wrote the notes—The Punisher. Her masked captor placed one hand on her arm and twisted it harshly behind her back. The other gloved hand clamped firmly over her mouth before she could cry out to Dante for help. Bright electric shocks shot through her blood, and the image of a snarling tiger burst into her mind. It was an Amoveo from the Tiger Clan.

It had happened in a split second.

One moment she's in the bathroom getting ready for their meeting with Jacqueline, and the next she's standing in a rundown bedroom littered with cages and lit candles. She knew it was the old house in the bayou. Joseph's house.

When they materialized in the dilapidated bedroom, her heart sank at the sight before her. Her kidnapper had collected a twisted menagerie. She struggled in vain against the iron-clad grip of her captor. The Punisher giggled lightly in her ear and yanked harder on her arm, sending red-hot streaks of pain up her arm. She bit back a cry of pain, and her eyes frantically scanned the scene around her.

A wolf and eagle stirred restlessly. She knew that the wolf was Samantha, and she could only assume that the eagle was Malcolm. They were both in their clan animals. Samantha stood in her wolf form, trapped in a massive steel cage in front of a crumbling fireplace. Her glowing blue eyes were filled with a mixture of fear and anger, a leather muzzle clamped tightly over her face. She locked eyes with Kerry and let out a low growl. Kerry tried to touch her mind to Sam's, but was met with an odd void.

Her confused and frightened gaze flicked to the enormous eagle tethered to a tall perch. It was Malcolm. It had to be. His head was covered by a blinding hood, and his leg tethered by a chain to the perch. Kerry tried to connect with him as well, but again, was met with absolutely nothing. Bile rose in her throat, and fear gripped her heart. What the hell was going on?

When they'd appeared in the room, he'd spread his massive wings out and screeched in anger. However, the chain on his leg kept him firmly on the wooden perch. One cage remained covered, and although the black drape over it fluttered, the occupant remained hidden. Two other cages stood empty, and she shuddered at the sight of them. She had the sinking suspicion they were meant for her and Dante.

Her mind raced. Of course, she could touch her mind to his. Dante. She had to find him—tell him where she was. She reached out to him with her mind and screamed as loud as she could. *Dante*. But it was as if she hit a mental block—an invisible brick wall.

Movement to the right caught her eye, and a vaguely familiar face stood in front of him. It was the sweet kid from the hotel. However, at the moment he didn't seem so freakin' sweet. What was his name? Brent? What in the hell was this kid doing here? He stood there frightened as ever with those big, dopey, puppy dog eyes, sweaty brown hair stuck to his pale forehead. He shifted his weight nervously back and forth and had something in his hand. Brent's gaze flicked between Kerry and her kidnapper, and he licked his quivering lips.

"Do it," the Punisher barked loudly in his ear.

Brent held out his hand. "I'm sorry," he whispered.

Before she could ask questions or demand answers, Brent blew a cloud of black powder into her face. It stung her eyes and burned her nostrils. Kerry coughed and sputtered at the unexpected assault, and her kidnapper released her abruptly. Without warning, her back arched, and her limbs flew out in front of her. Kerry's entire body shivered, and every single cell tingled. The lightning fast sensation bordered on pain as it zipped from the ends of her hair to the tips of her toenails.

She'd meant to cry out in confusion, but much to her surprise, a massive roar came out instead. Suddenly, everything seemed further away, and she thought for a moment she'd fallen down. Her body felt heavy and clumsy. She went to hold up her hand, and instead, found massive black paws. Paws?

She had shifted into her panther.

Snarling, she turned toward her captor and crouched low, instinctively preparing to attack. Her glowing yellow eyes darted toward Samantha, who sat growling loudly in her prison. Kerry tried to reach out with telepathy, but was met with a void. Confused, she looked to Malcolm and tried to connect with him. Still nothing. What the fuck was happening?

Kerry's bright yellow glare landed on their masked kidnapper. Before she could pounce, their kidnapper drew a gun, pointed it directly at her head, and motioned to the open cage behind her. Kerry didn't know a whole lot about being an Amoveo, but she was pretty sure that "bulletproof" wasn't in the job description. She was trapped, and she knew it. Growling, she reluctantly backed into the open cage and watched powerlessly as the door swung shut. The lock snapped closed with a sickening click.

Brent stood behind her jailor with a look on his face that resembled something like regret. The Punisher squatted down in front of the cage and finally removed the black ski mask. A long mane of dark hair spilled out, and Kerry found herself staring into the face of a vaguely familiar woman. She snarled. Was it Dante's sister? Her mind raced. Marianna was descended from the Bear Clan, like their father, and she'd seen a tiger when she'd touched this woman.

Realization dawned, and a low growl rumbled in her throat. It was the woman from the pictures at The Den.

It was Pasha Zankoff.

Her cold green eyes glittered cruelly at Kerry through the thick bars. "You may be a half-breed and only part Amoveo, but I'd say the binding powder worked quite nicely on you." A nasty grin cracked her face. "By the way, roar all you want. No one will hear you out here. Joseph finally left for the square, but when he comes home, now that's when the fun really begins." Then with a twisted, satisfied smile, she stood and covered the cage, leaving Kerry in darkness.

Kerry tried for what seemed like hours to connect with Dante, Samantha, and Malcolm. However, time and time again she was met with the same void. Nothing. Exhausted and frightened, she lay down in the massive steel cage. Being surrounded by absolute darkness, Kerry had no concept of time. She had fallen asleep, but had been unable to walk in the dream realm. How long had she been here? Hours? Days? Only one thought kept going through her head. Where was Dante?

Frustration simmered relentlessly as the reality of her predicament became more clear. She'd been alone before meeting Dante, but that was nothing compared to what she felt at the moment. The emptiness that haunted her now cut even deeper, because now she knew exactly what she was missing.

Chapter 17

BACK IN HIS OWN SUITE, DANTE SWORE LOUDLY AND threw the note across the room. He needed help. Who could he trust? There were only two other Amoveo left that he thought—no—he hoped, he could trust. Dante threw out a silent prayer that he was right. He held his breath and reached out to William and Steven, but this time, much to his relief, he found some success. Instead of a void, he discovered William's distinctly sharp energy and connected. Moments later William materialized next to him in the suite, but there was still no sign of Steven.

"Thank God!" Dante sank onto the couch and put his head in his hands. Relief had replaced some of the fear that had threatened to consume him.

"What on earth is going on?" William stood stiffly in his pinstripe suit and looked at Dante with thinly veiled disgust. "You look dreadful." He sniffed and looked around the room. "Where is Kerry?"

"She's gone. The Punisher has her out at the old house." Dante kept his head in his hands. Unable to look William in the face, he pointed to the note on the floor. "See for yourself."

William calmly went over, picked up the note, and read it. "Oh dear," he said quietly.

"I think he's got Samantha, Malcolm, and Steven as well." Dante stood quickly and paced the room. "I can't believe I let this happen. Son of a bitch!" He stalked toward William and grabbed him by the lapels of his jacket. "He came right in here and took her. I was in the next fucking room, and he took her," he shouted into William's emotionless face. "Some goddamn body-guard I am, huh? I'm her mate, William." He shoved William away from him and shouted, "How could I let this happen?"

Dante wondered if he sounded as helpless as he felt. He stood there defeated and half expected William to knock him senseless. At this point, he practically wel-comed it.

William straightened out his jacket and tie, but his face remained as serene as ever. "If you're finished having your pity party, I suggest we go and collect our friends. Really Dante, do get yourself together."

Dante shot him a contrite look—he knew William was right. "Have you seen or spoken with Steven today?"

"No." William shook his head, and his brow fur-rowed. "Still no word."

"Me either," Dante seethed. "Every time I try to create a mental link with him, I get nothing. It's the same with Kerry, Malcolm, and Sam. It's like… they're gone."

A sharp rap at the hotel room door interrupted them. Dante and William exchanged a puzzled look. Dante went to the door and looked through the peephole. It was Peter. Dante swore softly and ran his hand through his hair. The last thing he wanted to do was involve Peter. As a human, he didn't stand a chance against an Amoveo warrior. He couldn't just ignore him, so he'd have to make something up and send him on his way. Reluctantly, he opened the door.

Pete came right in, and immediately started giving

Dante the business. "Jeez, boss. I've been waiting for you two in the lobby for almost half an hour. I was starting to get worried." He stopped dead in his tracks and looked quizzically at William. Before Dante could say a word, the smile faded from Peter's face. "What's going on?" He pointed at William. "You're not Kerry. Hey, who's the stiff with the ponytail?"

William made a sound of disgust. "Stiff?"

Dante quickly closed the door. "This is an old family friend, William Fleury."

Peter and William shook hands briefly, and each sized up the other. Dante could see that they didn't trust each other. He couldn't blame them, and right now, he was having some major trust issues himself.

"Listen," Pete said. "I know something is going on. Where's Kerry?" He looked back and forth between the two men.

"She's in trouble," Dante bit out. He struggled to keep his anger under control. It took every last iota of resolve to prevent his eyes from shifting. "I need you to drive us back to the old house."

"Wait? I thought we were supposed to meet Jacqueline at her place," Joseph said through confused eyes. "I think that coot waving a shotgun around today made it pretty clear that he didn't want us there."

William's voice slammed into Dante's rage-clouded mind. *Why do we need him to drive us? He will just complicate matters. I don't want to baby-sit a human.*

Dante ignored William and gave his full attention to Peter. "I know, and as far as I can figure, Joseph is probably to blame for this mess. Listen, I can't explain. I just need you to drive me out there." He looked at his friend and found his serious face held nothing but acceptance and trust.

"Whatever you say, boss."

I'm quite serious, Dante. I don't think we should be bringing him. He's a human, and as a result—he's weak.

Dante silenced him with one deadly look. *You go ahead of us, and try to get a read on the situation. Kerry, who happens to be half human, hasn't learned how to use our form of travel.* He felt the need to remind William of Kerry's heritage. *That place is in the middle of nowhere, and I want options. Besides—I trust him.*

Well, I don't. The resolve in William's voice matched the determined set of his jaw.

"Hello?" Peter stood at the door of the suite. "Are you two going to just stand there glaring at each other?"

William brushed past Peter to the door. "I'll be taking my own means of transportation and will meet you there."

Peter rolled his eyes and let out an exasperated sigh. "Whatever, man. Let's get going. I can't imagine whatever she's gotten herself into is going to improve with time." Peter took out his gun. He checked to see that it was loaded and then shoved it back into his holster. "It's always good to have this old girl handy," he said, patting the lump in his jacket. "Especially out there, man. You never know what kind of creepy crawlers you could run into."

Dante and William exchanged a knowing look as the three men walked out the door.

———~~~———

"Can't this car go any faster?" Dante barked from the passenger seat of the Mercedes.

Peter continued to white knuckle the steering wheel and kept his sharp eyes trained on the dark highway. "I'm getting us there as fast as I can. We'll be there in a few minutes."

When you get here, Peter should stay outside. William's stern voice cut into Dante's mind with his usual razor-sharp precision. *We will need someone to keep an eye on the perimeter of the house.*

Dante knew he was right. *Fine. Do you see anything unusual yet?*

No. It's very quiet. Too quiet.

Dante cursed softly and glanced at Peter. "I'll need you on the outside and ready to get Kerry out of there as quickly as possible if things go bad."

"Boss, come on." He looked over at Dante, but the determined look on his face sent a clear message. Pete let out a frustrated sigh. "I suppose you won't want me calling the local cops on this?"

"I've already got a cop—a retired cop—but a cop." Dante forced a strained smile, but couldn't squash the ache in his chest. He'd kept trying to connect with Kerry, but nothing worked. The inability to touch her mind terrified him. It left him feeling empty and lost. He used this fear and frustration to fuel his anger.

Whoever took Kerry, whoever had the audacity to lay so much as one finger on her, would pay for it with life itself. Dante didn't consider himself a violent man, but right now, that was the one thing that dominated his thoughts.

They turned into the gravel driveway, and Peter shut

off the lights of the car. The bayou, blanketed in the early evening shadows, seemed to sense their presence and sounded unnaturally quiet. Peter stopped the car just inside the entrance of the driveway.

The two men got out as silently as possible and crept toward the seemingly empty house. Dante led the way along the edge of the drive, and crouching low, ran over and hid behind the crumbling fountain where William sat waiting.

Peter looked at William quizzically. "How the hell did you get here so fast?" He glanced at the empty driveway. "Where the hell is your car?" he whispered.

"That's not your concern," William muttered without taking his eyes off the house.

Pete flicked a glance of annoyance to William. "Really?" He scoffed audibly. "You sure are a dick."

"Can you two give it a rest?" Dante hissed. "We're here to find Kerry, not to have a pissing match."

"Point taken," Pete said without a second glance at William. He drew his gun and peered around the edge of the fountain. "Are you sure she's here?" He kept his voice low. "There are no cars, and I don't see any lights inside. If I hadn't been here earlier, I'd never believe that there was a photo shoot here today. I don't even think this place still has electricity."

Dante crouched between Peter and William, closed his eyes, and focused on the energy that surrounded them. That odd ripple he'd felt earlier that morning was still there. Whatever was causing it had to be coming from inside that house. Kerry was in there, and that's all that mattered. Rage bubbled up uncontrollably, and his body trembled. Before he could stop it, his eyes shifted and glowed brightly. He knew Pete would see it, and he didn't care. All that mattered was getting Kerry.

We are flying blind Dante, William thought to him bluntly. *Someone has put a mental shield around the house. I can sense it. We should call for help. We have no idea how many people are in there.*

Kerry's in there, and that's all that matters. Impatience and desperation clawed at him. *Besides, the only people we can really trust are probably with her.* He stood to run inside, but Peter grabbed his arm and pulled him behind the stone and brambles.

"Hey, boss," Pete whispered and gestured toward Joseph's cottage. "What about the old guy? We don't know if there's anyone in that cottage."

Dante did his best to keep his back to Peter, hoping he wouldn't see his shifted eyes. "I need you to stay out here and keep an eye out for him or anyone else," he said over his shoulder. "The last thing we need is more surprises. When Kerry comes out of the house, with or without me, you get her the hell out of here."

"Shit," Peter hissed. "If you think I'm going to leave you out here, you're fucking crazy."

William grabbed Peter's shoulder and spun him so they were now face-to-face. He locked his shifted, glowing black eyes on Pete's shocked face. "You have absolutely no idea what you've just been dragged into." His voice, low and deadly, stayed just above a whisper. "So, do as Dante tells you, and stay here. The last thing we need is human blood on our hands."

Peter's face flickered briefly with surprise, but without missing a beat, his usual steadfast gaze took hold. He held his ground along with William's harsh gaze. "I got your back... *boss*."

Dante, his eyes burning like two embers in a fire, turned to Peter and gave a nod of gratitude. A brief flicker, a mixture of confusion and wonder, moved over Pete's features when he saw Dante's eyes.

Peter licked his lips and slowly nodded his acceptance. "You just have to promise me that when this whole thing is over, you'll tell me what the hell is going on." He double-checked the ammunition clip in his gun and slammed it back into place. Somehow, checking the tangible gun in his hand helped confirm that this was really happening, and he wasn't having some kind of bizarre hallucination.

"William, go check the cottage and get an aerial view of the property. Give us a better idea of what's going on, and see who we're up against."

William gave Dante a curt nod and stood up. He spread his arms wide and kept his glittering black eyes locked on Peter. "*Verto*," he whispered.

Peter watched with genuine awe as William shimmered briefly and shifted into a large Gyrfalcon. His enormous white and brown flecked wings flapped as he hovered briefly above the ground. He shrieked loudly through a hooked beak and flew into the twilight sky.

"Holy shit," Pete whispered. "That guy has some creepy-ass eyes. They were all black, and I could swear they were edged with yellow. They fucking glowed in the dark, boss." He turned to Dante, and his eyebrows flew up. "So do yours, but for some reason, yours don't freak me out quite as badly."

"They are the eyes of our clan," Dante said simply.

"Uh-huh," Peter breathed. His gaze held Dante's, and he nodded slowly. "Like I said, explain it to me later."

The two men watched as William circled high above the property. Strong waves of shock and confusion pulsed from Peter. Dante had to admit he was surprised that Peter took it so calmly.

"Man, I thought I'd seen everything," he mumbled, his eyes still on the sky.

"Not quite everything." Dante kept his sights on William and watched as he swooped down to the cottage.

His sharp voice cut into Dante's mind. *He's not in the cottage. It's empty. There doesn't seem to be anyone else outside of the house except us—Amoveo or human.*

Can you get a closer look inside the house itself?

Of course. William flew behind the house and out of sight. Dante swore softly and glanced at Peter who was looking at him through narrowed eyes.

"What's going on, boss?"

"The cottage is empty," Dante said. He kept his glowing gaze on the sky. "William's going to see if he can get a closer look and see inside the main house."

"Uh-huh. And how do you know that?" Pete asked warily.

"Telepathy," Dante said in a very matter of fact manner. "It's how we communicate with each other when we're in our clan form."

"Of course," he murmured quietly. "Why didn't I think of that?"

Before Pete could ask anything else, William swooped down behind them. Startled, Pete swore softly and jumped involuntarily. William shifted back into his human form and squatted next to them. His intense, now human eyes, immediately landed on Peter. "Sorry if I frightened you." A smug smile played at his lips.

"You didn't scare me. You startled me. There's a difference." He eyed William's suit. "Aren't you a little overdressed for this?"

"Peasant," William mumbled.

Dante let out a frustrated sigh. "Could you two duke it out later?" He turned to William. "Did you see anything?"

• "Yes." William nodded, his mouth set in a grim line. "I'm sorry to say I did. Samantha, Malcolm, and Kerry are all in their clan form. The women are caged, and Malcolm is tied to a perch like some kind of house pet." His lip curled in disgust. "There is one human. A male. I didn't recognize his energy signature. There were definitely two others. I couldn't see or sense who they are, but they're definitely one of us."

"One of us?" Pete's brow furrowed in confusion.

William sighed and rolled his eyes. "An Amoveo, you simpleton."

"Simpleton? Who are you calling a simpleton, you birdbrain?"

"Both of you shut up," Dante hissed. He furrowed his brow in confusion. "Why wouldn't they shift? Malcolm and Sam could just transport themselves out of there. Damn!" He ran a hand through his hair and stared up at the ominous house. "What the hell is going on?"

"I'm not sure. However, I know that Samantha saw me. I tried to connect with her, but I was unable to create a mental link. It was as if…" He trailed off, a look of worry etched deeply in his face. "It was as if she wasn't there." His somber eyes flicked back to Dante. "Just as you said."

"I don't know what the hell is going on here... exactly," Peter hedged. William shot him a look of doubt, which caused Pete to let out a frustrated grunt. "Okay. I have no freakin' idea what the deal is, but I do know that Kerry is in there, and some sick son of a bitch put her in a cage. So how do you boys want to handle this? It's getting pretty dark in this creepy-ass swamp," he said in a loud whisper as his eyes scanned the surrounding area. "Can we please go get her, so I can go back to New York City and deal with the regular weirdos?"

Dante nodded and sharpened his focus. "Pete, you stay here, and keep watch on the perimeter. William, I want you to fly up to the second story, and wait for my signal."

"What the hell are you going to do," Pete asked incredulously. "Just walk up and knock?"

A slow, deadly smile spread across Dante's face. "Not exactly." He stood, spread his arms wide, and whispered, "*Verto*."

Peter watched with wide eyes as Dante shimmered and shifted into his clan form. Slowly, approval and something that resembled admiration spread over Peter's features. His gaze followed Dante as he trotted in his fox form noiselessly across the gravel driveway and whisked up the steps of the house in a dark red blur.

"Holy crap," Peter mused. "He's a fox?" He laughed softly and shook his head. "Well, the ladies always did say that about him." He turned to William, but his smile faded quickly at the look of his unamused face.

William's sharp dark eyes studied Peter intently.

"You have to know that he will die to save her," he said quietly. "His life will mean nothing if he loses her."

Peter turned to face him, a look of annoyance blanketing his face. "Look, I know. Of course he'd be upset. She's his client." Peter knew that they were more than just business associates, but this guy, whoever he was, didn't seem to be a big fan of human beings.

"She's his mate." William bit out the words, each one dripping with impatience. Peter's blatant dislike of William rolled off him in angry waves and was now compounded by major confusion. William rolled his eyes and let out an exasperated sigh. "Never mind."

William's head snapped up as Dante's voice captured his attention. *The door is open a crack. I'm going in. Which side of the house is that room on?*

The back far right corner of the house. The one closest to the water. I'll fly around back now. Don't do anything rash, Dante. Get your mate, and get out of there. I'll get Samantha and Malcolm.

Peter watched the intense concentration carved in William's face and suspected he was speaking with Dante. He glanced to the porch and saw Dante slip inside the open door. A soft whisper behind him and cool breeze brushed past, as William shifted into his gyrfalcon and took flight. Peter crouched low at the edge of the fountain and positioned himself, so he had a clean shot of the door. If anyone or anything came out of that house, it better be friendly, or it was going to end up dead.

He looked at the chipped cherub wrapped in vines. "Guess it's just you and me kid." Then he turned his full attention to the house. "Game on."

Dante stilled when he entered the enormous and oddly familiar front hall of the old house. His heart thundered in his chest as he inspected his surroundings. It was exactly as it had been in the dream realm Kerry created. Everything. Every detail of the mammoth gilded mirror and the faded pattern on the rug runner—all of it was just as it had been in the dream. She'd been right. She was definitely somehow connected to this place.

He closed his eyes, stuck his snout in the air, and drew in a deep breath. He picked up her exotic scent immediately. His body flooded with relief. It wasn't the mental link that he craved, but it was better than nothing. She was here.

He padded silently across the old wood floors and paused at the foot of the grand staircase. The floorboards creaking above him caught his attention. Footsteps? His large ears pricked up, and he stood stone still, straining to hear more. He closed his glowing amber eyes and concentrated on the energy signature that pulsed through the house. The ripple or disturbance in the energy field was even stronger inside, and it was coming from upstairs. William had been spot on—as usual. Someone had put a mental shield around the house, but it was coming from upstairs. Whoever did it had taken Kerry. His lips curled back, and a low growl rumbled in his throat.

Slowly, he crept up the curved staircase and paused just before he reached the top. His large bushy tail flicked behind him. The light sound of a woman giggling drifted toward him. A door creaked open and echoed through the halls. The snickering grew louder and bounced down the hallway from the right side of the house. He had to shift back to his human form. His fox was perfect for

stealth movements in the dark of night, but now he had
to be prepared for battle. Members of the Fox Clan were
well known for their abilities to slip in and out of places
without being noticed, but they were physically stronger
in their human form.

Dante whispered the ancient language and shifted. He
pressed himself against the wall and listened. He called
up the acute hearing of his fox and kept his eyes shifted
to take advantage of the sharper vision of his clan.
Dante peered around the corner at the top of the stairs
and found it empty, except for a soft light coming from
the last door on the right. He needed a weapon. A gun
would've been ideal, but that was far too complicated
to visualize—too many working parts. Only the oldest
Amoveo had the ability to do that.

In his mind's eye he visualized a large, steel hunt-
ing dagger with a leather-wrapped handle. Within seconds he felt the weight of it in his hand. Dante gripped
it tightly in his right hand and smiled at the cold steel
blade. Prior to connecting with Kerry, he never would've
been able to visualize a weapon like this, let alone do it
so quickly. Samantha kept saying he was the missing
piece to Kerry's puzzle, but the truth was that Kerry was
his. They fit. He wouldn't lose her. Not now. Not ever.

With the dagger gripped tightly in his fist, Dante
silently eased his way down the hall. He repeatedly
attempted to connect with Kerry, but each time found
nothing. He stayed close to the wall with its faded and
peeling wallpaper and inched his way up to the door
that stood open just a crack. Light flickered, and just as
Dante was about to kick open the door, an unfamiliar
female voice stopped him dead in his tracks.

"No need for violence. Come on in, lover," she purred. "We've been waiting for you."

Anger burned brightly in his glowing eyes. He held the dagger pointed out and swung the door open with his free hand. The hinges screamed their resistance as the room came into horrifying focus. Pasha Zankoff stood in the center of the gigantic bedroom bathed in soft, dancing candlelight. There must've been fifty candles lit and flickering throughout the decrepit room.

Pasha, surrounded by her captives, had a smug, satisfied smirk on her face. Dressed in black from head to toe, she looked every bit the villain she had become. Her hair, an untamed mass of dark curls, framed bright green eyes that glittered insanely back at him. Each hand held a gun. One was pointed at Samantha and the other at his beloved Kerry. His gaze flicked to Kerry, who paced restlessly behind the cold steel bars in her panther form. Her bright yellow eyes stared pleadingly back at him, and a low growl rumbled through the decaying room.

Dante held his ground in the open doorway and turned his harsh gaze back on Pasha. "Why are you doing this, Pasha?"

She made a soft scolding sound and shook her head slowly. "Now, now. Why are you asking questions that you already know the answers to?"

"You're a Purist," he spat.

"Yes, lover, I am. But you figured that out too quickly," she taunted. "Come on now, ask me something else. A higher level query, perhaps?"

"I don't want to play games with you." He took one step forward, but stopped when Pasha cocked both guns.

"No, no." She shook her head and smiled. "I don't want to have to blow their brains out quite yet."

He growled and gripped the knife tighter. "You sick bitch!"

She stamped her foot and pouted like a child. "Oh, you're no fun. Fine," she said with a huge exasperated sigh. "I guess I'll just have to show you."

Her gaze flicked to Dante's left. He caught movement out of the corner of his eye two seconds too late. He took aim and threw the knife at Pasha with incredible force, but she moved with lightning fast reflexes and avoided his blade. The knife flew across the room and shattered the glass in the French doors behind her. Seconds later, he was blinded and choking on some kind of powder. Coughing, his eyes tearing, he felt the shift come on beyond his control.

The familiar tingle and prickling sensation of shifting rippled across his skin faster than it ever had. His body contorted and twisted almost to the point of pain. Before he could leap on his attacker and rip her throat out, a tremendously heavy net came down on him like a lead blanket. Snarling and growling, he fought back. Dante snapped blindly, hoping to catch one of them with his razor sharp teeth. However, the unexpected trap was more than effective, and within minutes they tossed him into the empty cage next to Kerry's.

The heavy door slammed shut, and Dante looked helplessly at his mate as he wrestled out from under the tangled net. Kerry roared loudly and turned her attentions to Pasha. She snarled and threw herself at the steel bars, but to no avail. Pasha threw her head back and let out a loud cackle, but Dante barely heard it.

When he saw the man standing behind her, the whole world went out of focus. It was as if he was hearing everything underwater. The person helping her was the kid from the hotel—Brent. What the hell? He'd scanned the boy's mind, but found nothing. No evidence of Pasha or the Purists. All he'd seen was fear. Why would this wimpy kid be involved with Pasha? How could he have been so completely wrong?

The boy stood there shifting his weight back and forth and shuffling his feet nervously. He looked at Dante and Kerry through sympathetic eyes. It was as if he didn't want to be doing what he'd obviously helped her do. How the hell did this kid even know about the Amoveo?

"You see," Pasha began. "New Orleans is the perfect place for our people. It's colorful, loud, and possesses a good deal of magic. If you know the right people and have enough money, you can get a spell for just about anything." She practically sang it. "I have to admit this worked far better than I thought," she said, referring to the glass bottle in Brent's shaky hands. "The powder that's stinging those pretty eyes and burning the inside of your nostrils? Well, that's part of a binding spell. Although… I did have to be very careful not to breathe any of it or get it on my pretty skin."

She stood, grabbed the boy by the arm, and pulled him next to her. He looked at her with pure terror. "My boy Brent has been very helpful, to say the least."

She shoved him away from her, twirled in the center of the room, and let out a maniacal giggle. Breathless, she stopped and flopped herself on the rotting floral blanket on the four-poster bed. Dust puffed up around her. She sat up swiftly and struck an innocent pose on the edge of the bed.

"You are all bound in your clan forms with none of your abilities. So really... you're just animals." She laughed and then sighed dramatically. "Sadly, it only lasts a month. You see, this was the only way to keep you all in one place. This way you can all watch each other die."

Disbelief flooded his mind as he looked around the room. Dante shook his furry head and let out a low whine. This couldn't be happening. He wanted to scream at Pasha and the boy. To stand up and choke the life out of her and ask her how she could betray their people like this. His head swam with questions. First and foremost, how the hell were they going to get out of this? With all of his abilities gone, he was as powerless as a run of the mill fox.

Pasha's cold, calculating eyes peered at Dante. "You are really pathetic, you know that? Look at you. You are pissing your life away over this thing," she spat with a look of disgust at Kerry. Dante snarled viciously in response. "It's men like you that are killing our race."

Dante watched as rage and resentment bubbled under the surface and clouded her features. Bitterness tinged every word. Pasha stood up from the bed, sauntered over, and squatted down in front of the cage, putting herself eye to eye with Dante.

She threw a glance and nod toward the glass in the door. "By the way, if you think you're getting any help from William, you can forget it." She leaned in closely and lowered her voice. "That knife that went flying through the window—" She smiled. "It hit poor

old Willie. Yup, it knocked him right out of the sky."
She smacked her hands together. "Splat! He's probably
bleeding to death on the ground as we speak. Too bad
there's not a healer nearby who will help him." She narrowed her eyes and made a scoffing sound. "Well, not
one who can help him. He's... otherwise occupied."

Dante's eyes flared bright red. He snarled at the
mention of Steven. He scanned the room and quickly
focused on the cage that remained covered. Steven must
be in there, trapped like the rest.

She sauntered slowly over to Malcolm's perch.
"Polly wanna cracker?"

Malcolm, still blinded by the hood, shrieked and
flapped his wings desperately, attempting to claw at
Pasha with his razor-sharp talons. However, the short
chain kept him tethered to the post and garnered a cruel
laugh from her. Still laughing, she walked to the one
cage that remained covered. Dante couldn't believe that
this coldhearted, evil bitch had accomplished all of this
on her own.

Someone else had to be involved besides the snivel-
ing kid. It had to be her brother, Boris. He scolded himself. How could he have been so blind? His gut instinct
had told him not to trust Boris and Pasha. He looked
around the room at his mate and his friends, trapped and
helpless. Guilt flooded his heart. They were all here—in
this situation—because of him, and at the moment, it
looked as though they had no way out.

Pasha casually placed one of the guns on a wing chair
by the bed and slithered next to Brent, who flinched and
attempted to slip out of her embrace. He looked as though
he wanted to run right out the door. She wrapped one arm

around his waist and held the other gun against her belly. She glanced down at the covered cage and smiled.

"Shall we show them who else we brought to our party?" she said, placing a kiss on his trembling jaw.

Brent licked his lips nervously. "I guess."

"You guess?" she sang. "Come on. They'll love this." Smiling, she grabbed the cover with both hands and made a drumroll sound. With a great flourish she tore the drape from the cage and shouted, "Ta daaa!"

A massive striped tiger stood rocking back and forth, trapped within the cold steel bars. Thick muscles rippled under an orange and black streaked hide. A long tail flicked angrily, and large clawed paws swatted viciously through the bars. His burning golden eyes honed in immediately on Pasha, and he let loose a bone-shattering roar. It was Boris. Pasha was going to kill her own brother.

Chapter 18

THE SHATTERING SOUND OF BREAKING GLASS RUPTURED the wild quiet of the bayou.

"Son of a bitch," Peter hissed from his position by the fountain. Crouching low, he ran at full speed toward the house. Out of nowhere, Joseph Vasullus appeared in the open doorway. Peter skidded to a halt at the bottom of the porch steps as gravel spit out from under his feet. He aimed his gun directly at Joseph's tie-dyed-clad chest. He may have been well into his sixties, but he still looked damn strong. Pete had to admit he cut a pretty imposing figure, old or not.

"Don't move, you squirrelly bastard, or I'll shoot you where you stand," he said in a deadly voice. Sweat beaded on his forehead and trickled down his back. Peter eyed the wooden-handled shotgun, which dangled in the old guy's hand unthreateningly. If Joseph had wanted to shoot him, he could've done it before Pete had even seen him.

Joseph slowly placed one finger to his lips. "Shhh." He made a nodding motion toward the upstairs. Pete's brow furrowed with confusion. He opened his mouth, but the earth-shattering roar of a big cat interrupted the standoff. Pete took the steps in one leap, but Joseph refused to move.

"Get out of my way, old man. You have no idea who or what is up there," he said, trying to push past him.

With surprising strength and speed, Joseph shoved him against the wall next to the door. He held him there with one strong arm, preventing Pete from moving. Pete looked up and found himself staring into the bright yellow eyes of a cat. For a second, his thoughts went to that stupid black cat that Jacqueline always carried around, but it was pretty clear that Joseph was no house pet.

"Unfortunately, boy, I know exactly what is up there," he said quietly.

Pete nodded his head in slow disbelief. "Crap. Are you going to turn into a bird or something too?"

"No," Joseph whispered and cast a quick glance toward the inside of the house. He stepped back and released Peter. "I don't have time to explain. Go around the back of the house. There's a balcony outside the room they're in. I need you to climb up there. I'm too damn old and tired to go scaling walls. We'll have a better chance of getting them out of there if we cover the front and the back."

Joseph pulled a worn envelope from the back pocket of his jeans and handed it to Peter. "Here, take this. You give that to Kerry when this is all over."

Peter took the mysterious missive and slipped it into his pants pocket. He looked into Joseph's now human eyes and found them tinged with sadness. Pete had no idea what the hell was going on or what exactly these people were, but it became quite clear that Joseph was an ally.

"Normally, I'd argue with you, but the freaky-ass thing you just did with your eyes was all the convincing I needed."

The lines in Joseph's forehead deepened, and confusion flickered briefly over his face. "Whatever. Get going," he rasped.

Pete gave a quick nod, and as quietly as possible, headed around the right of the house. He crept slowly along the paint-chipped side and peered carefully around the corner. He looked up and saw the balcony Joseph was talking about. Soft light flickered in the window, confirming he was in the right place. He scanned the sky and didn't see any sign of that bird guy, William. Maybe he was waiting for him on the balcony? His jaw clenched, and he threw a quick glance to the sky. No time to wait around and find out.

A snarl of vines and ivy crawled all the way up the weatherworn clapboard of the mansion. The mass of greens had grown unchecked for years, and it seemed they had become a permanent part of the structure. It also created a natural ladder. Pete tugged on the thick blanket nature had provided and tested its strength. Satisfied, or at least hoping that it would hold his weight, he holstered his gun and grabbed a fistful of the bulky vines.

"Like rock climbing at the gym," he mumbled under his breath.

Just as he was about to begin his climb, a faint rustling to his left caught his attention. He pulled his gun back out, stilled and waited. The rustling emanated again from the back of the house, but this time was accompanied by the faint screech of a bird. Shit. Birdbrain? He glanced back to the light above him. He had to get up there, but if this bird guy was hurt, then they'd be down a man and quickly becoming outnumbered.

Peter inched his way to the corner and held the cool

steel gun tightly against his chest. He peered slowly around the back and swore softly at the sight before him. William, still in his gyrfalcon form, lay on the ground with a massive knife sticking out of his chest.

Peter, crouching low, ran silently to the wounded, feathered beast. As soon as William saw Peter, he tried to stand and steady himself, furiously flapping his uninjured wing. He stumbled, lost his footing, and squawked weakly as he landed again on his side. Blood stained the white feathers and seeped from the wound where the knife remained.

Peter shoved his gun back in the holster and ran a hand over his face. "Great. I get to be a fucking vet."

William's curt voice sliced into Peter's mind with the same cold precision as the knife in his chest. *If you would be so kind as to remove the knife, I believe I have enough strength to shift.* His voice wavered, revealing the severity of his wounds. *It will be easier to heal and slow the bleeding in my human form.*

Peter shook his head, and his mouth fell open. "Holy shit," he said in almost reverent tones. "I'll do anything you want, if you just promise me you'll get out of my head."

He stared down at the wounded animal with something that resembled awe and even respect. This arrogant shapeshifter needed his help, and Pete knew that he'd swallowed a big serving of pride to ask for it. Giving a quick nod of agreement, Peter placed one hand on William's chest and marveled at how unbelievably silky the feathers were. Warm and soft were not words anyone would use to describe this guy, he thought wryly.

Pete took hold of the leather-handled dagger and looked into William's glowing black eyes. "Ready?"

Do it, William shot back.

Peter, his mouth set in a grim line, took a deep breath and pulled the steel blade from his feathered chest. Blood immediately poured from the wound, and for a moment, he thought that he'd made a mistake. A split second later the bird shimmered, and static electricity surrounded them. Peter scrambled to his feet and stepped backward, needing to put some space between himself and the situation. By the time he was on his feet, the bird had become a man. Pete secured the knife in his belt and shook his head in disbelief.

"Dante has got a lot of damn explaining to do," he mumbled.

William, his suit dirty, bloodied, and torn, immediately placed his right hand over the bleeding wound in his chest. His long hair had come loose and fallen over his face. He looked up at Peter through his dark brown human eyes and gave him something that resembled a smile. "Thank you," he grunted.

"I bet saying *that* hurt more than getting stabbed," Pete said as he squatted to look at the wound.

"You have no idea," William murmured. He grabbed Peter's wrist and pushed him away. "I'll be fine, but unfortunately, I'm not going to be much use to you for the moment. I've lost quite a lot of blood, and I am uncharacteristically weak." His face twisted in pain, and he gave a fleeting look to the balcony. "You have to get up there. They need your help more than I do. The woman, Pasha, has at least two guns. She is Amoveo of the Tiger Clan—they are vicious and fierce fighters."

"Tiger? Shit, it's like a fuckin' circus up there." He sighed. "What else?"

"There's a human with her. A young male." He grunted, and pain flickered over his pale face. "I don't think he'll cause you much trouble."

"You're the boss." He gave William a pat on his good side and turned quickly to the house. Pete grabbed fistfuls of the vines and made his way silently and swiftly up to the balcony.

Joseph broke into a cold sweat the moment he set foot in the house. He hadn't been inside it for almost thirty years. When Jacqueline showed up at the square completely hysterical, he knew something was wrong. She came to him babbling that they hadn't shown up at her house, and they weren't at the hotel. He shook his head. There was always some kind of drama with that girl. At her behest, he went to the hotel in search of Kerry and Dante. The girl at the desk had been easily intimidated into telling him he saw Dante leaving with another man. She hadn't seen Ms. Smithson all evening. He knew they'd been lured here. It made sense.

This was where it all began.

Joseph crossed the large foyer and looked at himself in the antique mirror. A wry smile formed on his lips, and he shook his head at the wrinkled man looking at him. The eyes that stared back were surrounded by crow's feet and quite human. He'd been almost as startled as Peter when they'd shifted. He hadn't been able to do that or use any of his other Amoveo abilities for over twenty-five years. After he'd lost his mate, he became Vasullus.

For all intents and purposes, he'd become human.

Joseph placed the shotgun on the table in front of the mirror. The last thing he wanted to do was go in with guns blazing. He knew he had to keep the situation as calm as possible, and he figured that by going in as a harmless old man, it would buy him more time than someone wielding a gun. He climbed the steps quickly and noiselessly. Joseph moved silently down the hallway and paused just outside the door of what used to be his master bedroom— their bedroom. A sad smile formed at his lips as he allowed memories to flood his mind. Her long dark hair and smiling brown eyes were the most vivid. Even after so many years, he could still picture her vibrant beauty.

A sick, twisted laugh interrupted his walk through time. Joseph's face went dark at the sound of her voice— Pasha Zankoff. He should've known that bitch was one of the Purists. She had always hated him and made no secret about it. He'd never been certain if she'd gotten wind of who he really was—or who he had been—but he'd always had his suspicions. She always looked at him with contempt.

"Come on in, kitten" she called. "I knew you'd show up."

Joseph stepped tentatively into the doorway with his arms raised in a sign of surrender. Pasha stood in the midst of the bedroom surrounded by several caged Amoveo. She was clad in skintight black from head to toe. No one would deny she was smoking hot, but she was also one crazy-ass bitch. A young human boy he didn't know stood nervously next to her. Caedo maybe? Pasha had a gun pointed at Joseph and a satisfied smile on her face.

"Hello Pasha," he seethed. "Who's your friend?" He flicked a glance at the frightened kid.

"This is Brent. He's become something of a pet of mine." She ran one red fingernail down the side of his pale face. "I needed someone to help me, you see. He worked at the hotel the freak was staying in." Her voice was thick with disgust. "He's weak, which is so typical of humans, and easily intimidated." She shrugged.

Brent cowered, and his lips quivered. "Please. You said that once I helped you, you'd tell me where my girl-friend is. You didn't say anything about killing anyone or turning people into animals." Tears filled his eyes, and he crossed his own tightly over his pudgy chest. "This is crazy," he whispered with wild eyes. "I just want to get Penelope and go home." His voice shook and bordered on hysteria.

Pasha grabbed him by the back of the neck without taking her eyes or the gun off of Joseph. The boy whim-pered pathetically and squeezed his eyes shut. "Poor baby," she taunted cruelly. "I just want Penelope." Pasha made a sound of disgust and shoved him away from her. The boy stumbled and fell into a sobbing heap on the floor. "You'll get her back when I finish what I need to do here." Pasha's green eyes narrowed. "Stay." She pointed at him as if he were a dog. The boy obeyed.

Joseph, hands still in the air, kept his dark gray eyes on Pasha. "So, what's the deal exactly? To be more specific, Pasha, what's *your* deal?" His gaze flicked around the room at the various cages and stopped at Boris. "You even caged your brother." He scoffed loudly. "What. A. Bitch."

Pasha kept her gun on Joseph and wandered over to

Boris's cage. As she got closer, one large clawed paw swiped through the bars in a futile attempt to grab her. She merely hopped out of reach and laughed. Boris snarled, and a baritone growl rumbled through the room.

"I gave him the opportunity to help me. I thought he would be loyal to our people and want to keep our race pure. To keep more abominations like these two from being born," she said with a nod toward Kerry and Samantha. Their hackles raised, the two growled and snarled in response.

"When my brother confirmed he was indeed... pathetic," she spat toward Boris, "I had to find another helper. I tried to get Steven's help, but all he wanted to do was get in my pants. Sorry. Not my mate and not interested," she seethed. "Since he wasn't going to be any help at all, I decided to try the binding powder on him first." She giggled and leaned toward Malcolm, who still sat blinded on his perch, and lowered her voice to a whisper as though she was telling him a delightful secret. "And you know what? It worked."

Malcolm made a loud squawking sound and flapped his wings furiously, but to no avail. Joseph knew that he was never going to get out of those restraints on his own. None of them would. He glanced at the broken window on doors to the terrace. No sign of that Peter guy. Shit. Joseph looked at Brent, and his shoulders sagged with some defeat. If this kid was their only hope for help, then they were all in big trouble.

Pasha's voice snapped his attention back to her. "Bet you're wondering where horny Steven is?"

"Not really." Joseph shrugged. The less emotion he showed her, the better. "He doesn't mean a thing to me."

She stuck out her bottom lip in an exaggerated pout. "Oh, come on. You're no fun at all." She waved the gun at him and placed the other hand on her hip. "Well, I decided that he was such a dirty dog, he deserved to be with other dirty dogs." A slow smile cracked her harsh features. "Coyotes can be such nasty creatures. I sent him to a wild animal preserve." She giggled, but the smile faded quickly. "He'll get to see how it feels to be treated like a piece of meat."

"That's just mean." Joseph laughed. "I guess the preserve keepers will have quite a surprise in a few weeks when some strange guy wakes up in their habitat."

Pasha smirked and puffed her chest with pride. "Yes." She sighed, and a frown formed on her full red lips. "I should've put it in his drink. Then he would've been bound forever." She shrugged one slim shoulder. "Oh well. Live and learn." Her face relaxed when she looked over at Brent, who still sat shaking pathetically on the ground. "This human ended up being very helpful in getting all of the players in place for our little get together. He did need some convincing though. Hence, the whole 'give me my girlfriend back' thing," she said with a roll of her eyes.

"Please," Brent sputtered pathetically through a strained voice. "Please let me go, and tell me where she is."

"All in good time, my boy."

Joseph tracked Pasha as she sashayed nonchalantly over and stood between Kerry and Dante's prisons.

"As you can see, we've got several of the traitors, or would-be traitors, in my brother's case, and now I'm going to dispose of them." She turned her emerald green eyes on Joseph. "You are one of the original traitors. *You* are responsible for *this*," she said. Every word dripped with disgust as she looked down at Kerry. "You were a top-ranking member of the Panther Clan, and you threw it all away to be with a *human*." Pasha sneered.

She said "human" as if it were the lowest form of life.

"You, Lucas, and the others all disregarded our laws for your own pleasure," she shouted. Her anger filled the room, and the candles flickered in response. "Because of you, your friends, and all of your disgusting offspring, he didn't see me in the dream realm." She gestured toward Dante. Her eyes grew wild, shifted, and glowed bright orange.

Joseph's salt-and-pepper eyebrows flew up, and he flicked his gaze to Dante. The large red fox sat there with a look of shock and confusion on his white-masked face. If they weren't in such a dangerous situation, Joseph probably would've laughed out loud at the look on Dante's face.

"I called to him time and again, but he ignored me. Year, after year, after year! He never acknowledged me in the dream realm. Me? A pure-blooded Amoveo female," she pontificated. Disgust and rage dripped from every word and punctuated each syllable. "Do you have any idea what it's like to know that your mate has chosen a birth defect over you?"

Joseph looked at Kerry, who stirred restlessly in her cage as she listened. Her long black tail twitched impatiently behind her, and her bright yellow eyes were locked intently on Joseph. He had to do something. He had to get his daughter out of there.

It was time to shake things up.

He glared at Pasha. "I bet you think you're pretty clever, don't you? Typical Amoveo arrogance." He flicked a quick glance toward the Wolf and Eagle. "Let me guess," he said in the most condescending tone he could muster. "You've been to see old Beaumont down in the Quarter. Buy the binding spell from him by any chance?" A look of shock flickered across Pasha's face, and he laughed. "Don't you think that I, of all people, would want to know how to bind a shifter?"

Brent held the glass bottle out in a shaking hand. "Please take this. I don't want anything else to do with this stuff. I just want—"

"Penelope back," Pasha finished for him.

Brent shrank from her and almost dropped the expensive powder.

"Be careful with that, you idiot," she spat.

"You gonna let her talk to you like that, kid?" Joseph taunted. He hoped that maybe he could get the boy to muster up some courage out of peer pressure. He glanced at the gun Pasha had left on the chair, hoping that the boy would get the point and use it on Pasha. "Jeez, grow a set. Would ya? Some boyfriend you are." He shook his head and grunted his disapproval. "Penelope better not count on you for any damn help."

"Shut up," she barked. "I'll talk to him any way I please." Her glowing orange eyes landed on Brent, and a dangerously calm look came over her features.

Brent's mouth set in a determined line. "Without me, you wouldn't have been able to pull any of this off." He stood on shaky legs and shoved the glass bottle in his pocket. "I'm leaving now. Where's Penelope?" he said, sticking his chin out defiantly. "Tell me, and let me go. You don't need me anymore."

Uh-oh, thought Joseph… that was the wrong thing to say. He looked at Pasha, and his heart sank. The kid should've stayed on the ground crying. He glanced to the terrace. What the hell was Peter waiting for?

Her expression went blank, and her eyes grew cold. A slow smile cracked her devilishly beautiful face. Quicker than a snake, Pasha swooped in front of Brent, grabbed him by the back of the head, and placed a firm kiss on his mouth. The boy struggled in vain against the much stronger woman.

"You're right, lover. I don't need you anymore," she murmured the testament against his quivering lips and shot him in the stomach.

The blast echoed through the room, and she smiled as the bullet tore through the boy's soft form. His face registered shock, pain, and confusion as his body crumpled to the floor with a sickening thump and landed at her feet in a heap.

"You sick bitch," Joseph screamed, and the rest of them snarled and roared in protest.

Without missing a beat, Pasha pointed the gun back at Joseph. Smiling, she shoved Brent's limp body with a stiletto-clad foot and stepped over him, careful to avoid the quickly spreading pool of blood. Joseph made a move toward her, but stopped when she cocked the gun.

"Ah-ah-ah," she scolded. "He served his purpose." She sighed. "After all, I have your daughter, don't I?" She laughed softly, and without taking her eyes off of Joseph, turned the gun onto Kerry. "Say bye-bye to your baby," she whispered.

Rage bubbled up, scorched Joseph's blood, and triggered the most unexpected reaction. His gray eyes tingled and shifted harshly into the bright yellow orbs of his clan. Screaming with fury, his skin prickled, and the familiar, almost forgotten, electricity sizzled through every cell of his being as his timeworn body cracked, contorted, and shifted.

He wanted to scream in protest and tear this woman to pieces with his bare hands, but instead of a word, an earth-shattering roar ripped from his weary lungs. For the first time in almost thirty years, and without the ancient language, he shifted into his panther form. He didn't know how he was able to do it, but he'd never been more grateful for anything in his life.

Energized by the ancient, long-lost gift, and fueled by fear for his daughter's life, Joseph leapt onto a shocked Pasha with surprising speed. The gun fell from her hand and fired. The bullet ricocheted off Kerry's cage. She snarled, and her sleek body flinched, shrinking into the corner. The bullet bounced around the room, finally smashing into two pillar candles on the mantel. Within seconds, flames licked up the wall with frightening speed and began to engulf the room.

Joseph knocked Pasha to the ground. He pinned her there with his massive black paws and promptly sank his sharp teeth into the tender flesh of her throat. Stunned by his unexpected attack and with no time to shift, Pasha struggled helplessly, and her glowing eyes grew wide with shock. Driven by rage for all that had been stolen from him, Joseph tightened his grip and crushed her delicate neck with his vice-like jaws.

Her mouth moved as if to scream for help, but only

a gurgling sound came out, and a thick rivulet of blood dripped from her nose. Her eyes dimmed as the life was strangled from her body, and blood spurted from the wound in her neck as it snapped with a satisfying crunch.

Joseph growled, shook her violently, and tossed her lifeless body away from his precious daughter. He let out a bone-shattering roar through a blood-stained muzzle and stood triumphantly above her crumpled form.

Shaking with exhaustion and relief, Joseph padded over to Kerry's cage and stood with her for a moment, eye to eye. His glowing yellow eyes searched hers, and his breath came in heavy labored gasps. Joseph's heart squeezed excrutiatingly in his chest, and agony radiated down all four legs. In a flash of blinding pain, his body contorted, and he shifted back into his human form. Gasping, he clutched his chest and collapsed onto the floor in front of Kerry. She reached one paw through the bars and placed it tenderly on top of his limp, weathered hand.

Flames raced up the walls at incredible speed and quickly spread to the tattered drapes along the windows. Peter burst in through the fire-framed doorway with wild eyes and his gun drawn. Malcolm screeched and flapped his massive wings in an effort to free himself; next to him Samantha continued to whine and paced nervously. Pete ducked away from the heat and flames and ran over to Joseph, who lay on the floor in obvious discomfort.

"Don't waste time with me, you idiot," he wheezed as sweat poured down his face. "We have to get them out of these cages before this place falls down on top of us." He nodded toward Pasha's and Brent's bodies. "Check her pockets, and see if there are any keys." Each word came out more labored than the last.

With enormous effort he propped himself on one elbow and looked into the beautiful, glowing eyes of his daughter. "I'm so sorry, Kerry," he said as he searched her eyes for forgiveness. "I was a fool and a coward."

Pete frantically dug through Pasha's pockets. "Got 'em," he shouted.

"Well, what are you waiting for?" Joseph coughed as smoke filled his lungs.

Pete, eyes tearing from the thickening smoke, quickly undid the locks on the cages, beginning with Dante and Kerry. He made quick work of the wolf's cage and released the massive eagle from his confines.

The tiger roared loudly with impatience, but Peter hesitated at its cage. "If I let you out of here, you better not fucking eat me," he wheezed. He undid the lock, swung open the door, and stepped aside, releasing the beast from its prison.

"Get over here," Joseph gasped.

Pete stumbled blindly through the smoke. He took off his shirt and held it to his mouth, trying to keep out the toxic fumes of the burning house. Peter thought Dante and Kerry would run out as quickly as the others, but both had gone directly to Joseph. Kerry bent her large black head to Joseph and nuzzled him with her nose. She licked away the stream of tears that flowed freely down his face.

"Come on, old man, we have to get out of here. This whole place is going to come down around us," Pete shouted above the roar of the fire. Joseph lifted his hand from his side, and Pete saw it was covered with blood. "Shit. You got hit in the ricochet."

"Get my daughter out of here," he bit out. His face was twisted in a mask of pain.

"She and Dante can get themselves out. Come on. I've got you."

Peter picked Joseph up and followed Kerry and Dante out of the room. The fire licked at them relentlessly, and the smoke threatened to overcome them as they ran down the stairwell. They raced through the smoke-filled foyer and burst out into the Louisiana night. Their lungs burning with smoke and effort, they ran to the decaying fountain a safe distance from the raging inferno.

William, still wounded and bleeding, sat on the ground, leaning against the fountain. The golden eagle sat on the stone edge just behind his shoulder in a protective stance. The massive tiger and the gray wolf stood there as well, waiting for them.

Peter laid Joseph on the ground and breathlessly sat down next to him. He coughed and wiped at the tears streaming down his face as he leaned in to get a better look at the wound on Joseph's side. He cursed at the sight of it and exchanged a deeply concerned look with Dante.

"Don't do that, boy. I know I'm a dead man," he wheezed. Peter opened his mouth to protest, but Joseph grabbed his hand tightly. "Go to The Voodoo Room in the Quarter and ask to see Beaumont," he closed his eyes and grunted. "Use my name. Go get Jacqueline, and take her with you—she knows. You have to get the antidote for the binding spell." He coughed up blood, and his wrinkled face twisted in a mask of pain.

Peter licked his lips nervously and looked at the unusual menagerie. Even the imposing and ferocious tiger sat next to them quietly and waited. Peter shook his head and shrugged. "Absolutely," he said with a wry smile. "I don't think Dante can write my paychecks with those furry mitts."

Peter eyed the enormous black panther as she lay down next to Joseph and tenderly placed her head on his chest. Dante moved in and nuzzled her neck in a gesture of love and support as Joseph placed a blood-stained hand on her head and stroked her smooth black fur gently. Ears flattened back, tears shimmered in her glowing yellow eyes as she gazed lovingly at her father.

"I have loved you every day of my life," Joseph whispered haltingly. "I hope you'll remember that every day of yours."

The bright orange glow of the burning inferno flickered brightly in the bayou as Joseph took his last shuddering breath. Kerry lifted her head and let out a grief-filled roar. William and Peter looked on as the rest of them, feeling her loss, lifted their heads toward the night sky and howled, roared, and shrieked to the heavens. The energy in the bayou swelled with their sorrowful cries as the old house came crashing down in a fiery heap.

Chapter 19

DANTE PULLED KERRY CLOSER INTO THE CROOK OF HIS arm and took a sip of his beer. After the events over the past few days, he never wanted to let go of her or let her out of his sight ever again. He stroked her upper arm with the tips of his fingers and smiled as she leaned into him, resting her head on his shoulder. She was safe. They were safe—for now.

Joseph's funeral at the old cemetery, although just attended by their intimate circle, had been poignant. He was buried in the crypt with Victoria, Kerry's mother. Richard had even left his pregnant wife Salinda in order to perform the ceremony and give him the burial of an Amoveo warrior. The Purist Network was no longer a secret. Richard called a gathering of the Council and made it clear that anyone involved with the Purists would be dealt with quickly and harshly.

It looked as though Pasha had been involved with other Purists. However, the cold, hard truth was that they just didn't know who they were. Was this what their lives would be? Looking around every corner and only trusting the select few who knew about this conspiracy from the beginning? Looking at Kerry's lovely fair skin, and stroking her long soft arm, he realized it didn't matter. As long as they were together, it would be alright.

"Dante," William barked from the wingback chair across the room. "Are you listening?"

"Of course I am, William," he said without taking his eyes off of Kerry. She arched her neck and looked up at him with a smile tinged with sadness.

Jacqueline and Peter came back in the room with a tray of cheese and crackers and two bottles of wine. Jacqueline placed the tray on the coffee table and instantly scooped up Jester, who'd been standing patiently at her feet waiting to be put in the familiar cradle of her arms. Peter poured more wine for Kerry and then for Samantha and Malcolm who sat on the other sofa.

"He's not listening to you, bud. I think he's permanently punch drunk on love," he said with a wink to them both.

William let out a loud sigh. "Then would you mind answering the question," he said with his typical impatience.

Dante's gaze flicked to William, and an amused smile curved his lips. "You're still pissed about the whole knife thing, huh?"

William straightened his back, and pain briefly flashed over his features as he smoothed one lapel. "No." He sniffed. "I know it was an accident. Besides, I'm practically healed. Now, please answer the question. Has Boris connected with you yet? I was very surprised that he wasn't at Joseph's funeral today."

Dante nodded his head. "Yes. He's been busy with the police. Pasha had stashed that Penelope girl in the basement of their bar. He's had to give his statements and so on. Pasha is getting the blame for all of this with the humans. The fire, murders, kidnapping… the whole ball of wax." He looked lovingly at Kerry and played with a silky strand of her long hair. "They think that she was an obsessed fan of Kerry's. She coerced Brent by kidnapping his girlfriend and then made the poor kid help her lure Kerry out to the house. Joseph came home early, surprised them... and well, we all know how it turned out."

Everyone nodded somberly in agreement.

"At least the girl is okay," Kerry murmured. "I saw her at the police station that night and had a chance to touch her. She doesn't remember much, and the grief of losing Brent overwhelmed her," she said with tears shimmering in her eyes.

"I can't imagine how she feels." Dante squeezed her tighter and kissed the top of her head. "I don't know what I'd do if Pasha had achieved her goal and taken you away from me," he whispered.

"I have to be honest," Kerry said quietly. "There's a part of me that actually feels sympathy for Pasha."

Everyone in the room looked at her as though she'd lost her mind.

"Why on earth would you feel sorry for her?" The lines in Dante's forehead deepened.

Kerry shrugged one shoulder and wiped at the condensation on her wineglass with her thumb. "I think I can understand how frustrated and sad she must've been." She looked around the room at each of her friends. "Can you imagine? She thought she'd found her mate, but he ignored her and had chosen someone else?" Kerry sighed softly. "I know what true loneliness feels like, and I wouldn't wish it on anyone."

Jester mewed loudly, breaking the melancholy mood of the room.

"Apparently, Jester feels the same way." Jacqueline smiled at them. "I, for one, am very glad to have found you, Cousin," she said to Kerry through a shaky voice.

William's stern expression cracked with confusion. "What on earth are you talking about, woman?"

"Uh-oh," Pete sang. "Looks like somebody isn't the smartest kid in class today."

William shot him a look that was a mixture of boredom and doubt. "I had some things I needed to follow up on." He looked at his watch. "In fact, I'll be leaving shortly to attend to my... business."

Kerry laughed softly at William's obvious confusion and annoyance at being behind the curve. "Jacqueline is the daughter of my mother's late sister. Her only child— and my only real family."

"Hey," Dante said, feigning injury.

"Oh, you know what I mean, Tarzan." Kerry elbowed him playfully in the gut. He grunted softly, and laughing, pulled her tighter to him.

"We still have to find out where on earth Pasha dumped Steven," William said calmly. "Although, I do find him to behave inappropriately on most occasions, I certainly do not relish the idea of him living amid wild animals."

They all nodded in agreement. "Good to know that you're on our side," Pete said, popping a cube of cheese into his mouth.

William looked at him through narrowed eyes. "*Our* side?"

"I did save your life," Pete pointed out. "In case you already forgot."

"Peasant," William mumbled.

"Birdbrain," Pete shot back.

The two men glared at each other briefly, before Peter burst out laughing, and William actually cracked something akin to a smile. Dante breathed a sigh of relief at their playful rivalry. Thank God these two were getting along, because now that Peter knew about the Amoveo, there was no going back. Although he would remain in Dante's employ, he would also be made an honorary member of the Vasullus family. The truth was that they there were going to need all the help that they could get.

Kerry stood outside in the rooftop garden of her Manhattan apartment building and looked out over the bustling city lights glinting brightly in the dark. She rubbed the worn envelope between her fingers and held the letter to her heart. Peter had given it to her the night of the fire. The cool, early November wind blew her hair off her face. She closed her eyes, reveling in the brisk sensation. Tears threatened to spill over as she thought of Joseph—her father. It had only been a little over a month since she'd found out who she really was, but it felt like an eternity. She sniffled and opened the letter to read it for the thousandth time.

> *My Dearest Kerry,*
>
> *Today I sent you to live with your new parents—your new family—a human family. This was the hardest decision of my entire life, but one I had no choice but to make. Your mother, Victoria, and I naively thought that our love, our destiny to be together, would overcome the prejudice of my people. We were*

gravely mistaken. We lived in fear after the deaths of Jane and Lucas Logan, rarely leaving the house here in the bayou. We knew that their deaths were no accident. Like us, they were a mixed couple, and as a result—outcasts.

After Victoria was murdered, I knew that you would never be safe with me. I knew they wouldn't stop until you were dead.

I have entrusted my old friend Davis to help place you with a loving family. He too lost the woman he loved to the Purists and would do anything to help protect you. I do not want to know where you are. It is safer for you if I don't. Everyone in the Purist Network thinks you were killed in the same incident that killed your beloved mother. It is best if they continue to believe that.

I am now considered to be a member of the Vasullus Family. This is the great secret that is revealed eventually to each generation. I have lost my mate, and as a result, will slowly lose all of my Amoveo abilities. I can feel my body aging as we speak. I, for all intents and purposes, will become human. Most Amoveo look at this as the ultimate death sentence. However, I count it as a blessing, because to have to live without you and your mother for eternity would be unbearable.

I worry for you and your future. I do not know what your unique heritage will bring. You are Amoveo and human—but your mother was not your average human. She had the gift

*of sight and could read people with one touch.
It frightened her, but empowered her as well.*

*I think of you as I try to sleep each night and
wonder if you will have her gift. I try to find you
in the dream realm, but I seem to be walking
there less and less with each passing day.*

*If you do someday discover your heritage,
and by some miracle you have an Amoveo mate
who finds you, please be wary. We suspect the
corruption goes all the way to the Council, possibly even to The Prince himself.*

*You should take comfort in knowing that you
are not alone. There are other hybrid children.
There are rumors that some of them even know
who and what they are, but they are being
raised in secret and away from our people. I
continue to hope that you may find the others
like yourself... or that they will find you.*

*I love you my darling daughter, and I will
carry you in my heart, my Amoveo heart, for
the rest of my days.*

Your Father—Joseph

Tears dripped heavily on the timeworn paper in her
shaking hands. Kerry wiped at her wet face as Dante's
strong arms wrapped tightly around her waist, and the
fox image burst into her mind. He murmured soft musings in her ear and placed a warm kiss on her neck. She
clutched his arms against her and held him close, allowing herself to be swallowed by the honeyed warmth of
his touch. He rocked her slowly, but said nothing.

"I wish I could've known them." Her voice shook, and she let out a shaky breath. "He died to save us, Dante."

"I know." He sighed.

"There are others like Samantha and I, Dante. That night, Pasha mentioned that there were others who had mated with humans, and my father confirmed it in his letter." She shuddered and leaned even further into his embrace. "We have to find them before the Purists do," she pleaded. "Promise me we'll find them. I know how lonely I was, how out of place. I hate the idea of others out there suffering like that. I was so lonely and in so much pain." She sighed softly and smiled. "At least until you found me."

Gently, he turned her around to face him and tilted her chin up, forcing her to look into his glowing amber eyes. She studied his handsome face and wanted to commit every line, every curve, to memory. His warm eyes, the ones that filled with passion almost every time he looked at her, flared brightly in the dark night. His strong forehead and high cheekbones came together to create an incredibly beautiful man. Her man. Her mate. Her heart fluttered in her chest and literally took her breath away. She'd almost lost him, and she still hadn't told him that she loved him. She still hadn't said those three little words out loud.

"We'll find them," he whispered and placed a feather-light kiss on the tip of her nose. "I promise. Who knows? Maybe they'll find us."

Kerry stilled. "Do you think what he said was true? That there are hybrids out there who know what they are?"

"Maybe," Dante said softly. "At this point, nothing would surprise me. All I know is that I'm grateful we found each other."

Dante ran his strong hands along her arms and down the curve of her hips. She shivered from the exquisite effect of his touch. Her glowing yellow eyes looked up at him from under thick black lashes as her tongue darted out and moistened her lips. She knew her energy levels had quickened and felt him adjust his body in response. He pulled her even tighter into the shelter of his arms.

Kerry rested her cheek on his shoulder and curled her arms around the broad expanse of his back. She adored the feel of his muscles as they rippled beneath her fingers. His heart beat strongly in time with hers, and their energies mingled deliciously through the air.

Dante stroked her hair down the length of her back and held her close. "Your father sacrificed everything for you from the day you were born because he loved you, Kerry. I know how he feels, princess."

Her heart skipped a beat, and she pulled back to look him in the eyes. "Me too," she whispered. Silence stretched between them with several beats of their hearts. "I love you, Dante."

That lopsided smile she'd grown to adore cracked his handsome face. "I know," he said in the most infuriatingly calm manner.

Kerry slapped his arm and laughed out loud. "You big Neanderthal!"

He laughed with her and took her face delicately in his strong hands. "I love you, Kerry. I've loved you from the moment I laid eyes on you that day at the

beach." He stroked her cheek with his thumb, and it left
little trails of fire in its wake. "I will honor his memory
by spending every day, every minute of my life, making
you happy and keeping you safe. And I promise you,"
he said as his voice dropped to a husky whisper, "we'll
find the others."

Kerry smiled as he placed a soft, warm kiss on her
lips and moaned contentedly. She nuzzled his neck and
pulled him close once again. Now, more than ever, she
needed to be connected with him, with his touch.

Music drifted in the breeze from the speakers strate-
gically placed throughout the garden. Amy Petty's song
"Honey on the Skin" floated in the air around them, and
they rocked slowly to the tantalizing melody. His wickedly seductive voice slid into her mind and around her
heart. *I told you we'd dance.*

READ ON FOR A SNEAK PEEK AT

Untamed

NEXT IN THE AMOVEO LEGEND SERIES
BY SARA HUMPHREYS
COMING NOVEMBER 2012
FROM SOURCEBOOKS CASABLANCA

WHY WOULDN'T HER LEGS GO ANY FASTER? HER LUNGS *burned with effort and sweat dripped down her back as she stumbled blindly through the fog laden woods. He was right behind her. Always. His energy signature rolled around her in the mists. Behind her. Above her. In front of her. He was everywhere.*

Powerful.

Unrelenting.

He seemed to surround her but still—she couldn't see him.

Layla's breath came in heavy labored gasps and a bare branch caught in her long, curly red hair as she tripped over a log. She pulled the tangled strands away, swore softly and ducked behind the large trunk of giant old elm tree. Layla pressed herself up against it, praying he wouldn't see her there. In response to her silent plea, the fog in the dream realm thickened and provided additional shelter from her relentless hunter.

She'd been able to avoid him so far, but tonight it felt as if he was dreadfully close to finding her—and claiming her. His energy swamped her and stole from her lungs what little breath she had left. She squeezed her eyes shut and prayed that the tree and the fog would swallow her up. Could she do that? Could she control the environment of the dream that much? Just as she was about to try, an unfamiliar voice tumbled around her.

Why do you run from me? *The smooth, deep baritone flooded her mind and filled every ounce of her being in a shockingly intimate way. The sharp pang of desire zipped through her and made her breasts tingle. The sudden onslaught caught her off guard and had her head spinning.*

Layla froze.

He'd never spoken to her before. She could barely hear him above the rapid pounding of her heart and wondered for a moment if she'd imagined it.

You did not imagine it. *His voice had become irritatingly calm.* Please answer my question. Why do you run away from me? *That distinctly male voice rumbled around her and through her. It reverberated in her chest just like the deep bass beat of one of her favorite songs.* Why are you afraid of me? *Amusement laced his voice and flickered around her in the fog.*

That did it. Now she was pissed. He was laughing at her? First he haunts her sleep every night for the past two weeks and now he's making fun of her? Oh, hell no! Layla's eyes snapped open and she expected to find him—whoever he was—standing right in front of her. However, she was met only with the thick fog she'd created.

I'm not afraid of you. *She placed her hands on her hips and looked around at the swirling mist. Layla tilted her chin defiantly.* I just don't want anything to do with you. So why don't you piss off!

Rich, deep laughter floated softly around her. You make it sound as if there is a choice in the matter.

You bet your bossy ass there is. *Layla shouted boldly into the gray abyss.* I decide my fate. Me. Layla

Nickelsen. *She pointed at her chest with her thumb.* Me. Not you or anybody else.

She waited. The beautiful sound of silence encircled her. Was he gone? She sharpened her focus and found him quickly. No. His energy still permeated the dream but had lessened somehow. He had backed off? Interesting.

Layla stepped away from the tree and the fog ebbed back in response. She steadied her breathing as her heartbeat slowed to a more normal pace. A victorious look came over her face as she found herself gaining more control. She tucked her thick hair behind her ears and watched the familiar woods where she had grown up come slowly into focus. A satisfied smile curved her lips, she nodded her head and made a hoot of triumph. Fate can kiss my ass.

The words had barely left her mouth when two strong arms slipped around her waist and pulled her against a very tall, hard and most definitely male body. Stunned and uncertain of what else he might do, Layla stayed completely still and glanced down to discover that her hands rested on two much larger ones. She could feel his heartbeat against her back as it thundered in his chest and thumped in perfect time with hers.

He dipped his head and warm firm lips pressed an unexpectedly tender kiss along the edge of her ear. Luminous heat flashed through her with astonishing speed, making her breasts feel heavy, and sending a rush of heat between her legs. It took every ounce of self-control to keep from sinking back into his strong, seductive embrace. Her body's swift reaction was positively mortifying. She shivered, bit her lower lip, and fought the urge to turn around and kiss him. Why and how could she be turned on like this? Layla stiffened with disgust at her lack of self-control and her body's obvious attraction to his.

You cannot outrun your destiny. *His surprisingly seductive voice dipped low and his breath puffed tantalizingly along the exposed skin of her neck. She closed her eyes and tried to fight the erotic sensations but it was like trying to stop the tide as it ebbed and throbbed through her relentlessly.* And for future reference, Firefly, the only one kissing your ass—or anything else on your beautiful body—will be me. *He released her from the confines of his embrace and disappeared with the mist.*

The shrill ring of the motel's wake-up call tore her from her sleep. Without even looking, Layla picked up the receiver and slammed it down harder than necessary. For the first time in a long time, she hadn't wanted her dream to end. That was a switch. She pushed herself up onto her elbows and blew the bed-head hair out of her face. She looked around the cheap motel room and squinted at the sun that streamed so rudely into her room.

"Why can't the damn curtains ever close all the way in these places?" Her sleepy mumble echoed through the empty room. The memory of last night's dream was still fresh and raw, which was painfully evident by the heat that continued to blaze over her skin. Layla flopped back down and threw her arm over her eyes. It looked like her bossy stalker was right. There was no escaping fate.

"Shit."

―∿∿―

Layla swung the old jeep into the driveway of Rosie's farm and instantly felt safer. The tension headache that had been eating at her since she left New Orleans began to ease back, and she let out a long slow breath. The drive from New Orleans to Maryland had been relatively smooth but still seemed to take forever. She desperately wanted—no—needed to be home, now more than ever. The tires crunched along the winding dirt driveway as the old jeep bounced along and rattled her around, but she barely felt it. A huge smile cracked her freckled face the moment that the old farm house came into view. It looked exactly the same as it had all those years ago, when she had first seen it.

Layla slowed the open air jeep to a halt at the bottom of the hill and pulled the hand brake. She grabbed the roll bar, stood up in the seat and closed her eyes. A gust of wind blew the stray strands of long red hair off her face as she took a deep breath and reveled in the crisp, sweet familiar scent of the farm. The cool fall air filled her nostrils and seemed to capsulize each individual smell, allowing her to pinpoint every one. The sweet smell of the hay and the freshly mowed grass mixed with a hint of manure from the stables. The combination of the weather and the smells instantly brought her back to the day she'd first arrived.

The first twelve years of her life had been spent being bounced around between her mentally ill mother and various foster homes. She always tried to fit in, to keep her mouth shut, but sooner or later, she would let a secret slip. After that it was only a matter of time before the foster parents asked that she be relocated. Layla grimaced. The last home she was placed in had been particularly unpleasant.

If it hadn't been for an unexpected visit by a new social worker, she would likely have wound up dead. The horrid memories threatened to creep in and steal her serenity, but the wind brought a reprieve and the familiar scent of Rosie's apple pie. She smiled and opened her big green eyes to gaze upon the only place that had ever really been home.

Layla plopped her butt back into the beat up leather seat, released the brake and threw it into first gear. Woodbine farm was a safe haven for her, just as it had been for her foster brother and sister. No one and nothing could hurt her here. Not her mother, not the crazy people she photographed, and not her dream stalker. Driving up the gravel driveway all she could think was, thank God for Woodbine and thank God for Rosie.

The jeep came to a shuddering stop in front of the house, and within seconds Rosie came lumbering through the screen door to greet her. She was a sight for sore eyes. Her salt and pepper braids hung all the way down to her waist and the plaid shirt and overalls were stained from gardening. With arms wide open and a huge grin on her well-tanned face, Rosie practically flew down the stairs. Layla barely had time to get out of the car before Rosie tackled her in a welcome home bear hug. Her big soft form enveloped Layla's much smaller one with minimal effort.

"Layla Nickelsen," she bellowed into her ear and rocked her back and forth. "You are a sight for these old eyes." She pulled back and eyed her at arm's length. "What the hell have you been doing, girl? You are skin and bones! You're swimmin' in that damn jacket."

Leave it to Rosie to point out the obvious. Suddenly

self-conscious, Layla pulled the big cargo jacket closed. She had always been thin but the sad fact was that lately she was downright skinny. Stress from the last job in New Orleans had really rattled her cage and nightmares haunted her sleep every night since then. The combination of bad dreams and stress had killed her appetite.

She shrugged her slim shoulders, "Hey, I've been working like crazy. What can I tell ya?" Layla looked away quickly, and grabbed her duffle and camera bag out of the back of the jeep. She couldn't look Rosie in the eye and lie to her. Never could. Why would time have changed that? The cold hard truth was that she might be almost thirty years old, but around Rosie she was always that little girl looking for a safe haven.

For the first time, in a very long time—she was scared. Layla gritted her teeth and shut her eyes against the long-forgotten feeling. Years ago, she'd promised herself that she would never allow herself to be afraid again. Ever. Fear was a dangerous, weakening and self-defeating feeling. Monsters could smell fear and that's how they picked their victims. Victims were weak and she would never be a victim—or victimized—ever again. She opened her eyes and let out a slow breath.

She was home and she was safe.

Rosie took Layla's now quivering chin in her hand and forced her to make eye contact. Those familiar warm brown eyes softened and her voice dipped low. "You can't lie to me, girl."

Layla nodded almost imperceptibly as the tender sound of Rosie's voice threatened to push her over the edge. She swallowed hard and fought the pathetic urge to cry. No tears. She hadn't cried once since she'd arrived at Woodbine and she wasn't about to start now. No matter how freaked out she was there would be no more tears.

"Everyone else may buy your tough girl routine, but I know better." Rosie gave her cheek a pat. "Now, why don't you come on inside and get settled in your old room. We'll talk about whatever is botherin' you over some pie and coffee."

She winked and wrapped her arm around Layla's shoulders, which immediately loosened the knots in her stomach.

"Come on. Your brother should be back soon. You know that boy," she sighed loudly and looked over her shoulder, "one whiff of my apple pie and he comes runnin'. Too bad he don't come runnin' like that when it's time to muck out the barn," she chuckled.

Layla walked up the steps wrapped in the safe shelter of Rosie's embrace. Even the familiar creak of the old steps helped to put her at ease. She threw a glance across the rolling fields and her gaze slid to the barn looking for any sign of her brother Raife. The horses grazed lazily and the chickens clucked loudly in the distance, but no sign of Raife. She smirked and shook her head. Raife loved the farm and had stayed on to run it, but what he really loved was to roam in the woods that surrounded it.

She and Raife's twin sister Tatiana used to tease him relentlessly about it. Raife and Tatiana were Rosie's niece and nephew and had been raised on the farm since they were babies. For all intents and purposes they were her siblings—blood or not, they were the only family she ever knew. Once Layla arrived at the farm it didn't take her long to realize that the universe had thrown them together for a reason. It turned out that they had a lot in common. They were all orphans, they were all damaged and they were all hybrids.

That first forkful of cinnamon spiced apples and buttery crust burst in Layla's mouth with explosive sweetness. Eyes closed, she savored the comforting flavors and made a shamelessly loud yummy noise of satisfaction. Rosie's hearty laugh bounced through the country kitchen and she clapped her hands. That rich, familiar sound warmed Layla's spirit as much as the steaming coffee warmed her body.

She shrugged sheepishly and swallowed the mouthful of pie. "You still make the best apple pie on the planet, Rosie." Layla sat back and wiped her mouth with the red checkered napkin from her lap. "Believe me. I've tried apple pie in every single town I've been to, all over the world, and none of them hold a candle to yours," she said with a smile.

Rosie nodded her head and stared at her through narrowed eyes. "That's fine and dandy. But you and I both know that you didn't come all the way home, after all this time... just to have my pie."

She pulled out one of the wooden chairs and the sound of it scraping on the floor brought back memories of various lectures Layla had gotten at this table. Most of them were for getting into fights at school. Tough-Girl-Talks, that's what Rosie called them.

Layla rubbed the smooth ceramic mug with her thumb and straightened her back in an effort to gather her waning courage. "He found me," she whispered. Her breath caught in her throat because it was the first time she'd said it out loud. She'd barely been able to admit it to herself. The only thing that she had truly feared happening—had finally happened. She drew in a shaky breath and forced herself to look Rosie in the eye. "My mate found me."

Acknowledgments

Writing a book is a solitary process, but actually, publishing one is anything but that. I have so many people to thank, namely the collaborative and creative folks over at Sourcebooks. Deb Werksman, my editor, has a sharp eye and an open mind. I value her opinion and advice more than she'll ever know, and I'm immensely thankful for her guidance. The PR that Sourcebooks does for their authors is second to none! Danielle Jackson works tirelessly for all of her authors and busts her butt to get our books in front of the masses. The covers that the SB art department puts out are nothing short of gorgeous.

As always, I must extend thanks to my agent, Jeanne Dube, for taking me on and sticking with me. You are the best!

Thanks as well to the talented Amy Petty and her record label, Red Pill Entertainment, for allowing me to use Amy's music in my book trailers. I mentioned her song "Honey on the Skin" because the moment I heard it, everything about Kerry's story clicked for me. Amy is still my muse, and I strongly suggest you check out her music on her website: www.amypetty.com.

However, I must thank my husband above all others. He is my rock and the voice of reason in my sometimes chaotic creative process, and quite frankly, I don't know what I'd do without him. He inspires me every day with his thoughtfulness and unconditional love, and in the process, sets an excellent example for our sons. He may not understand the whole shapeshifter attraction, and I may not agree with his politics... but that's where unconditional love comes into play. When I get my head in the clouds, he helps me keep my feet on the ground.

Last, but not least, thank you to my readers! I read every single email that I receive and do my best to respond to all. Thank you for coming along on this journey, and I hope you continue to enjoy the Amoveo Legend.

Dream on...

About the Author

Sara Humphreys is a graduate of Marist College, with a BA in English Literature & Theater, and her initial career path after college was as a professional actress. Some of her television credits include *A&E Biography*, *Guiding Light*, *Another World*, *As the World Turns*, and *Rescue Me*. For the past several years Sara has been a professional public speaker and speaker trainer. Her career began with Monster's Making It Count programs, speaking in high schools and colleges around the United States to thousands of students. For the past several years, Sara has worked with the College of Westchester in New York as the director of high school and community relations.

Untouched is the second book in The Amoveo Legend series, following *Unleashed*. Sara has been a lover of both the paranormal and romance novels for years. Her science fiction/fantasy/romance obsession began years ago with the TV series *Star Trek* and an enormous crush on Captain Kirk. That sci-fi fascination soon evolved into the love of vampires, ghosts, werewolves, and of course, shapeshifters. Sara is married to her college sweetheart, Will. They live in Bronxville, New York, with their four boys and two ridiculously dopey dogs. Life is busy, but never dull.

A SEAL in Wolf's Clothing

by Terry Spear

Her instincts tell her he's dangerous...

While her overprotective brother's away, Meara Greymere's planning to play—and it wouldn't hurt to find herself a mate in the process. The last thing she needs is one of his SEAL buddies spoiling her fun, even if the guy is the hottest one she's ever seen...

His powers of persuasion are impossible to resist...

Finn Emerson is a battle-hardened Navy SEAL and alpha wolf. He's a little overqualified for baby-sitting, but feisty Meara is attracting trouble like a magnet...

As the only responsible alpha male in the vicinity, Finn is going to have to protect this intriguing woman from a horde of questionable men, and definitely from himself...

Praise for Terry Spear:

"High-powered romance that satisfies on
every level."—*Long and Short Reviews*

"Hot doesn't even begin to describe
it."—*Love Romance Passion*

For more Terry Spear, visit:

www.sourcebooks.com

Dreaming of the Wolf

by Terry Spear

He'll protect her
or die trying…

Alicia Greiston is a no-nonsense bounty hunter determined to bring a ring of mobsters to justice. Her dogged pursuit of the crime family has forced her to avoid relationships —any man would only become a target for retribution. Luckily, Jake Silver is more than a man, and his instincts are telling him to stop at nothing to protect her.

However, the mob isn't entirely human either, and soon Alicia must flee for her life. When Alicia and Jake's passion begins to spill over into their dreams, Jake learns he will have to do more than defend her—he'll have to show his mate the way of the wolf.

Praise for **Dreaming of the Wolf***:*

"Riveting and entertaining…makes one want to devour all of the rest of Terry Spear's books." —*Fresh Fiction*

"Sensual, passionate, and very well written…another winner of a story." —*The Long and the Short of It*

For more Terry Spear, visit:

www.sourcebooks.com

Heart of the Highland Wolf

by Terry Spear

———

It's a matter of pride...
And a matter of pleasure...

Julia Wildthorn is sneaking into Argent Castle to steal an ancient relic, but reluctant laird Ian MacNeill may be the key to unlocking the one answer she really wants discovered...

From brilliant storyteller Terry Spear, modern day werewolves meet the rugged Highlands of Scotland, where instinct meets tradition and clan loyalties give a whole new meaning to danger...

———

Experience for yourself the sensual, action-packed, critically acclaimed worlds of Terry Spear, author of a **Publishers Weekly** *Best Book of the Year:*

"Crackles with mystery, adventure, violence, and passion." —*Library Journal*

"A thrilling, engaging, wonderful ride." —*Seriously Reviewed*

For more Terry Spear books, visit:

www.sourcebooks.com

Wolf Fever

by Terry Spear

—∿—

Her true nature now is devastating...

Carol Woods would do anything to go back to the time before a wolf bite changed everything. Now her pack won't let her out of its sight, especially not when a sexy stranger starts coming around...

As if he didn't have enough to worry about...

Gray pack leader Ryan McKinley is on a mission to a neighboring pack. With unrest growing, a mysterious illness spreading, and a couple of his guys going rogue, he definitely doesn't need a beautiful unmated female causing him even more problems.

So then why does he decide he's the only one who can teach her to embrace the new wildness within?

—∿—

"A terrific suspense... enough action to keep a reader fascinated and interested."—*Night Owl Romance* Top Pick

"A riveting and entertaining novel, *Wolf Fever* is a lot of fun and makes one want to devour all of the rest of Terry Spear's books."—*Fresh Fiction*

For more Terry Spear, visit:

www.sourcebooks.com

Seduced by the Wolf

by Terry Spear

—⁓—

His first priority is to protect his pack...

Werewolf pack leader Leidolf Wildhaven has just taken over a demoralized pack. With rogue wolves on the loose causing havoc and the authorities from the zoo suddenly zeroing in on the local wolf population, the last thing he needs in his territory is a do-gooder female, no matter how beautiful and enticing she is...

She'll do anything to help wolves...

Biologist Cassie Roux has dedicated her life to protecting wolves in the wild. On a desperate mission to help a she-wolf with newborn pups, the last thing Cassie needs right now is a nosy and entirely too attractive werewolf pack leader trying to track her down...

With rogue wolves and hunters threatening at every turn, Cassie and Leidolf may find their attraction the most dangerous force of all...

—⁓—

"Terry Spear's best wolf book so far... This fast-paced book will suck you in right away." —*Fangtastic Books*

"Spear has once again created an entirely believable and fresh take on her werewolf society." —*Star-Crossed Romance*

For more Terry Spear, visit:

www.sourcebooks.com

Legend of the White Wolf

by Terry Spear

A family mystery leads her into an unimaginable world...

Faith O'Malley travels to the frozen wilderness of Maine determined to discover what her father saw in that same region ten years ago. But her quest attracts the attention of two very different men, one a private detective with his own mystery to solve, and the other a werewolf pack leader who holds secrets for them both...

And a danger they must face together...

Private Detective Cameron MacPherson's search for his lost partners leads him down the same path as Faith's—and soon the two of them are thrust into the wilds of a forbidden, icy world.

When Faith and Cameron encounter a mythical creature, they must decided to face their enemies together, or perish on their own...

"If you like your werewolf stories with a bit of a bite, then pick this series up now."—*Night Owl Romance* Top Pick

"One of the best, as far as I'm concerned, when it comes to shifter stories."—*The Good, The Bad and The Unread*

For more Terry Spear, visit:

www.sourcebooks.com

To Tempt the Wolf

by Terry Spear

—◆◆◆—

She's fascinated by wolves—
but they are obsessed with her

Tessa Anderson doesn't know why wolves are attracted to her,
and she certainly doesn't know that werewolves exist. Now
she's being stalked—but is her stalker wolf or man? And who
is the gorgeous stranger whose life she saved, who now swears
he'll protect her?

He's an Alpha without a pack,
facing a deadly enemy

Hunter Greymere is a lupus garou, a gray werewolf. His
pack has abandoned him after losing their homes in a raging
wildfire. When he encounters Tessa, he's alone and injured,
but he quickly realizes the danger to her is much worse than
anything threatening him...

—◆◆◆—

"Perfect reading for those who love to mix their romances
with paranormal adventure, suspenseful intrigue, and
a couple who knows how to heat the sheets and our
hearts."—*Long and Short Reviews* Best Book of the Week

"Packed with action, mystery, and romance, all woven
together to make it a thrilling read."—*Bitten by Books*

For more Terry Spear, visit:

www.sourcebooks.com

Destiny of the Wolf

by Terry Spear

All she wants is the truth

Lelandi is determined to discover the truth about her beloved sister's mysterious death. But everyone thinks she's making a bid for her sister's widowed mate…

He's a pack leader tormented by memories

Darien finds himself bewitched by Lelandi, and when someone attempts to silence her, he realizes that protecting the beautiful stranger may be the only way to protect his pack… and himself…

"Terry Spear weaves paranormal, suspense, and romance together in one nonstop rollercoaster of passion and adventure."—*Love Romance Passion*

"Readers who enjoy a werewolf tale with a slightly different twist should definitely check out *Destiny of the Wolf*."—*BookLoons*

For more Terry Spear, visit:

www.sourcebooks.com

Heart of the Wolf

by Terry Spear

—w—

Their forbidden love may get them both killed

"Red werewolf Bella flees her adoptive pack of gray werewolves when the alpha male Volan tries forcibly to claim her as his mate. Her real love, beta male Devlyn, is willing to fight Volan to the death to claim her. That problem pales, however, as a pack of red werewolves takes to killing human females in a crazed quest to claim Bella for their own. Bella and Devlyn must defeat the rogue wolves before Devlyn's final confrontation with Volan. The vulpine couple's chemistry crackles off the page, but the real strength of the book lies in Spear's depiction of pack power dynamics…her wolf world feels at once palpable and even plausible."—*Publishers Weekly*

—w—

"A solidly crafted werewolf story, this tale centers on pack problems in a refreshingly straightforward way. The characters are well drawn and believable, which makes the contemporary plotline of love and life among the *lupus garou* seem, well, realistic."—*RT Book Reviews*

"I highly recommend this book for anyone who loves a good paranormal, romantic suspense, and shape-shifter story!"—*Fallen Angel Reviews*

For more Terry Spear, visit:

www.sourcebooks.com